CUTTHROAT

CUTTHROAT

BY
STEVE BREWER

BLEAK HOUSE BOOKS

MADISON | WISCONSIN

Published by Bleak House Books,
an imprint of Big Earth Publishing
923 Williamson St.
Madison, WI 53703

Set in Times New Roman

ISBN 13 (trade paper): 978-1-932557-62-6

FIRST TRADE PAPER EDITION

Library of Congress Cataloging-in-Publication Data has been applied for.

Printed in the United States of America

11 10 09 08 07   1 2 3 4 5 6 7 8 9 10

Cover and Book Design by
Von Bliss Design — "Book Design By Bookish People"
http://www.vonbliss.com

For Kelly

CHAPTER 1

•••••••••••••••••••

Flickering pink neon spelled out "Hotel," but the sign might as well have said "End of the Line." The two-story building was a concrete cube with Spanish pretensions, as if Frosted-Flakes stucco and a frill of snaggle-tooth tile could persuade potential guests: "This is no concrete cube. This is a Mediterranean villa!" Out front, two weary palm trees leaned over the littered sidewalk, throwing sunset shadows up against the wall.

The seedy hotel stood at the intersection of two decayed East Oakland streets. Nearby storefronts were boarded up, except for a busy package store, its windows plastered over with colorful advertisements for Old Milwaukee and Schlitz Malt Liquor.

From the back seat of the black limousine, Solomon Gage studied the arrangement of buildings and streets, measuring distances, calculating how many drunken pedestrians were run down here every year.

Across the street, two winos already were bedding down for the night, snagging prime doorways. In a parking lot in the next block, some tough-looking hombres sat on the tailgate of a pickup truck painted the color of a sunburn.

The other dozen or so people Solomon could see were engaged in the commerce of the streets. Hypes and pushers and hookers and cruisers prowled the sidewalks and lurked in doors. Homeboys in track suits and baseball caps worked the corners, tending the pharmaceutical needs of crackheads and knuckleheads and Saturday shoppers picking up a little something for the long ride home.

The street dealers watched the limousine warily. A limo could mean easy money, or it could mean an Uzi snaking out a tinted window to rake the sidewalks clean. Somebody's idea of style.

After the limo parked in front of the hotel, the dealers went back to their business, but they remained watchful, anxious about the strange vehicle in their territory. With their macho alliances and deadly hardware, the dealers undoubtedly ruled this area. If trouble erupted, they would settle it with lethal quickness. Nobody around here would call a cop, ever.

All in all, about the worst possible place for a linebacker-sized white man to go flashing a gun and kicking in doors. Solomon hoped he could handle the situation quietly, but he had a bad feeling about this street.

He never would've found his way here if it hadn't been for the limo driver, a round-faced black man named Carl Jones. They'd worked together for three days now, prowling Bay Area backstreets in search of Abby Maynes, showing her photo to junkies and hookers and street rats. Carl seemed competent and experienced and loyal to Sheffield Enterprises. But how would he react if the neighborhood suddenly crackled with gunfire? Solomon didn't want to run out to the curb, Abby flung over his shoulder, to find that the limousine had vanished.

"You going to be okay here, Carl?"

The gray-haired driver met his eyes in the rear-view.

"You sure you want to do this?" he asked. "She's been in there this long, she could wait until the cops get here."

"I'll handle it," Solomon said. "If it goes wrong, call 911."

Carl swiveled around to face him. "I'll be out here in the car. How will I know if anything's gone wrong?"

Solomon opened the jacket of his lightweight gray suit and gave Carl a glimpse of his shoulder holster, black nylon straps barely visible against black turtleneck, and the butt of the .45-caliber Colt Commander.

"You'll know."

Carl faced forward, his hands at ten and two. Ready to do his job, or to run like hell?

Solomon popped open the door and slid out into the fading evening light. He paused beside the open limo door to adjust the drape of his jacket and glance up and down the street. Ran a hand over his shaved head, the scrape of blond stubble evidence of what a long day it had been already. And he was just getting started.

He closed the limo door as quietly as possible, a sudden bang being the last thing anyone needed here in Dodge City. He crossed the sidewalk in three quick strides and jangled his way through the hotel's finger-smeared door.

The lobby was a naked square of grimy tile floor surrounded by two closed doors, some worn stairs, and a counter with a thick window of what looked like bulletproof glass. A crescent-shaped slot was cut in the glass at counter height, for passing keys and currency. A round hole was cut higher, so guests could shout through to the skinny old man beyond. Solomon thinking: It's bulletproof glass, and they leave a hole big enough to poke a gun through? A robber could angle a pistol around, spray the entire office.

The manager's name, according to a tag pinned to his purple cardigan, was Rufus Broxton. His furrowed face was the color of fresh loam, plowed through the middle by a glinting grin rich in gold dental work. Broxton took his time rising from his threadbare La-Z-Boy and shuffling over to the window.

"Help you?"

Solomon reached inside his suit jacket and pulled out the employee photograph of Abby Maynes.

"Have you seen this girl?"

Broxton's smile went cagey. "Who wants to know?"

"Benjamin Franklin."

Solomon dipped his hand into the pocket again and pulled a crisp hundred-dollar bill from a deck he carried there. He slid the bill across the counter. The manager deftly swept it off into his pants pocket.

"Upstairs. Room 217. They were making a helluva racket, few hours ago. I could hear 'em down here."

"'They?'"

"The girl, a couple of gangbangers, this frog-eyed Mexican. They come and they go. I can't keep 'em sorted out."

"How many are there now?"

"How many more Benjamins you got?"

Solomon shook his head. "That's not the way I work. The first time I reach inside my coat, I pull out money. Presto."

The manager nodded. "A fine trick—"

"The *second* time I reach inside my coat, I pull out a pistol. The conversation takes a different direction."

The golden smile of Rufus Broxton winked off. He swallowed hard.

"I think they're all up there," he said. "Your girl, another crack whore, and three men. I saw the Mexican go up a little while ago."

"Everybody uses these stairs? Right past your window?"

"That's right."

Solomon turned away from the old man and lightly trotted up the creaky stairs to the second floor. The narrow corridor was empty, but scratchy music played and people talked behind the closed doors.

Solomon listened at the room labeled "217." A man's voice murmured inside, then a woman's, too low to make out what they were saying. Solomon pulled the pistol from its holster and held it down by his thigh, pointed at the floor. He rapped on the door.

Nothing for a few seconds, then footsteps inside the room. The door was snatched open by a squat, copper-colored man with bulging black eyes, a wide mouth and a thin mustache.

"You must be the frog-eyed Mexican," Solomon said.

"What did you say?" The man's eyes twitched and blinked. Some heavy drugs at work inside his head. Solomon didn't like that. Drugs made people unpredictable, made them forget about consequences and caution and risk.

Better to keep it simple.

He jammed the muzzle of the .45 against the crotch of the Mexican's saggy pants. The man's eyes got even wider at the sudden contact with his valuables.

"Do I have your attention?"

The Mexican nodded.

"There's a woman here, Abby Maynes."

"I don't know, bro. I just—"

Solomon jabbed with the gun. The man's face puckered briefly in pain. Sweat glistened on his forehead.

"I want her to come out. Make that happen."

"Uh."

"Who is it?" A man's reedy voice came from inside the room. Solomon looked past the Mexican's head, but he couldn't see anyone else. The door opened into a narrow entrance hall, the bathroom to one side and a blank wall to the other. The other occupants were around the corner, out of view.

The Mexican glanced back over his shoulder.

"Tell him everything's fine," Solomon said.

"Everything's fi-i-ine," he called. "There's a dude here. Wants to talk to Abby."

"What dude?"

"Some white dude."

A pause.

"You a cop?" the voice called.

"No," Solomon said.

"Who are you then?"

"I work for Abby's grandfather."

Rustling in the hotel room. Solomon still couldn't see anyone back there.

"What you want?"

"I need to talk to Abby."

Another pause. Whispering, but Solomon couldn't make out what they were saying.

"Hell, let the man in, Jorge." The suddenly friendly voice dragged out the Mexican's name, made it sound like *Whore-hey.* "We got nothing to hide."

Jorge swallowed. Solomon gave his gonads one last prod with the pistol, then nodded. The Mexican backed up, keeping his hands in sight, smiling and twitching and trying his damnedest to look reassuring.

Solomon kept the gun close by his body as he followed Jorge into the room. The entry was like a cattle chute, the worst kind of trap, but there was nothing to do but barge ahead. Now that he'd located Abby, there was no turning back.

He reached the end of the short wall, where the room opened up, and a pistol jabbed into the side of his neck.

"That's right, muthafucka," said the gunman, close by his ear. "You best be still."

CHAPTER 2

•••••••••••••••••••

Standard hotel room, beaten down by years of abuse and neglect. Grimy carpet and cigarette-scarred furniture and walls the color of tooth decay. Two rumpled beds jutted from the far wall with a nightstand and a cockeyed lamp between them.

On one narrow bed sat Abby Maynes, pale and gaunt, her hair pulled back into a tight ponytail as black as an oil slick. Drugs lit her eyes from within, so bright that Solomon half-expected to see smoke trailing from her ears. Her feet were dirty and bare, but at least she was dressed, in greasy jeans and a soiled yellow T-shirt that hung limply from her narrow shoulders.

The black woman sprawled across the other bed was naked, her crumpled hair snarled across her face. Out cold, and nobody here with enough decency to throw a blanket over her.

The lanky homeboy jabbing the gun into his neck was nearly as tall as Solomon's six-foot-four. He was maybe twenty-five, with watery brown eyes and coarse features. A darker, smaller man stood just beyond him, holding a pocket-sized semi-automatic at arm's length, pointing it at Solomon's face. They both wore red tracksuits with white stripes down the sleeves. Baseball caps and bulky Nikes and chunky gold jewelry.

A mustard-yellow sofa sat against the wall behind them, facing a TV that silently played a Bugs Bunny cartoon. The coffee table was crowded with silver Coors Light cans and pizza crusts and overflowing ashtrays. The centerpiece was a brass tray covered in hypodermics and glass pipes and razor blades and crank and crack and a baggie with something black inside.

The Mexican backed all the way to the foot of the bed where the unconscious woman lay. A smile spread on his face, making him look even froggier.

"Who's got the hot dick now, huh?" he said. "Who's the man *now*?"

"Shut up, Jorge." Close by Solomon's ear. "Drop that gun, muthafucka."

"Or what?"

"Or bang, you're dead."

Solomon thumbed a button, and the clip dropped out of his Colt and fell to the floor. Better to never hand your opponents a fully loaded weapon. Especially after they've been thoughtful enough to bring their own.

Still one in the Colt's chamber, but he didn't clear it. He hoped to manage this without anyone firing a shot, but if not, that bullet might come in handy. He bent his knees and let the pistol drop to the worn carpet. The gun at his neck didn't waver as he straightened up.

The lanky one poked him with the gun. "Now who the fuck did you say you were?"

"Solomon Gage. I work for the Sheffield family."

"I don't know no Sheffields."

"Abby's grandfather is Dominick Sheffield. A very influential man."

"But her last name's something else." The lanky one scowled, trying to remember.

"Maynes," Solomon said patiently. "Her mother is Dominick Sheffield's daughter."

"S'that right, Abby?" The gunman glanced over at her, giving Solomon an opening. He could've taken the pistol away, snapped the man's wrist. But there was the problem of the smaller guy, who still had his gun pointed at Solomon's head. He squinted down the barrel, as if he could miss at this range.

"Hey, Tyrone, you know who this fucker looks like?" the short one said. "That guy on TV. Mr. Clean. You see that? Bald head and those funky white eyebrows. This muthafucka is Mr. Clean."

Tyrone grinned, looking Solomon over. "Sure as hell ain't Uncle Ben."

While they got a good laugh at that, Solomon was busy calculating risks. He could get hold of Tyrone's gun fast enough to shoot the short guy. Get the guns out of action, then do the rest by hand. But what if Jorge was concealing a gun? What if Abby caught a stray bullet? Better for now to keep these morons talking. Maybe they'd make a mistake.

"Abby's mother is named Dorothy Sheffield Maynes DeAnza Burton," he recited. "She's been married three times, and is currently engaged to a shipping magnate. They are to be married in July. Abby is invited to the wedding, but has not sent in her RSVP. Abby's been missing for two weeks, and her bank account has been drained. They sent me to find her."

As he spoke, Solomon felt some of the pressure ease from the gun at his neck.

"What the fuck, Abby?" Tyrone said. "You didn't tell us you came from money."

"It doesn't matter." Her voice was strung tight. "It's not my money. It doesn't do me any good."

"Shit, baby, we coulda cooked something up," Tyrone said. "Turned you into some profit."

"I told you we shoulda turned that white girl out," said the little guy, whose cap sat so far back on his round head, the bill pointed at the ceiling.

"Naw, Jamal. I mean some real money. Your granddaddy rich as this man here's lettin' on?"

"He's richer than God," Abby said flatly. "He's got the whole family on his payroll. And thousands of employees all over the world. Including this asshole here."

"You know Mr. Gage?"

Tyrone stepped back, took the gun away from Solomon's neck. Jamal lowered his gun, too, but both kept the weapons pointed his general direction.

"I know him," she said bitterly.

Tyrone's voice went suddenly chilly. "Did you know he was *lookin'* for you?"

Abby hesitated. "Solomon always shows up eventually. That's his job."

"Ever occur to you, bitch, that you shoulda mentioned this shit? Might've saved everybody a lotta trouble if we'd known Mr. Gage was coming. Now we got to do it the hard way. Act like low-class criminals."

Jamal snickered. Jorge, still keeping out of the way, laughed and said, "No! Not us!"

"You coulda fucked us up," Tyrone said to Abby. "He coulda brung the cops."

That thought pulled Tyrone up short. "Did you? Did you bring the cops?"

"No police," Solomon said. "The family wants to keep this quiet."

Tyrone smiled. "Maybe we can work something out."

"I hope so."

"You better hope so," Jamal blustered. "I am, personally, still enthus-i-*as*-tic about the idea of poppin' a cap in your white ass."

"Shut the fuck up, man," Tyrone said. "I'm tryin' to think here."

They all stood around, watching Tyrone think. It apparently was hard work that involved elaborate screwing up of the facial features. Quite a show, but Solomon finally said, "Let me help."

They looked at him. Abby, still sitting on the edge of the bed, rolled her eyes. The naked girl hadn't twitched, and Solomon was beginning to wonder whether she was dead. That could complicate matters.

"I want to get Abby out of here, take her to a hospital, get her some care."

"Oh, for shit's sake—"

"Shut up, woman!" Tyrone shouted. "You brought this down on us. You can fuckin' sit still through it."

Abby clamped her lips together so hard, they went pale. Her eyes burned with cold ferocity. Solomon wished he'd found this place when they all were on the nod, when he could've slipped in quietly and spirited her away. Instead, they seemed amped to the gills, twitchy and wired.

Tyrone focused on Solomon. "Why should we let you take her? That's good pussy right there. She been showin' us a good time."

Solomon knew he was being baited. He kept his face expressionless. As long as Tyrone believed he was a simple errand boy, there was hope of settling this thing like businessmen.

Tyrone apparently was thinking the same way. "How much money you got?"

Solomon answered without hesitating. "Five thousand dollars, give or take a few. Inside pocket of my jacket."

Tyrone's face did its writhing thing again.

"You won't get a better offer from the Sheffields," Solomon said calmly. "Abby's not a big deal to them. I'd say we're at take-it-or-leave-it right now."

"Bullshit!" Abby screeched. She bounded across the room to Solomon and stabbed her finger at his chin. "They want me back! They need to keep an eye on me. I know plenty, buddy. I've been working with Uncle Mike. I know all about the Africa deal. More than you—"

"Yes, ma'am," Solomon said. "But you're not yourself right now. Let me take care of this little problem and we'll be on our way."

"Listen to you! My God, you're a fuckin' robot! You're so well-trained—"

"Yes, ma'am. Can we talk about that in the car?"

"Hold on, muthafucka," Tyrone said. "I didn't say you were goin' anywhere."

The track stars pointed their guns at Solomon's head.

"Take my money, Tyrone," he said. "Five thousand bucks. Let Abby and me walk out of here. I've got a car waiting."

Tyrone thrust out his skinny chest. Jamal tried to look taller. Even Jorge drifted a couple of steps closer.

"We let you go," Tyrone said, "and you'll have the cops here in minutes."

"No cops," Solomon said. "You walk away with five grand. I walk away with Abby. Everybody gets to keep breathing."

Tyrone tilted his head, closing one eye, sighting down the barrel of his pistol. "That your final answer?"

"Good as it gets. They won't go higher for Abby."

Tyrone laughed. "Ain't just Abby we talkin' about. We got both of you now. How much they pay for the two of you?"

"Nothing for me," Solomon said. "I'm strictly an employee, like she said. And they're not willing to pay more for Abby, either. Far as they're concerned, this is her last shot. Go into rehab or be a full-time crack whore."

Abby shrieked and swung at Solomon's face. He leaned back far enough to make sure she missed.

"The fuck you doin', bitch?" Tyrone said. "Get out of the way."

He shoved her aside. She stumbled, and Jorge caught her by the arms. They didn't fall, but they were tangled up, Abby screaming curses.

Tyrone's gun was pointed at Solomon's face, so close he could smell stale gunpowder from the muzzle. Jamal's aim had strayed as he turned to watch Jorge and Abby dance around.

This, Solomon thought, is probably as good as it's going to get.

He grabbed Tyrone's gun hand at the wrist and twisted, bending the wrist back, turning him halfway around. Tyrone squeezed the trigger, but by then the gun was pointed away from Solomon. White plaster dust exploded from the wall.

Solomon folded Tyrone's arm at the elbow and swung it up into a hammerlock with such sudden force that Tyrone bent double at the waist, wailing.

His gun hand was between his own shoulder blades, the pistol pointed toward his wide-eyed partner. The pistol boomed and Jamal's gaping mouth caught the bullet. The baseball cap blew off the back of his head in a sudden spray of blood.

Tyrone screamed. Abby screamed. Jorge said, "*Dios!*"

Solomon struck upward with his left knee and caught Tyrone squarely in the bridge of the nose. Tyrone's head snapped back, and he made a sound like a leaky balloon as he crumpled to the floor. Solomon wrested the gun from his hand as he fell.

Solomon whirled toward Jorge and Abby, raising the gun, but the frog-eyed man was quicker than he looked and he'd already thrown her out of the way and charged. Solomon crashed into the wall, Jorge crushing into his chest. Tyrone's gun flew out of his hand and tumbled end over end through the air, landing on the yellow couch.

Solomon jabbed the rigid fingertips of both hands into Jorge's short ribs. The Mexican gasped and reeled backward. Solomon swung for his chin, but hit nothing but air as Jorge flung himself sideways, scrambling for the blood-spattered couch, going for the gun.

Abby had stumbled to the space between the beds and fallen to the carpet. About the safest place she could be, and she didn't seem in any hurry to get up. Tyrone writhed blindly on the floor, his hands over his face. Jamal's body lay between the sofa and the coffee table, afloat on a spreading pool of blood.

Solomon couldn't see Jamal's gun. Might be under him, or it might've slid under the furniture. Solomon's own gun was where he'd dropped it, and he threw himself to the floor and grabbed it up. He rolled onto his knees, his gun pointed at Jorge, who lay on his side on the sofa, Tyrone's pistol in two hands, aimed at Solomon's face.

Standoff.

Solomon's mind raced. He could hear noises outside in the hallway. Hotel guests scrambling for the exits. Time was running out.

A smile oozed across Jorge's froggy face. "You're bluffing."

Solomon waited.

"Your gun ain't loaded. You took out the clip."

"Very good, Jorge."

Solomon pulled the trigger. The Mexican's left shoulder exploded. Jorge screamed and dropped the gun. He grasped his bloodied shoulder and curled up on himself on the sofa.

"Still one in the chamber." Solomon leaned over and plucked the magazine off the floor. He slammed it into the butt of the Colt, and racked the slide. Kept the gun trained on Jorge while he squatted and picked up his smoking brass.

He dropped the spent cartridge into his pocket, then crossed to the beds, grasped Abby's upper arm and pulled her to her feet.

"Let's go."

She yanked at her arm, but couldn't get free. "I'm not going with you. You can't make me."

"Let's go *now*." He gave her skinny biceps a squeeze, hard enough to make her yelp.

"Get your hands off me!"

Solomon made sure Jorge and Tyrone were busy with their injuries, then he holstered the .45 and reached into another pocket for the handcuffs he'd brought.

When Abby got a look at the cuffs, she said, "You wouldn't dare!"

He snapped them on her.

"That hurts, you fucker!"

"Quiet," he said. "Or I'll make you wear them behind your back."

"Fuck you, you bastard! When I tell Uncle Mike what you did—"

Solomon tuned her out. He'd heard it all before. He steered her out of the hotel room, closing the door behind them.

He marched Abby quickly to the staircase. People peeked out of rooms up and down the hall, but quickly shut their doors when they saw them.

Abby stumbled as they went down the stairs, but Solomon kept her from falling. She used the moment of imbalance to try to claw at his face. He said, "Stop that."

The hotel manager was in his chair behind the bulletproof glass. He made a point of not looking up from his reading as Solomon and Abby went past, out the front door, into the humid evening air.

The limo was at the curb, the engine running. Solomon looked neither left nor right as he and Abby crossed the sidewalk. After the gunshots in the hotel, he felt sure homeboys brandished weapons up and down the street, waiting for somebody to make the wrong move. He wanted no part of that.

Solomon shoved Abby into the back seat of the limo. He went in right behind her and slammed the door. He shouted to Carl, "Go!"

Carl went. The limo leapt from the curb.

Solomon looked out the back window at the darkening street. Business as usual along the sidewalks. Hell, on that street, shoot-outs probably *were* "the usual."

"Everybody okay?" Carl asked, checking them in the rear-view.

"Not everybody," Solomon said. "But we're all right."

"I called 911. When I heard the shooting."

"Good job." Solomon paused, listening, but heard no sirens yet. "Glad we didn't need the help."

He took a deep breath and settled back into the seat. "You know where we're going, Carl."

"Yes, sir."

"Where?" Abby demanded. "Where are you taking me?"

"You'll see soon enough," Solomon said. "Relax. We've got a long ride ahead."

"Fuck you."

"Yes, ma'am."

CHAPTER 3

●●●●●●●●●●●●●●●●●●

Abby rode in silence for the longest time, but she couldn't stand it anymore. The drugs in her system made her want to move, talk, *do* something.

"You know what we used to call you?" she said. "My cousins and me, when we were kids?"

"You're still a kid," Solomon Gage muttered, not even bothering to look over at her.

"I am not," she declared. "I'm twenty-four years old. What are you, thirty?"

"Thirty-three."

"See? Not that much older. I've dated men older than you."

His chiseled features and taut skin made it hard to tell his age. The way he shaved his tanned head, you couldn't tell if he was balding or what, and he had those sun-bleached eyebrows, which made him look older. He'd always seemed a watchful adult, even when he first started working for Grandpa, and that was more than ten years ago. There was a weariness to his posture that made him seem positively ancient. And the way he always knew what was coming, like other people were chess pieces to be moved around on a big checkered board—well, that was maddening at any age.

"So what?"

"So don't come on like you're the grown-up and I'm the little girl," she said. "I guess I know a thing or two. I guess I've been around the block a few times."

"I wouldn't brag about it, if I were you."

That stung. She hissed, "You bastard."

They rode in silence for a few minutes, sitting at opposite ends of the wide back seat, staring out the limo windows. They'd passed out of the urban clutter and into the hills of the East Bay. In the twilight, the hills seemed to undulate under their grassy skin, but Abby was pretty sure that was the drugs in her veins.

Her nose kept running, and it was difficult to discreetly clean it up with her wrists cuffed. She sniffled and shifted in the seat, tucking her bare feet up under her, trying to get comfortable. She felt edgy and unbalanced.

Headlights glowed in the oncoming lanes, and she squinted against the glare. Where the hell was Solomon taking her?

•••

Solomon didn't want to talk. He was busy rerunning the hotel shootout through his mind, checking for mistakes, for evidence they'd left behind. He thought they were in the clear, though lots of witnesses had seen them. Nobody in that hotel would volunteer information to the police. Abby no doubt had left fingerprints everywhere, but he didn't think the police had them on file. Solomon might've left prints on Tyrone's gun, but Jorge probably smeared those.

The shootout remained vivid in his mind, a slo-mo replay that captured every detail. He knew it would live forever in his brain, a movie starring Jamal's exploding head. He'd try to forget it, but the dead ones always stayed with him.

Abby sighed and squirmed, distracting him. She faked a coughing fit.

He gave up, and said, "Okay, what did you call me?"

"What?"

"When you were kids. I take it you had a nickname for me."

"We did. We called you 'the Archangel.'"

"Really?"

"Grandpa's like God, right? And who sits at God's right hand? You. When there's a problem, somebody gets in trouble, he sends you to take care of it. You're like his, um, his—"

Troubleshooter, Solomon thought. Messenger. Envoy, representative, surrogate, proxy. Fixer, bag man, hatchet man, lethal right hand.

"Emissary," he said.

"Whatever. He thinks something and you make it happen. You're his archangel, swooping in to fix everything."

Solomon said nothing.

"That's what we thought, anyway," she said.

"When you were kids."

"That's right. We'd be like: 'You better put out that joint, man. The Archangel is watching you.'"

"That's what I was? The bogeyman?"

"Sort of. But also like a guardian angel. We knew no matter how badly we screwed up, Grandpa would send you to save us."

Solomon sighed, thinking about Abby and the other grandchildren of Dominick Sheffield. The Third Generation, as he thought of them.

The First Generation, that's the one in which a family gets rich, the self-made men like Dom who carve fortunes out of a hostile world. Suddenly, there's a pot of gold, and everyone wants to gather round.

The Second Generation, the sons and daughters of those money men, always come up short. They don't have to claw their way to the top; they start at the top. They tend to be soft, weak, flawed. To crack easily. The Second Generation was plagued by divorce and failure and waste. Starving at fat farms and drying out in jitter joints and trying to escape daddy's shadow. Never quite living up to anyone's expectations, including their own.

The Third Generation, who came out of those broken homes, seemed set on self-destruction, to prove some point about wealth and privilege and neglect and need. Solomon didn't even pretend to understand them. He just tried to keep them all moving through the revolving doors of graduate schools and rehab and do-nothing jobs and ill-fated start-ups without anyone getting crushed.

He hated to think what the next generation would be like.

•••

A sudden flush warmed Abby's face, a fever wave breaking across her brow. The drugs? Or was she embarrassed at her thoughts about the huge man next to her?

She remembered high school slumber parties with her cousins, where the subject of Solomon Gage always came up. Abby was an only child, regularly shipped off to see various Sheffield cousins on the pretext that she should spend more time with kids her own age. She knew now that her mother merely needed a place to dock her kid while she sailed off after the next husband, but at the time, Abby bought it and did her best to endure her fluff-brained, spoiled-rotten, glue-sniffing cousins.

The cousins were scared of Solomon. They thought he was some kind of demon, the way he popped up at the worst possible times, catching them in various misdemeanors. Spooky. Abby had been the first to call the Archangel, with his hard muscles and icy blue eyes, a "hunk," which made the other girls squeal.

She sneaked a look at him now. Strong jaw, smooth forehead, eyes in the shadow of his white brows. Aryan-looking, despite his Jewish-sounding name. She wondered why he was staring at her, what he was thinking. She straightened, reached up awkwardly with her cuffed hands to smooth her hair. She knew she looked terrible. She hadn't slept in days, hadn't eaten or washed. Just wallowed in one drugged state after another—zonked on Ecstasy or hopped on crank or smacked out on whatever Tyrone slipped into a hypodermic. No idea what day it was or where she was or how the hell she got there.

Fucked, in every sense of the word. Tyrone and his friends going at her all the goddamned time. Abby doing whatever they wanted to keep the drugs flowing. It had been a parade of cocks. Fucking and sucking and getting slapped and spitting blood and jism everywhere and—

"Jesus," she gasped. "Stop the car. I'm gonna be sick."

•••

Solomon stood by the limo's back door while Abby heaved into an oleander at the side of the road. He kept an eye on her, making sure she didn't decide to make a sudden break. He was concerned about her bare feet; shattered glass on the shoulder of the road sparkled in the red glare from the taillights.

The slipstreams of passing cars snapped at his clothes. No one seemed to take much notice of the long black limo or the hand-cuffed woman puking in the bushes. Just another Saturday night in California.

He stooped and peered into the car. Carl sat behind the wheel, determinedly facing the windshield. He guessed the chauffeur had been in this exact position before, perhaps even with Miss Abby Maynes playing an identical role.

Solomon straightened as Abby wiped at her mouth with the backs of her cuffed hands.

"God," she sputtered. "My God."

"You all right?"

"Do I *look* all right?"

She was pale and sweaty and goggle-eyed. She had a stream of thick drool down the center of her chin.

"You've looked better."

"Thanks." She spat on the ground a couple of times, then twisted her head around to wipe her chin on the shoulder of her T-shirt.

"You can travel now?"

"I guess," she said. "How much farther is it?"

"We're almost there."

She climbed into the car and slid across the seat to make room for him. After he got in, she said, "Where the hell are you taking me?"

"A lovely rehabilitation center called Willow Glade."

"Sounds like air freshener."

"Exactly. You're going there to get your air freshened. Get the drugs out of your system. Get your life back on track."

Moaning, Abby let her head fall back against the seat.

"Why," she whined, "didn't you just let Tyrone kill me?"

"The option crossed my mind."

She raised her head and stared at him with feverish eyes. "You would've been doing me a favor."

"I don't think so. Get through rehab. You've still got a good future ahead of you."

"You're sure about that?"

"Absolutely," he said. "I know things. See, you were wrong about my name. Solomon, in the Bible? He wasn't an archangel."

"No? What was he?"

"A wise king."

She snorted. "That's you? You're *wise*?"

"I'm trying."

CHAPTER 4

•••••••••••••••••••

Solomon spent most of the night getting Abby checked into Willow Glade, filling out forms and making sure she was placed in a secure wing. Orderlies wheeled her away on a gurney, straps across her chest. Silent tears crept down her cheeks, and she wouldn't look at him. He hadn't expected thanks, but he wished she'd shown some sign of embracing rehab. Wished he felt better about her chances.

A bleary Carl drove him to the Oakland airport, and Solomon watched Sunday dawn over the hills while he waited for a Sheffield Enterprises helicopter to get fueled and checked out for the hour-long flight to the family sanctuary called Cutthroat Lodge. It was a fine day for flying, and he enjoyed watching the landscape slip past as the chopper zoomed north over Sonoma County's stitch-work of vineyards and Mendocino County's oak-studded hills. Took his mind off Abby and what had happened in East Oakland.

It was past 8 a.m. by the time they arrived, the Bell Ranger swooping past the steep sides of the hanging canyon where Dominick Sheffield's land nuzzled up to Mendocino National Forest.

Oaks grew like thick fur on the hillsides. Here and there, clumps of evergreens stood tall, tufts the barber missed. Solomon spotted the grove of even taller trees up ahead, the coast redwoods that grew near the lodge. Rare this far south, protected by Dominick Sheffield.

Past the redwoods, a teardrop-shaped lake shimmered in the morning light. A catch basin for the runoff from surrounding mountains, it fed the stream that tumbled downhill from Dominick Sheffield's property. The cutthroat trout that populated that creek were legendary among fly fishermen.

The airstrip, long enough to accommodate corporate jets, cut a perfectly straight slash through the oaks, pointing to the small lake. From the air, the combination looked like an exclamation point. The redwood grove stood between the airstrip and the oaks and gray pines that surrounded Cutthroat Lodge.

This time of year, early May, the tangled meadows alongside the airstrip were awash in wildflowers, a vivid abstract painting in purple and gold and red and orange and green. Before Solomon's eyes, the splotches of color became individual flowers as the chopper neared the ground.

The pilot set down beside two hangars that stood near the midway point of the airstrip. Solomon thanked him, then hurried over to one of the company Jeeps parked nearby. The keys were in the ignition, as expected. The vehicles were always available to ferry employees and visitors the mile to the lodge.

The paved private road roughly paralleled the airstrip, but with undulating curves to accommodate the topography. The tree-lined road ran along the edge of a mesa, the land to the right dropping away to a wooded valley. Dominick Sheffield had found the one flat spot in this rugged landscape, and had built Cutthroat Lodge there. No neighbors for miles, most of the land around his two thousand acres belonging to the U.S. Forest Service. The nearest town was Willits, thirty miles away over a winding county road. Dom had all supplies flown in, and most visitors came and went the same way. Sheffield corporate security kept guards on duty at the far end of the two-mile-long private drive, where it met the county road, but they never had much to do.

Dom had purchased all the isolation twenty million dollars could buy. He'd gotten sick of people during forty years in the shark pool of international business. These days, he rarely left the lodge and its surrounding property. You wanted to do business with Dominick Sheffield, you came to him.

Not that most people minded. It was a spectacular location, with views of the Coast Range, blue skies and a wide swath of green valley.

The lodge was built of cedar shingles and native stone and glass. Its two long wings were low, with shadowy eaves, but in the middle a pitched roof soared above a great room. Windows stretched twenty feet high on either side, so it was possible to see right through the house. Inside, a giant chandelier constructed of deer antlers dangled from the ceiling, above heavy leather furniture, rustic tables and Navajo rugs. At one end of the great room towered a free-standing fireplace, its river-rock chimney jutting through the pitched roof. Behind the fireplace, more tall windows looked into a dining room that separated the great room from the kitchen and servants' quarters.

Solomon jogged up the flagstone steps to the wood-plank deck that stretched across the front of the house. The house had a similar porch out back, so reclining Sheffields always had their choice of sun or shade.

The maid, a red-haired Irishwoman named Fiona, met him at the door and told him Dom was right where he would've expected on a Sunday morning—at his favorite trout hole on Cutthroat Creek.

Solomon couldn't call Dom there—the surrounding mountains made cell phones worthless—but he didn't mind hiking to the trout stream to find him. After the night he'd had, a walk in the woods might be the perfect thing.

A trail led from the long back porch and forked after fifteen yards. The right fork took visitors to three A-frame cabins that formed a curving line down to the shore of the lake; Solomon called the middle one home. The left fork meandered through evergreens and oaks, past a jumble of giant boulders, to a wooden footbridge over the creek. A narrower trail ran alongside the creek, a path worn by anglers and thirsty deer.

Dom's favorite spot was a hundred yards up this side trail, around a couple of curves, so there was no view of the bridge or buildings or anything else that might signal Man. Just towering trees and sparkling water and rounded stones. And, in the shadowy pools, fat, wily trout.

Solomon took his jacket off. It was a warm day, with little wind, and his black shirt was damp with perspiration. He carried the jacket slung over his shoulder, a finger hooked in the collar. Birds twittered in the treetops, and sunlight sliced through the trees to reflect off the tumbling water. He felt himself relax more with every step.

The narrow trail dog-legged through a stand of eight-foot-tall reeds. He stopped when he emerged on the other side.

Dominick Sheffield was thirty feet away, knee-deep in the gurgling stream, his dripping line catching the light as it whipped back and forth over his head. The old man had great form, his shoulders level under the suspenders of the chest waders, his posture perfect. His arm was a study in straight lines, but his wrist was loose. He dropped the fly into the exact center of a downstream pool.

Dom was hatless, and his silver hair swept back onto his collar. He squinted against the glare on the water, his leathery face creased into a sunburst of lines and arcs and concentration.

"That you, Solomon?" he called without turning around.

"Yes, sir."

"I thought I heard the chopper. Come tell me."

"I don't want to disturb you. If this is a bad time—"

"Don't be silly. They're not biting anyway."

•••

Dominick Sheffield reeled in his line. He watched as Solomon selected a boulder beside the creek and brushed it off before sitting. Solomon had his jacket off, which was unusual. Normally, he didn't want people to see the hand cannon he carried in that black shoulder holster. Solomon was almost always armed. Knowing that had, at times, been a source of great comfort to Dom.

Solomon dressed the same way every day—lightweight gray suit over a black, short-sleeved pullover shirt. Never a necktie. Years before, during a fistfight, he'd nearly been choked to death with his own tie. A lesson never to be forgotten.

The mock turtleneck covered a three-inch-long knife scar left by an importer in New Orleans who objected when Solomon informed him that Dom had put him out of business. Dom still felt bad about that incident. Even having the importer slain later hadn't made him feel any better. That was business: always a few regrets mixed in with the victories.

Dom waded to the bank, carefully placing each foot among the jumbled stones of the creek bed. He was out of breath by the time he climbed to the path and sat on a flat rock near Solomon.

"So," he said as he slipped the strap of the empty creel off his shoulder, "how's Abby?"

"I got her checked into Willow Glade. They've flushed her system by now and she's probably sleeping. They like to ease them into it there. You remember how it was, when Bobby was there last year."

Another of Dom's grandchildren. What was with these kids and their drugs? What was the matter with them? Wasn't life exciting enough without going around juiced up all the time?

Solomon told him, in his usual staccato manner, about the shootout at the Oakland hotel, which sounded plenty exciting itself.

"Any way that could come back on us?" Dom asked.

"The men knew Abby's name and I told them mine, but I don't think they'll go to the police. They'll get treatment for their wounds, and hold a funeral for the dead man. Then it should get real quiet."

"I'd rather not deal with the police. We don't need the attention."

"Of course."

"If we need to make the survivors—this Tyrone and what was the other one's name? Jorge?—if we need to make them disappear, just let me know."

"I think it will be all right," Solomon said.

"Sounds like you did a good job. I'm glad you and Abby weren't hurt."

"Thank you, sir."

•••

Solomon followed Dom back to the lodge, letting the old man set the pace. Dom had removed the clumsy waders and carried them over one shoulder, which threw off his balance a little. Solomon had offered to carry them, but his boss always said a man didn't deserve to fish if he didn't tend his own gear.

Solomon stifled a yawn as they reached the clearing around the lodge, and Dom said, "Why don't you take the afternoon off? Take a nap. Come to dinner tonight. Chris is flying in and Juanita's making enchiladas."

Solomon kept his face blank. "Just the three of us, sir?"

"If you're there, maybe Chris and I won't talk business the whole evening. You know Chris. One-track mind."

Christopher Sheffield was a perfect example of Solomon's theories about the Second Generation. Twice-divorced, self-absorbed, always trying to prove himself worthy of the name and the big inheritance. The eldest of four children born to Dom's late wife, Chris was fifty-two, but acted like a spoiled child, with enormous appetites for food, drink, money. Those appetites were slowly eroding his health, but Chris showed no sign of changing his ways. Solomon sometimes wondered whether Dom might outlive his son.

"I don't know, sir. I might be intruding. If you and Chris need to talk—"

"Nonsense," Dom said. "We've got no secrets from you. I'd like you to be there. You've been away a lot lately. We can catch up."

"Yes, sir."

Dom cocked an eyebrow. "Come on, Solomon. Sunday dinner! Juanita's enchiladas! Show some enthusiasm."

"Yes, *sir*."

Dom grinned. "That's more like it."

CHAPTER 5

••••••••••••••••••••

Solomon slept four hours and woke feeling refreshed. Dressed in gym shorts and a tank top, he made coffee and did some stretches while it percolated. Thought about taking a run around the lake or lifting barbells at the weight bench he kept on the cabin's covered back porch, but decided to skip both. He could exercise in the morning, at the coolest time of day. Besides, he had work to do.

He poured a cup of black coffee and opened his laptop computer on the butcher-block counter that served as his dining table and desk. He booted up so he could update Abby's file to include the rescue and rehab.

Solomon tilted the laptop's screen away from the sunshine that streamed through the windows. The A-frame cabin had tall windows front and back, but none on the sides because the eaves came almost to the ground. Another window, high above the front door, spilled light into the sleeping loft. Solomon's natural alarm clock.

He kept the small cabin as uncluttered as a boot-camp barracks. The downstairs was an open room with a kitchenette in one back corner and a compact bathroom in the other. The living area was large enough for a sofa, an armchair, a coffee table and a TV/stereo cabinet. Solomon kept his gray suits and other clothes in a small closet squeezed between the bathroom and the back door.

Pegs in the wall by the front door provided a place for jackets and rain gear.

Solomon had lived here for a decade, always turning down Dom's offers for more spacious accommodations. The cabin suited him, and the setting, with the lake in one direction and the lodge the other, couldn't have been more scenic.

He'd made adjustments over the years, installing a locking gun cabinet in the sleeping loft and adding the workout gear to the back porch. His cabin was wired with high-speed Internet connections. The phone lines and electric cables that served the cabins were buried so that no wires or satellite dishes marred the scenery. The cabins, with their weathered walls and mossy roofs, did their damnedest to disappear into the woods, and Dom wouldn't screw that up for the sake of technology.

The other two cabins sat empty much of the year. Assorted Sheffields used the one nearest the lake as a vacation getaway, and the one closest to the lodge was the official residence for visiting dignitaries. Most of the time, though, the only noises were natural ones—chirping birds and skittering squirrels and the wind whispering through the trees.

When traveling for business, Solomon stayed in swank hotels or in ritzy apartments that Sheffield Enterprises owned around the world. Nice, sure, but they couldn't compete with the Mendocino County forests. It could be lonely at times, out here in the woods, but Solomon compensated by taking "people baths" whenever he was in cities, the sights and sounds washing over him. He enjoyed the company of the women he dated, but was never tempted to bring one home. The cabin was his quiet sanctuary, his hideout from the wider world.

He punched in a series of passwords to reach his computer files. Solomon kept detailed records on every member of the family, plus various corporate officers and business partners. A typical entry included address and phone numbers, a summation of careers and connections, the subject's place in the Sheffield family tree or corporate dynasty, and Solomon's notes about strengths and weaknesses, bad habits and personal peccadilloes.

He clicked on a directory and Abby's file filled the screen. He scanned the information, and found nothing that made him feel better about her chances in rehab. He typed a few paragraphs about Abby's needs and Willow Glade and the shootout in Oakland. It was still so fresh, it seemed he could never forget any of it, but he knew better. Careful records were the secret to doing his job well; you can't always rely on your memory, especially when business deals are falling apart or bullets are flying.

Keeping track of all the Sheffield industries was difficult. The family owned scores of companies in a dozen different fields, from shipping and mining to logging and finance.

Take Sheffield Extraction Industries. Solomon had files on the corporate officers, the board of directors, and all key employees. The company, headquartered in the same San Francisco skyscraper as the family's umbrella corporation, pursued mining projects all over the world, everything from oil to diamonds. Solomon was expected to have more than a passing familiarity with coal mines and oil wells and open-pit copper mining, so he was prepared when Dom sent him to solve a problem.

On his computer, he clicked his way over to the organizational chart for Sheffield Extraction Industries. The company was headed by Michael Sheffield, Dom's younger son, who traveled the world, overseeing the mines. Abby's "Uncle Mike." Michael was two years younger than his brother Chris and in better shape, not so much given to gluttony and drink, but he had a weakness for exotic women. Solomon had been sent to more than one foreign locale to buy off an unhappy hooker or bust a blackmail ring. Michael never expressed remorse over these entanglements. He saw them as the cost of doing business.

Abby was listed as a "special assistant" on the organizational chart. Solomon put a question mark beside her name and a link to her personal folder. It would be a long time before she was back to work, and even longer before she'd be trusted with important tasks and data. Smart businessmen don't share secrets with drug users.

Despite what he'd told Tyrone and friends, Solomon knew the family would never give up on Abby or any other Sheffield who got in trouble with the law or suffered through an addiction or got sued. The Sheffields closed ranks around their weak, wounded and lost.

Dom gladly would've paid a fortune to get Abby loose from those drug dealers, and he'd put Tyrone and Jorge in the ground if he ever learned the details of her lost two weeks. Solomon often had to protect Dom from his own impulses. The old man wasn't beyond the occasional indulgence in vengeance.

Solomon had killed for Dom before—seven times, every one fresh in his mind. The redneck oilman who pulled a hogleg pistol out of his briefcase and tried to shoot Dom. The fat Chinaman who sent assassins after them in Hong Kong. The Seattle lawyer Solomon threw out of a high window. A crooked Teamster in Cleveland. Two mooks who tried to rob Dom on a Brooklyn street. And now Jamal. Every time, it was kill or be killed. Justifiable homicide. At least that's what Solomon told himself when he lay awake at night, the dead dancing around his bed.

Most of the time, he avoided violence. Mention of the Sheffield name was enough to open doors and close inquiries. But Solomon always stood ready to protect the family.

He had no family of his own, or none close enough to count. An aunt and some cousins back east, but he'd lost touch with them. He never knew his father, who was one of the last MIAs to vanish in Vietnam, when Solomon was a baby. He was only fourteen when his mother died in an auto accident, her car plunging into a canyon not far from the lodge.

She'd been executive assistant to Dominick Sheffield at the time, and Dom had taken her skinny, sullen son under his wing, had seen to it that Solomon was educated in business, the humanities and the special skills (martial arts, firearms, evasive driving, risk analysis, etiquette) that made him the perfect right-hand man.

Over the years, Solomon's relationship with Dom had grown into a friendship, almost a father-son connection. His privileged position often caused friction within the family. Solomon had enemies among the Sheffields, and he sometimes worried about his future. Dom was in good health now, but he wouldn't live forever. What would happen once the old man was gone? Solomon had worked his whole life to become an expert in one area—the Sheffield family and its industries. What other job, what other life, could he possibly find?

He straightened at a sound outside. A distant buzz, getting louder. A plane coming into the private airstrip. That would be Chris, arriving for his dinner with Dom.

He checked the clock and was surprised to find two hours had passed. Still, Chris was early, probably eager to start kissing his father's ass.

Solomon shut down his laptop and put it away. He stood and stretched his thick arms over his head, shifting his weight from one bare foot to the other, getting out the kinks. He poured a last cup of coffee and went to the closet for a clean suit.

Time to dress for dinner.

CHAPTER 6

●●●●●●●●●●●●●●●●●●

Solomon paused at the lodge's back deck, and used his handkerchief to clean dust off his black leather shoes. He was dressed as usual, suit and mock turtleneck, though he'd left his shoulder holster at the cabin.

Fiona opened the door and gave him a curt nod. She was frowning, but Solomon knew it wasn't aimed at him. Fiona was one servant who made no bones about who she disliked, and Chris Sheffield topped that list.

"They'd be in there by the fireplace," she said, Irish disdain in her voice. "Better hurry if you're planning to drink with them. Christopher might suck it all down before you get a sip."

Solomon grinned at her. "Just water for me. We're having Juanita's fiery enchiladas."

"This I know," Fiona said as she stepped aside. "The kitchen's been reeking of it all afternoon."

Solomon turned a corner and the great room opened before him. Dom and Chris stood by the huge river-rock fireplace that dominated the far end of the room, thirty feet away, their backs turned toward the flickering flames.

Both men had highball glasses in their hands, but there the resemblance ended. Dom was lean and tanned; Chris was fat and florid. Dom was dressed casually in khakis and a plaid shirt; Chris wore a blue Savile Row suit, crisp white shirt and striped tie, black loafers with tassels. Dom's hair swept back from his face; Chris wore his thinning brown hair combed forward in a Caesar cut. Dom's nose was an aquiline beak, but his son's upturned nose looked more like a snout with every pound he gained.

"There he is," Dom said when he spotted Solomon. "I was beginning to think we'd have to send someone to your cabin to wake you."

"I've been up a while," Solomon said as he crossed the room. "Got some work done."

Chris had a glint in his eye that Solomon didn't like. They didn't shake hands.

"I was just telling Dad, if I'd known we were inviting the hired help to dinner, I wouldn't have made Bart wait with the plane."

Dom frowned, but Solomon didn't let the rudeness faze him. He said, "Bart's got lousy table manners."

Chris laughed, an abrupt sound like the bark of a seal. "That's true. You want to know what Bart had for lunch, look at the front of his shirt."

That broke the ice a little. Dom's face relaxed, and he slipped Solomon a wink.

"Bart does a good job for us," Chris continued. "But you can't take him anywhere. His idea of a fancy meal is a burger with extra cheese. I think he spent too much time in the Third World before he came to us."

Chief of corporate security for Sheffield Enterprises for the past three years, Bart Logan was a wide-bodied forty-year-old with a military crewcut and narrow eyes and a square jaw that jutted forward like an invitation to an uppercut. He frequently traveled with Chris, who was grooming him to be his personal assistant, the way Dom had groomed Solomon. Another sign of trouble once Dom retired or died. Solomon liked Logan even less than he liked Chris.

"Speaking of cheese," Dom said, glancing at his Rolex, "I think Juanita's ready to feed us those enchiladas. You want a drink first, Solomon?"

"No, sir. I'm fine."

Chris gulped his bourbon so fast the ice rattled against his teeth. "I'll take another," he said quickly. "Carry it to the table with me."

While Chris went to the bar in the corner, Solomon and Dom walked around the free-standing fireplace. The dining room was on the other side, through a swinging door. The back of the fireplace formed one of the dining room's walls, and warmth emanated from its surface of rounded stones.

"Any news on Abby?"

"I called Willow Glade a few minutes ago," Solomon said. "They said she slept all day. She's probably got a lot of catching up to do."

Juanita came out of the kitchen, pushing a serving cart. The dishes were covered, but smelled heavenly, and Solomon inhaled deeply.

"Ah, Juanita," he said, "I hope you made a lot. I'm starving."

The cook smiled at him and brushed a strand of black hair back from her damp forehead.

"Plenty," she said. "If any is left, I'll send a dish home with you."

"Now I'm torn," he said. "Should I eat it all now, or save some for later?"

Dom chuckled. "You forget I'm helping you."

"True," Solomon said. "Then there's Chris."

Dom rolled his eyes but said nothing as his son waddled into the room. Solomon knew what he was thinking; Dom often complained about Chris being a slave to his appetites.

"Hey, Juanita," Chris said. "Damn, that smells great. Let's eat."

The mahogany table could accommodate twelve, but the place settings were grouped at one end. Dom sat at the head of the table with Solomon to his left and Chris to his right. Juanita lifted lids off chafing dishes and scooped food onto Dom's plate. Dom leaned back, giving her room, and said over her head to Solomon, "I told Chris about your difficulties in Oakland."

Solomon nodded but said nothing. He didn't discuss family matters in front of the help.

Juanita served Chris next, and he said, "More," before she even finished. By the time she turned away, his plate was heaping with chicken flautas and cheese enchiladas and rice and beans. Chris didn't wait for Solomon to get served. He dug in right away, lifting forkfuls into his mouth, breathing heavily through his piggy snout while he chewed.

After she filled Solomon's plate, Juanita rolled the cart back into the kitchen. Dom waited for the door to stop swinging before he said, "Chris is worried Abby might've revealed company secrets while she was loose on the streets."

Solomon shook his head. "The people she was with didn't even know who she was. The first time they heard the name 'Sheffield' was when I mentioned it."

"Hmm," Chris said through a mouthful. "You made a mistake there. You shouldn't have said anything about the family."

"Not much choice," Solomon said. "I was talking us out of a bad situation. I had a gun pressed to my neck at the time."

Chris gave a so-what shrug.

"I don't want this thing coming back on us," he said. "Abby works pretty closely with Michael in the mining sector. I'm sure she knows things that would help our competitors."

"Like what?" Solomon said.

Chris simply shook his head. The spicy food was making him perspire.

Dom looked from one man to the other, his brow furrowed. "What's the matter with you, Chris? You afraid to speak in front of Solomon?"

"It's not that—"

"Because you know," Dom continued, "there's no one I trust more than Solomon."

Chris frowned and sucked at a tooth.

Solomon didn't want to get caught between them. He said, "Abby wasn't talking about business. The only thing she mentioned, as I was getting her out of there, was some deal in Africa."

"Africa?" Dom said. "We don't do business in Africa. Too much instability. Every time somebody does make a success there, a petty dictator nationalizes everything and the government takes it away."

Chris stared at his plate. Solomon used the pause to take his first bite of the enchiladas. Delicious.

"What's Michael up to?" Dom asked Chris.

"You'd have to talk to him. You put him in charge of Sheffield Extraction Industries, remember? Over my objections. I've kept my nose out of their operations."

Dom silently stared at his son.

"Maybe it's nothing," Chris said. "Abby was zonked on drugs at the time, right? She was probably just raving, out of her head."

"Maybe so," Dom said, but he didn't look convinced. Solomon wasn't buying it, either. No matter what drugs Abby had pumped into her system, it wasn't likely she'd mention Africa out of the blue.

Chris used a flour tortilla to mop up the red sauce on his plate. The other two had barely made dents in the meal, but Chris already was eager for seconds. He rang for Juanita.

"Damn," he said. "That's some good chow. I'll have to be sure to tell Bart what he missed."

Dom launched into a smiling ode to the wonders of Juanita's cooking, and Solomon thought Chris looked relieved at the change of subject. He made a mental note to look into Michael's activities, to see whether the mining subsidiary was digging around in African soil.

Perhaps he'd go see Abby, as soon as she could have visitors, and ask her. Give her a chance to curse at him some more. He could sit still for that, if it meant he'd get the information.

Once she was detoxed, Abby might talk to him. Might even be grateful to him for getting her out of that Oakland flophouse.

But he wouldn't count on it.

CHAPTER 7

●●●●●●●●●●●●●●●●●●●

After the meal, the men returned to the great room and sprawled on the leather furniture under the intricate architecture of the deer-antler chandelier. The fire burned down to glowing embers. Dom had another drink and Chris had two. They talked business and family, fishing and golf, but Solomon barely listened, still caught up in his thoughts about Abby and Oakland and Jamal's exploding skull.

As the evening wore on, Chris made less sense. The drinks had gone to his head, and his round face was red, and he blustered and guffawed. Dom recognized the symptoms, and asked Solomon to drive his son to the airfield. It said something about Chris' condition that he didn't object.

Solomon went onto the front deck and breathed the cool night air and waited while Chris finished his good-byes. Whenever Chris and Dom met, it was a strange cross between friendly visit, filial duty and corporate board meeting. Solomon's ears were tired.

A canvas-topped Jeep was parked near the porch, and he strolled over and climbed behind the wheel. He started the engine, hoping the noise would draw Chris out the door.

The fat man moved slowly down the flagstone steps to the driveway. Dom watched from the deck, making sure his unsteady son managed the twenty feet to the Jeep. Solomon fought off the urge to rev the engine.

As soon as Chris was buckled in, Solomon threw the Jeep into gear and swung onto the sinuous driveway. Chris said, "Whoa," and grabbed hold of the door.

Solomon raced along the familiar road, getting the Jeep up to fifty miles per hour, though he had to cover only a mile.

"You in a hurry?" Chris shouted over the engine's roar.

"Aren't you?"

The brakes squealed as Solomon slowed for the turn to the airfield. The hangars were dark, but the landing lights along the airstrip were lit, their round white heads marching away into the distance.

A six-seat Cessna waited on the taxiway and a couple of shadowy figures loitered nearby. The Jeep's headlights washed across the men. One was Bart Logan, dressed in khaki head to toe, as if he were on a safari rather than a quick business trip to Mendocino County. The other man Solomon recognized as the pilot, a lean, leathery type who wore his plaid sleeves rolled up above his elbows.

"Finally," Logan said as he opened the car door for Chris. "We were beginning to think we'd have to bed down here for the night."

"I told you it would take hours," Chris said. "Don't act like it was a big surprise."

"You could've sent some food. We're starving."

"You'll live," Chris said. "An hour from now, we'll be back in the city."

Solomon, stepping out of the Jeep, couldn't pass up the opportunity to tweak Logan. "We had Mexican food at the lodge. Juanita's terrific enchiladas. Too bad you missed it."

Logan glowered at him. "Don't rub it in. I haven't eaten since lunch."

"Oh, stop your carping," Chris said. "Let's get this bird in the air."

The pilot went around to the far side of the Cessna and climbed into the cockpit for his last-minute checks. Logan opened the door on the near side and held it open for his weaving boss.

"Chris," Solomon called.

Chris looked back over his shoulder. "Yeah?"

"Will you talk to Michael? About what we discussed at dinner?"

"That stuff Abby said? Don't worry about it."

Chris hitched at his pants and squinted against the headlights.

"Will you talk to Michael?" Solomon repeated.

"Yeah, yeah. I'll talk to him. All right? Shit, give it a rest, Solomon."

Solomon let that float on the night air for a moment before saying, "Yes, sir."

"What are you two talking about?" Logan demanded. "Is this a security issue?"

Chris shook his head, annoyed, but Solomon said, "Might be. Abby certainly was a security risk when she was running loose in Oakland, talking to anybody who'd supply her with drugs. Why didn't your people track her down?"

Logan's eyes narrowed to slits and his heavy jaw thrust forward. "We would've, given half a chance. But we were ordered off the hunt once you took over."

Solomon tried not to let surprise show on his face. Dom hadn't mentioned that he'd waved off Logan's security people. It had been the smart thing to do; Solomon hadn't needed the interference. But still.

"We got her into rehab at Willow Glade," he said. "That's the most important thing. This stuff she mentioned just made me curious."

"I'll talk to Michael," Chris said. "If there's anything to worry about, I'll let Dad know."

Solomon wanted to say more, but he could see it would be a waste of breath. Instead, he got back in the Jeep and wheeled it around toward the lodge.

Better that he not watch Logan pack Chris' fat ass into the Cessna. Not even Solomon could keep a straight face through that.

As he drove back to the lodge, he caught a glimpse of a black-tailed deer as it bounded off the road into the trees. He slowed. Lots of deer in these woods. Last thing he needed was a buck coming through the windshield and landing in his lap.

Most of the lights had been turned out at the house. Folks tended to turn in early at Cutthroat Lodge. Surrounded by wild land and with few night-time diversions available, people shifted their rhythms to something more natural—up at first light, to bed at full dark.

Solomon parked the Jeep and killed the headlights. As he climbed out, he spotted a shadowy shape on the deck. An orange light glowed bright for a second, a mere dot of color in a field of darkness.

A cigar.

CHAPTER 8

••••••••••••••••••••

At the airstrip, Chris and Bart Logan watched the Jeep's taillights until they disappeared from sight.

"Son of a bitch," Logan snarled.

Chris laughed. "What's the matter with you?"

"I've never liked that guy. He thinks he's better than the rest of us. Always so fuckin' smart, like he knows everything you're thinking before you even finish thinking it."

Chris nodded and wiped a hand over his forehead. It was cool out on the tarmac, but he still sweated from Juanita's fiery food.

"I think it's what they call a defense mechanism. He's always on the outside, looking in, so he acts like he knows everything already."

Logan looked him up and down. "Who are you, Dr. Phil?"

Chris laughed again. Logan was always good for a laugh, even if that wasn't his intention. The security man was dead serious about everything, which made it funnier. He acted like a military officer, with the crewcut and the khaki uniforms and the stick up his ass. His head was shaved around his small, twisted ears. The strip of dark hair on top, flat as the deck of an aircraft carrier, seemed to get narrower with every trim. He was the only man Chris had ever seen who was going bald from *the sides*.

"What was that he was saying? Did Abby let the cat out of the bag?"

Chris shook his head. "She blurted something about Africa, but no details. I told them it must've been the drugs talking."

"Stupid little bitch."

"Hey," Chris said. "That's my sister's kid you're talking about."

"Sorry. I meant stupid little *rich* bitch."

"That's more like it. I told Michael he shouldn't have hired her. That kid's been nothing but trouble since she started walking."

"Then why—"

"It's a family thing, Bart. You wouldn't understand."

"I don't need to understand," Logan said. "As long as she doesn't do us any damage, flapping her lips."

"She doesn't know enough to hurt us. Besides, she's locked up in rehab now. Who's she gonna tell?"

"I don't know." Logan scratched at his jutting jaw. "Solomon seemed pretty damned interested."

"I told him it was nothing," Chris said. "He doesn't have any reason to pursue it."

"Doesn't mean he won't. You know how he is."

The pilot was settled into the cockpit, illuminated by the glow of the dashboard dials as he flipped switches and checked readings. He called, "Ready when you are."

"Give us a minute." Logan cocked his head to the side, squinting at Chris like he was peering through smoke. "You want to trust it'll go away on its own?"

"Maybe you're right," Chris said. "Solomon gets a burr up his butt about this, he'll never leave us alone."

"That's what I'm saying."

"Fuckin' Solomon," Chris muttered. "Studies my family like we're bugs in a laboratory."

Logan stared up the road where the Jeep had disappeared, chewing on his lower lip. Then he said, "The next few days are critical. We don't need Solomon poking his nose in it."

Like Chris didn't know that already. He said, "Keep an eye on him. If he starts getting close, we'll have to do something about him."

For the first time all night, Bart Logan smiled.

CHAPTER 9

•••••••••••••••••••

Dominick Sheffield drew deeply on the Cohiba, the fragrant smoke filling his mouth before he blew it toward the night sky. Ah. Doesn't get much better than this. A big meal, a few drinks, a Cuban cigar. Simple pleasures.

Solomon came up the flagstone steps and onto the wooden deck. Barely making a sound, moving with his usual grace. He was remarkably agile for a big man; Dom credited the martial arts training. A memory flashed: A TV show he'd seen once, where a kung fu master walked on delicate rice paper without leaving a trace behind. Solomon could do something like that. The man weighed two hundred and fifty pounds, but it looked as if he floated just above the ground.

"Nice night," Solomon said.

"Sure is. Come sit with me."

Dom smiled as Solomon moved upwind of the cigar and settled into one of the Adirondack chairs lined up along the deck. Solomon disapproved of his smoking. But, hell, the occasional cigar wouldn't hurt him. He'd made it to seventy-six in good health. Why quit now?

Dom took another drag and let the smoke slip away on the light breeze. He felt relaxed and happy, despite the way Chris had behaved at dinner, despite the usual business problems his son had dumped in his lap. The corporate world seemed far away from this peaceful forest.

A noise broke the silence, the drone of an airplane engine. Dom said nothing as the racket grew more intense. The engine whined, working hard, as the plane lifted off the ground. Within a few seconds, the noise faded away, leaving behind a quiet that seemed more complete than before.

Dom hated to break the silence, but Solomon patiently waited, and it was getting late.

"Interesting dinner," he said. "Chris seemed anxious."

Solomon said nothing.

"He always drinks too much when he's nervous about something. What do you suppose it is?"

"I was wondering the same thing, sir. He seemed off."

Dom puffed on the cigar, thinking. Had it been the discussion about Abby that put Chris out of sorts? Or was he already nervous when he got here? Hard to tell now, thinking back on it.

"He's got a lot on his plate right now," Dom said. "Business deals. Acquisitions. Lot of travel."

"Yes, sir."

"Listen to me. Still apologizing for my son. That's the story of our whole relationship right there. Chris acting strangely, and me trying to explain it away."

Dom couldn't make out Solomon's expression in the darkness, just his silhouette against the glint of moonlight on the glass behind him. Wouldn't have mattered if it had been broad daylight. Solomon was good at hiding what he was thinking.

"Chris told me about something I want you to handle. You know that shipping operation we've got in Alameda?"

Dom could picture the place, though he hadn't seen it in years. Creosote-coated wooden docks jutting into the gray waters of San Francisco Bay, long warehouses with barred windows, asphalt yards surrounded by chain-link fences, two towering steel cranes.

"Yes, sir," Solomon said. "Bayside Lading."

"That's the one. Chris tells me we've got a problem. Shipments going out light, goods disappearing."

"Theft?"

"Looks like it," Dom said. "Logan's people discovered the foreman is behind it. Mick Nielsen. You know him?"

"No, sir. Need me to investigate?"

"The security people already did all that. It's him all right. Chris was telling me, before dinner, that they planted bugs in a shipment of TVs before they were unloaded off a ship. Most went onto trucks to where they were supposed to go. But not all. Guess where one of them ended up."

"At Mick Nielsen's house."

"Good guess. They've got him cold. We're firing him tomorrow."

"Handing him over to the police?"

"No. We'll simply get rid of the problem."

"Yes, sir."

"Why don't you chopper down in the morning, be there when they let him go?"

"Think there'll be trouble?"

"Not really. But handle it with some delicacy, or we'll end up spending a ton on lawyers and grievance proceedings. We can't trust Logan to be diplomatic."

"Yes, sir."

Dom puffed on the cigar. He had another chore for Solomon, but it pained him to mention it.

"While you're in the city," he said finally, "there's something else I want you to do."

Solomon leaned forward.

"It's Michael's wife. I've been hearing things about her."

"Yes, sir?"

"The servants." Dom didn't need to explain. The family retainers were loyal to their households, sure, but they knew who was behind the Sheffield fortune. Their attempts to curry favor with Dom often proved invaluable.

"They tell me Grace is unhappy, and drinking heavily."

"Really?" Solomon sounded surprised. Dom knew he hated to think that anything involving the Sheffield clan could get past him.

"It's a recent development," Dom said. "Michael's been traveling a lot, and she doesn't like that. Some women don't respond well, being left alone. I'd like you to look in on her while you're down there."

"Yes, sir."

"Chris tells me that Michael's out of town at the moment, so you can get her alone, talk to her."

"Yes, sir."

"I've always liked Grace," Dom said. "Oh, not when she and Michael were first married. She was the second wife, and she's much younger than him, and that always has the potential for problems. But she won me over pretty damned quick. Smarter than hell, well-spoken. Just the kind of woman I went for when I was younger."

He thought, in fact, that Grace looked a lot like Solomon's late mother, Rose. Same pale blond hair and clear blue eyes and killer figure. He remembered the first time he'd seen Rose, more than twenty years ago now, when she'd first come to work for him, how she'd taken his breath away. He wondered if Solomon had ever seen his own mother in Grace.

Dom shook his head to clear the thoughts. If he let himself remember Rose, it wouldn't be long before he relived the night she died in a car crash, the sirens and the blood and the loss—

"Just see if you can help her," he said. "I hate to hear that my daughter-in-law is unhappy. And we sure as hell don't need Michael in the middle of another divorce."

"Yes, sir. Anything else?"

"No, that'll do it." Dom snuffed the cigar in an ashtray at his elbow, then wrestled his way out of the low chair. Solomon sprang to his feet.

"Good night, Solomon. Get some rest. You've got a long day tomorrow."

Dom felt a little unsteady as he walked the length of the deck to the French doors that led to his bedroom. He looked back before he went inside. He couldn't see Solomon's silhouette anymore, but he could feel him watching.

CHAPTER 10

•••••••••••••••••••

Robert Mboku stood at the edge of the strange forest, reveling in the camouflage of his own blackness. He blended into the night, the only possible exception the whites of his eyes, which he kept narrowed to slits. Even the machete dangling from his right hand was painted a flat black, all except the razor-sharp edge.

No one could see him, not even the unfamiliar forest animals he'd heard skittering through the underbrush as he'd made his way to the lodge. He was invisible.

Motionless, he watched the two men who sat outside the big house. He'd waited through their long meal with the other man, the fat, red-faced one Robert had secretly named the Warthog. The building's tall windows had given him a full view of the three men around the table, and of the dark-haired woman who served them. Robert's nostrils had picked up the aroma of the exotic food, which made it feel even more as if he was right in the room with them.

The big, bald man had driven the Warthog away after dinner, apparently had taken him to the airfield because Robert heard a plane fly away a short time later.

He was surprised and delighted when the silver-haired man turned off most of the lights before he came outside to smoke the cigar that Robert could smell from where he stood. The darkness was like a warm blanket, and he felt it wrap tighter around him as one light after another clicked off. Still, he'd kept to his hiding place behind the spongy trunk of a giant tree until he'd seen the big man return in the Jeep.

Once the two men were sitting on the porch, though, Robert sneaked closer, moving one step at a time, his bare feet silent on the thick carpet of the forest floor.

Now, he stood right at the edge of the clearing, not twenty meters from the men. Close enough to hear them speaking in low voices, though he couldn't make out the words. Robert didn't know much English. He spoke fluent French and several African dialects, but English sounded harsh to his ears, like someone shaking gravel in a can.

The machete weighed heavily in his hand, and he rested its sharp tip on the ground. He'd like to use the big knife. He could slip up to the porch, slash the blade across the men's necks, the way he'd done so many times before. The satisfying thunk of blade through flesh, the sudden stop as it hit bone. It had been some months since Robert had last taken a life; he missed it.

The old man would be easy. His reflexes would be slow and his dried-up old neck would snap like a chicken's. The other man looked more formidable. A man who would try to fight back. The thought of it made Robert want to smile, but he didn't expose his white teeth in the darkness.

Unfortunately, his orders were to merely watch them and report to Jean-Pierre. The Frenchman had a plan, and Robert knew it eventually would get them what they wanted. Jean-Pierre's plans always bore fruit.

The old man stubbed out his cigar, and the pair rose from their chairs. They exchanged a few more words, then the silver-haired one tottered along the porch, walking toward Robert, who remained perfectly motionless.

The bald one watched the old man, too, or so it seemed in the darkness. He stood still, his broad shoulders and round head a mass of black, like a target in a shooting gallery, facing this direction. Had he sensed Robert's presence?

No. Once the old man went inside, the big one disappeared around the corner of the building. Robert strained his ears and finally was rewarded with the crackling of twigs from the far side of the house. The big man was marching toward the dark cabins Robert had seen on his initial reconnaissance.

Everyone calling it a night. It was time Robert did the same. He slipped away through the trees.

The forest was different from the tangled jungles of his youth. The trees were so tall they blotted out the stars. Apparently, they blocked out the sun, too, because there was little underbrush growing around them. The forest floor was thick with fallen leaves and prickly needles.

Soon, Robert found the game trail he'd used earlier to approach the house. He padded along it, confident now that he wouldn't stumble over something in the dark or smack face-first into a tree. Making good time.

The trail dipped, going down the steep hill he'd climbed on his way into these woods. Almost back to the highway now, where Jean-Pierre waited.

Robert struggled against gravity as he picked his way down the hillside. He leaned backward, and fought the urge to run. Took his time, silently putting one bare foot in front of the other.

Moonlight spilled into the gap between the trees and onto the paved road. Jean-Pierre's rented truck was parked along the shoulder, its silver paint glinting. Robert approached the passenger side and snatched open the door.

"*Merde!*"

Robert smiled at his trick, surprising his boss this way.

"Very funny," Jean-Pierre said in French. "You nearly made me piss myself."

Robert laughed, a silent exhalation.

"I could've shot you!" Jean-Pierre said.

Robert climbed into the truck, his lithe body barely making a dent in the seat cushion, and gave his report: "No sign of the one we're seeking. A fat man arrived on a plane and ate dinner with the old man and a big bodyguard. They talked, then the fat one flew away."

"No Michael?" Jean-Pierre said. "Perhaps we missed him in the city. We'll go back there in the morning. But first we must return to that shithole motel. I'm exhausted."

Robert slipped the machete into the gap between the seat and the door. He crossed his arms over his chest.

Jean-Pierre faced forward, his beak of a nose silhouetted against the night beyond, his scraggly beard like white fuzz in the moonlight. He turned the key and the truck's engine leapt to life.

"For Christ's sake, Robert," he said, pronouncing the name the French way, Ro-*bair*. "Would you put your clothes on? I can't be seen driving around with a naked man. What if we encounter a policeman? What if we—"

He kept talking, but Robert stopped listening. He smiled at the dark forest as the truck lumbered onto the highway.

He felt they would come back here. Soon.

CHAPTER 11

• • • • • • • • • • • • • • • • • • •

Michael Sheffield's hangover was easing. Every day he spent in this dusty outpost, he woke with the most excruciating hangovers, the only available remedy liberal application of Bloody Marys.

His host, General Erasmus Goma, Supreme Military Commander of the Republic of Niger, insisted every night on toasting everybody and everything. Some nights, they got all the way down to favorite cows Goma remembered from his youth before the fat general toppled from his chair.

Diplomacy required that Michael match the general drink for drink, and manhood required, apparently, that the drinks be shots of Chivas Regal. Nothing else would do. Michael was more of a wine man; that was one reason he loved Northern California. But Goma had declared, "Wine is for women! Men drink whiskey!" End of discussion.

A couple of Bloody Marys the next morning, and Michael was ready to go again. He was feeling better already.

The night before, he'd been too drunk to fully enjoy the gifts General Goma had left in his room. One woman was wide-hipped and full-breasted and as coal-black as Goma himself. The other was a slender Asian girl who Michael suspected had been purchased from the slave trade that still operated in this part of the world. Both exquisite, and they proved eager companions. When Michael left the bedroom this morning, the women were snuggled together like puppies under a red satin sheet. He looked forward to joining them there shortly, as soon as the tribal drums in his head abated.

He sat on a balcony that jutted from the second floor of Goma's whitewashed ranch house, a canvas umbrella angled to keep the glaring sun off him. A nervous servant stood by the arched door, ready to fetch another Bloody Mary if Michael gave him the nod. The view from the balcony was of a vast plain, gold and brown, dotted with gnarly trees and a few bony cows. Dust hung in the air, a yellow smudge on the horizon, but the sky above was a bright blue that was beginning to fade with the heat of the day.

Michael's phone chirped discreetly in the pocket of his borrowed bathrobe. It amazed him that he could get cell service out here, so far from the capital. He reminded himself to send a commendatory memo to the technical services department, which supplied his phones and other electronic gear. Those fucking nerds did a top-notch job.

"Hello?"

"It's Chris. Can you hear me?"

The reception was staticky, but Michael could make him out.

"Yeah, Chris. What are you doing up? It's what, one o'clock in the morning there? Two?"

"Who (*crackle*) a shit? (*snap, crackle*) talked to Dad. He's asking about (*pop*)."

"You're breaking up, Chris. Say that again."

"Dad knows something's up."

That came through loud and clear. Michael felt a stab of pain at his temple. Son of Hangover.

"How did that happen?"

"Abby. On her way to rehab, our niece mouthed off about Africa. No specifics. But Solomon, naturally (*crackle*) to Dad. Now Dad wants to know what you've been up to."

"Shit."

"That's right, shit. You'd better get back home."

Michael rose from the umbrella table and paced around the balcony. The nervous servant danced in place, not sure what to do. Michael went past him, into the house, the phone at his ear.

"Can't you handle this, Chris? Stall 'em. It'll be over by Sunday night. We need me to stay over here, make sure everything goes smoothly."

"Stall Solomon? How would you suggest I (*crackle*) that?"

"Give him something else to keep him busy. Send him out of town or something."

"And Dad?"

Michael stopped in the shadowy corridor. Maybe Chris was right. Michael was better at smooth talk and stonewalling, especially with Dom.

Home would be safer, too. It had occurred to him the night before, while Goma was bellowing drunkenly about the swift victory to come, that it might actually be dangerous for a Sheffield here in Niger, once the shit hit the fan. What safer place than the far side of the world? What better alibi?

"All right, Chris. I'll arrange a flight home later today. But I'll have to talk to Goma first. Might be Tuesday morning before I get there."

"Fine. (*crackle*) as possible."

Michael threw open the bedroom door. The girls were awake, and the black one sat up. The satin sheet poured off her bosom like red wine.

He smiled at the women. They smiled back.

"Gotta go, Chris. Before I head home, I've got a couple of things to do."

CHAPTER 12

•••••••••••••••••••

Solomon rose early Monday morning, so he'd have time to run three miles along the forest trails before he showered and dressed. He took the trails at a fast clip, pushing himself, until he reached the last half-mile, the broad path through the redwoods that stood between the lodge and the airstrip. He always ended his runs here, slowing to a walk, cooling down in the shade, the redwood grove as quiet as a cathedral.

Later, during the cramped helicopter ride to San Francisco, he was glad he'd made time to exercise. His muscles felt warm and taut under his skin.

The Golden Gate Bridge still was shrouded in fog, and it looked as if a blanket of cotton had unrolled from the ocean, covering the western half of the city. The downtown office spires glinted in sunshine as the helicopter came in low over the bay.

Solomon leaned over to watch the Embarcadero flit past. He still marveled at how this section of the city had changed since the first time he'd seen it, when he was just a kid. Before the Loma Prieta earthquake, an elevated freeway had wrapped around the waterfront, dumping tourists at Pier 39 and Fisherman's Wharf. But the damaged roadway was razed after the quake, and city officials had seen an opportunity. In place of the double-decker highway, they built a broad boulevard with wide sidewalks and rows of palm trees. The old Ferry Building was renovated into a fresh-food market full of trendy shops and little cafes. Now, the area was so scenic, with its spacious plazas and its views of the Bay Bridge, it was featured in romantic television commercials.

The Sheffields owned real estate in this part of the city, and Solomon felt sure Dom had helped engineer the facelift to increase his property values. It certainly had improved the surroundings for employees at the headquarters of Sheffield Enterprises, which was housed on three upper floors of the easternmost of Embarcadero Center's office towers. The bay views from the executive offices were much better without the ugly concrete freeway, and the plazas, with their fountains and sculptures, were ideal for al fresco lunches.

A company car picked Solomon up at the family helipad north of San Francisco International Airport, and fought its way into the city on Highway 101. When they got within a few blocks of Embarcadero Center, he told the driver to let him out. He felt like walking in the sunshine along the waterfront.

The breeze coming off the bay kept it from being too hot, and wraparound sunglasses diminished the glare off the choppy water. Seagulls hovered and shrieked, and antique streetcars clanged as they hummed along tracks nearby. A day like this made Solomon want to forget his duties. Made him want to slip out of his jacket and stretch out on a bench and stare across the water at the giant cranes replacing the superstructure at the far end of the Bay Bridge. Watch the sailboats flit past. Doze a little.

He checked his watch. His 11 a.m. appointment with Bart Logan and Mick Nielsen was only ten minutes from now. He picked up his pace.

Solomon shifted his brushed-aluminum briefcase to his other hand. It held his laptop and his shaving kit and assorted documents and a paperback spy novel to read during lulls. On overnight trips, the five-inch-thick briefcase doubled as suitcase. In a pinch, it made a dandy weapon.

One of the benefits of private aircraft—no worries about metal detectors or airport security. No one to search the briefcase or question the big pistol he carried in his shoulder rig. He didn't expect to need the gun today, but he didn't feel complete without it. Solomon hurried across a plaza with a huge sculpture in its center. The sculpture was constructed of giant concrete tubes, jumbled into a heap, and they always made him think of a pile left behind by a dog.

By the time he reached the cool confines of Embarcadero Center, a light sweat had broken out on his freshly shaved scalp. He used his handkerchief to pat it away, then folded the handkerchief neatly and put it back in his pocket.

Embarcadero Center is a four-block-long, two-story mall with four office towers on top of it. Solomon passed a women's wear shop, a shoe store and a crowded café before he reached the elevators that would take him skyward to Sheffield Enterprises.

The elevator was crowded. Solomon stood near the back, trying not to loom over his fellow passengers. He took up a lot of room in such close quarters, and people did their best not to press against his bulk. The elevator emptied as it climbed, until only a few passengers were left. The door opened onto the thirtieth floor, and Solomon stepped out into the tidy lobby of Sheffield Enterprises.

Three well-dressed receptionists sat behind a maplewood counter, chattering into headsets. The company's ornate "S" logo filled the powder-blue wall behind them. The carpet was the same color, so plush it seemed to absorb all sound.

A glass security door to the left led into the corporate offices. A gray-uniformed guard—one of Bart Logan's men—sat in a chair beside the door, ready to pounce on intruders. Solomon gave him a wink. The guard glared at him.

The guard's outstretched legs were in front of the door. He made no move to get out of the way. Solomon kept his face expressionless as he stepped around the guard's feet, but he made a mental note of the man's name badge. Davis. He'd see to him later. A word in Dom's ear.

The corridors beyond the reception area were hushed and dimly lit. Most of the inner office doors were closed, concealing the manic activity that kept a billion-dollar corporate umbrella standing up to the gales of commerce. The top executives occupied this floor, and Solomon found it interesting that the security chief had managed to land space at one end of the long corridor that bisected the floor. Chris definitely was grooming Logan for bigger things.

Solomon checked his watch as he reached Logan's office. Right on time. He rapped twice on the door, opened it and went inside.

Logan sat behind his desk, his back to the window, which looked out at another sunlit skyscraper. The shaved areas around his ears glinted, made it look like his head had shiny fenders. Logan was dressed in his usual khaki, and he leaned back in his swivel chair, frowning.

Two uniformed guards stood near the door, displaying perfect posture, trying to look bigger than they were. Solomon immediately could see why. The guest who occupied the chair across from Logan was a huge man, and he looked angry as hell.

Mick Nielsen had orange hair and a freckled face that currently glowed bright red. He'd put on a brown sports coat for his visit to corporate headquarters, and it stretched tight across massive shoulders. He got to his feet as Solomon entered the room. It was rare that Solomon found himself looking up at anyone. Nielsen was at least six-and-a-half feet tall, maybe two hundred and eighty pounds. Forty years old, developing a roll of fat around his midsection, but he still had the bulky muscles of the longshoreman he once had been. No wonder the guards looked ready to piss themselves.

Logan made a point of looking at his watch, but Solomon knew he wasn't late. If they'd had an uncomfortable few minutes, waiting for him, it was their own damned fault.

"Finally!" Nielsen blurted. "Are you the one who can tell me what this is about?"

Solomon nodded and waved the big man back into his seat. Better that he be sitting when he got the bad news. Solomon took the other guest chair, casually turning it before he sat so that he was facing Nielsen. Six feet of space between them, which wasn't enough if the redhead went crazy, but it would have to do.

"Mr. Nielsen," Solomon said. "We asked you to come here today so we could inform you that your services are no longer needed by Sheffield Enterprises."

Nielsen flushed brighter. "You're shittin' me."

"Not at all." Solomon kept his voice low and calm. "We have evidence of thefts from Bayside Lading. We know you're behind them. Rather than take the matter to the police, we're terminating your employment, effective immediately."

Nielsen leaped to his feet, his fists clenched. "You're sayin' I'm a *thief*?"

"That's exactly what I'm saying."

The redhead vibrated with anger. Solomon thought of a tuning fork.

"You got any proof?"

Solomon turned to Logan, who looked pale behind his desk. If he leaned any farther back in his chair, he'd topple over.

"You want to explain it?"

Logan cleared his throat and said, "You've got the proof right in your own house."

Nielsen's eyes narrowed. "The hell are you talking about?"

"You have a new plasma TV?" Logan said, wincing as the words leaked out of his mouth. "Forty-two-inch screen?"

"Yeah? So?"

"It came from a shipment that passed through Bayside Lading. Several TVs went missing from that shipment, as we had expected."

"I don't know anything about that," Nielsen snapped. "You can't prove that my TV—"

"We put tracking devices on those televisions while they were still aboard ship," Logan said. "All four-hundred of them. Cost a fortune, but it paid off. We tracked the TVs as they left the warehouse. One of them went to your place."

Solomon kept his eyes on Nielsen, measuring the looming man, calculating whether his rage would overcome his good sense.

"You think you can fire me just because—"

"That's right," Solomon interrupted. "You serve at the pleasure of the corporate officers. They are not pleased."

"You son of a bitch."

"Steady, now." Solomon casually crossed his legs and sat back. "This is business. Treat it like a businessman. You'd rather walk out of here unemployed than be taken in handcuffs to the city jail."

Nielsen hesitated, but he was still flushed and shaky, barely under control.

"Hand over your employee ID card and walk away," Solomon said. "Don't go back to Bayside Lading for any reason. This is over. Understand?"

"What about my paycheck? I should get severance pay."

"No. You can keep the TV. But that's it."

Mick Nielsen clearly couldn't stand it anymore. His tightly strung body demanded that he take some kind of action. His hands came up on their own accord, clutching and trembling, and he lunged at Solomon.

Solomon uncrossed his legs and planted a foot squarely in his midsection. Nielsen said, "Oof!" and staggered backward a couple of steps.

Solomon sprang to his feet just as Nielsen swung a haymaker. Solomon stepped inside the punch and blocked it with his forearm, windmilling his arm so that it came up under Nielsen's elbow. The redhead's fist was caught in Solomon's armpit, and his thick arm bent backward at the elbow. He went up on his toes, grunting at the pain.

Using the heel of his hand, Solomon popped him hard, just above the eyebrows. Nielsen's head snapped back and his eyes rattled around in their sockets. Solomon released him, and he staggered in a circle like a stunned ox.

Out of the corner of his eye, Solomon saw that Logan had pulled a pistol from his desk. The guards by the door were going for their guns, too.

"Stop," Solomon commanded. Everybody froze. "No shooting. We want this handled quietly."

Logan hesitated, then dropped the pistol back into his desk drawer. He slid the drawer closed. His men holstered their weapons as well.

Solomon stood still, waiting for Nielsen to focus. It took a few seconds.

"You," Nielsen said, but he didn't seem capable of completing the threat. Solomon imagined that his brain was still sloshing around inside his head.

"Try it again," Solomon said, "and we no longer have an agreement. We can have the police here in five minutes. Get out, and I mean right now, and we let you walk away."

It took one long, tense minute for Nielsen to make up his mind. He stood clutching his elbow, looking from Solomon to Logan and back again. Finally, he reached into his shirt pocket and pulled out his laminated ID tag and threw it onto the desk.

"There. I hope you fuckin' choke on it."

He turned toward the door. The guards edged away.

Solomon straightened his lapels. As he expected, Nielsen couldn't go without a final word. He turned when he reached the door.

"Fuck you," he snarled. "All of you."

Solomon said nothing. He and Nielsen locked eyes.

"If I ever see you again," Nielsen said, "you're a dead man."

Then he snatched open the door and stalked away.

"Follow him," Solomon said to the guards, "but keep your distance. Make sure he leaves the building."

Once they were out the door, Solomon turned to Logan, who looked sweaty and pale.

"Well," Solomon said. "That went okay."

"You think so?" Logan scowled. "Didn't you hear that man threaten to kill you just now?"

"Nothing I haven't heard before."

CHAPTER 13

•••••••••••••••••••••

Solomon instructed Bart Logan to have all the locks changed at Bayside Lading, just in case, then he left the security chief's office. No sign of Mick Nielsen or the guards in the corridor. Solomon took a deep breath, glad to have the firing behind him.

The main hall stretched all the way to the offices of Chris and Michael Sheffield, who, naturally, held the suites with the best views of the bay. A door opened at the far end, and four black men in suits emerged from Chris' office.

Chris shook hands with the tallest of them, a long-faced man who wore a green-white-and-red sash diagonally over his double-breasted suit. Some sort of dignitary, but Solomon didn't recognize him or the others.

Big shots regularly trooped through these halls. Government officials, company presidents, Washington lobbyists and high-priced attorneys, all coming to pay obeisance to the Sheffields, trying to curry favor or earn contracts. But that sash made Solomon think the black men were foreigners, perhaps Africans. And coming so soon after Abby mentioned a deal in Africa.

The tall man with the sash led the way toward Solomon. Two of the others, whip-thin men with ebony skin, fell into step behind him. Errand boys.

The fourth man interested Solomon most. He was well-built, maybe six feet tall, and he had large eyes and graying hair clipped close to his head. He wore an olive-green suit, cut so that most people wouldn't notice he wore a shoulder holster. His eyes fixed on Solomon as he shepherded the tall man and the two flunkies along the corridor. They turned a corner toward the reception area, and the bodyguard gave Solomon a look of wary recognition before he disappeared around the corner, too.

Chris still stood in his office doorway. His piggy face reddened when he spotted Solomon looking his way. He ducked back inside and shut his door.

Solomon hurried along the hall and around the corner to reception, trying to catch up with the delegation, but they'd gotten lucky with the elevators and were gone. He filed Chris' odd behavior away in his brain. Maybe he'd mention it to Dom when he got back to Cutthroat.

The surly guard still sat in his chair beside the door. Solomon ignored him, turning to the receptionists, asking one of them to summon him a car. He needed to grab a quick lunch, then get across town to his next stop. Get that chore accomplished, so he could go home.

He allowed himself a frown. He wasn't looking forward to seeing Grace.

CHAPTER 14

 • • • • • • • • • • • • • • • • • • •

Michael and Grace Sheffield lived in a three-
story, Mediterranean-style mansion in the
exclusive neighborhood of Sea Cliff, which perches atop the
San Francisco peninsula like a parrot on the shoulder of a pirate.
Sea Cliff was only six miles from corporate headquarters, but it
seemed farther because the limousine driver kept getting caught in
traffic jams on the congested streets. The swarthy driver was new,
and he showed no interest in chatting, which suited Solomon.

Unlike most of San Francisco, where homes and apartment
buildings crowd together, sharing walls, the mansions of Sea Cliff
are separated by driveways or narrow strips of lawn that give the
illusion of space. A smooth concrete driveway climbed the slope
between Michael's stucco house and the Italianate monster next
door. The bottom of the limo scraped as it lumbered into the narrow space.

"Wait here," Solomon said as he climbed out of the
back seat. The chauffeur touched the bill of his black cap in
acknowledgment.

Flagstones set into the tidy lawn formed an ellipsis that reached
to the front door. Solomon crossed the lawn, climbed the narrow
stoop and rang the bell. The door was dark, oily wood, banded
with iron, looked as if it might've come from an old church. He
expected a haunted-house squeal when it moved on its hinges, but

it was absolutely silent when it opened. Solomon found himself looking down on a five-foot-tall albino dressed in black.

"Yes? May I help you?"

Solomon didn't recognize the butler; he must be a recent hire. The man blinked his white eyelashes at Solomon and glared, as if daring the larger man to stare at his pink skin and rabbit-like eyes.

"Solomon Gage to see Mrs. Sheffield."

The white-haired man looked Solomon over. "Do you have an appointment?"

"Do I need one?"

The butler bristled. Solomon added, "I work for Dominick Sheffield."

"Ah." The albino stepped out of the way and bowed Solomon into the house. He might be new, but he knew who Dom was.

"I'll see if Mrs. Sheffield can have visitors now. Earlier, she was feeling, um, indisposed."

He pronounced the word as if it were a new acquisition. Solomon guessed that Grace Sheffield was often "indisposed" lately.

The butler hurried away. Solomon waited in the foyer. The house, what he could see of it, looked the same as the last time he'd visited here with Dom, with one exception. On the right-hand wall hung three large wooden masks. They were shaped like footballs, pointy on the ends, with narrow slits for eyes and protruding round mouths.

"Solomon Gage, as I live and breathe."

He turned to find Grace coming down a corridor from the back of the house. She wore a pale blue caftan that dusted the floor as she floated toward him, and she carried a cigarette in one hand and a martini glass in the other. Solomon resisted the urge to look at his wristwatch.

Her silky blond hair was pulled back from her face and twisted into a knot behind her head. She'd pierced the knot with a decorative chopstick to keep it in place.

Grace Sheffield always reminded Solomon of the movie stars favored by Alfred Hitchcock: Kim Novak. Janet Leigh. Grace Kelly. Blond hair, perfect skin, trim figures. Plus, she had a Southern accent like warm molasses. A beautiful lady, trapped in a marriage with a womanizing rat.

"Hello, Grace. How are you?"

"Just peachy, sugar. If I were any better, they'd have to bottle me and sell me."

She took a deep drag off the cigarette and blew the smoke toward the high ceiling. "You caught me in my housedress. I haven't even made up my face today."

"You always look beautiful, Grace."

She batted her eyelashes at him. "Why, thank you, Solomon. Bless your heart. You always know the right thing to say. Dom has trained you well."

He let that go, pointing instead at the masks on the wall. "These are new."

Grace made a face. "God, they're horrid, aren't they? Michael picked them up in his travels, and insisted on hanging them there. I think he's trying to scare away visitors."

"Are they African?"

"That's what he told me. From Niger."

She pronounced the name of the country the French way, "Ny-zheer," with the emphasis on the second syllable. Solomon tried to picture a map of Africa. He thought Niger was a Saharan country, north of Nigeria and south of Libya and Algeria, but he couldn't swear to it.

"Michael's been in Africa?"

Grace took a last deep drag on her cigarette, then tossed it onto the marble floor.

"Step on that for me, will you, sugar? I'm barefoot."

She must be drunker than he'd thought. He bent over and picked up the burning butt and carried it across the room to an ashtray that sat on a small table.

"Oh, I didn't mean for you to do that," she said. "Stomping on it would've been fine."

"Might damage the finish on the floor."

"Like I give a shit, pardon my French. I'm tired of this house. It's like living in a museum. I'm alone here most of the time, except for the servants. And these old paintings and statues and shit that Michael buys, all of 'em staring at me."

She knocked back the last of her drink. Solomon took the glass from her hand before she could throw it to the floor, too.

"Thank you," she said, leaning into him. "You are a gentleman. Perhaps you'd like a drink?"

"Maybe some coffee."

She gave him a little pout to show he was no fun, then smiled and said, "Come on back. I'll have Charles bring you some."

Solomon followed her toward the rear of the big house, trying not to stare at the swing of her hips under the caftan.

"Charles is the new butler?"

"I hired him last week, after Michael went out of town. I can't wait for him to get back and find that I've hired a gay albino midget. That oughta put a twist in his shorts."

Solomon hoped Charles was out of earshot.

"Charles!" Grace called. "Where are you, darling? *Charles*!"

The butler scurried through a swinging door. He was scowling, but Solomon didn't think he'd heard Grace's blunt description. More like something important had been interrupted. What did the albino have going in the kitchen?

"Yes?"

"Solomon would like some coffee. Would you bring it back to the sunroom? And fix me another drink, sugar."

The butler gave her a quick nod and ducked back through the swinging door. Grace waited until the door was closed before loosing a musical laugh and saying, "Oh, yes, Michael's going to *love* that boy."

Solomon followed her into the sunroom. The back wall was mostly glass, offering a prime view of the Golden Gate Bridge and the dark, choppy water where ocean meets bay. A blanket of fog still hid the tops of the bridge's orange towers. They looked like ladders to nowhere.

As if to combat the gloom outside, the room was furnished with rattan lounges with bright tropical cushions. Grace curled up on one, tucking her bare feet under her. Solomon sat across from her, gently lowering his big body onto the creaking chair.

"When does Michael get back?"

"Tomorrow," she said. "I've got a big ole surprise to welcome him home."

"The butler?"

"Much bigger than that." She smiled broadly, but her blue eyes looked cold. "That son of a bitch is in for a huge surprise."

"What is it, Grace? What's going on?"

"Michael's finally going to get what's coming to him."

Solomon didn't like the sound of that. "What do you mean?"

"As soon as his feet touch American soil, my husband will be greeted by a lawyer, handing him a summons."

Uh-oh. He said nothing, waiting.

"I'm divorcing him, Solomon. I've had enough of his shit."

"Aw, Grace, you don't—"

"Don't try to talk me out of it. I know where your loyalties lie. You and the rest of the family retainers. You'd say anything to keep me from breaking up my unhappy home."

The butler opened the sunroom door and came inside. He carried a tray with a steaming mug of coffee, sugar bowl and creamer, and a new martini.

"That was quick," Solomon said, but the butler didn't even look over at him. He set the tray on the coffee table and hustled from the room before they could thank him.

Solomon cocked an eyebrow.

"He's a brusque little shit, isn't he?" she said, sounding delighted.

"Fast with a cup of coffee, though."

"You'd better taste it. It's probably been sitting on a burner for hours."

He took a sip. She was right; the coffee tasted scorched.

"How is it?"

"Hot." He set the cup down. "Talk to me, Grace. Surely there's some other way. Counseling, or a trial separation or—"

"Hah! We've been trying separation for years now. Michael's always traveling on business, leaving me here, rattling around this big ole house, bored out of my skull. You and I both know about his 'business' overseas. Just an excuse for whoring around."

Solomon tried hard to keep his expression blank.

"You know it's true," she said. "Hell, the whole family knows it. The man's never been able to keep his peter in his pants."

She lifted the drink and took a healthy gulp without the slightest wince or shiver. Like she'd been getting a lot of practice.

"He comes back from these trips, and he brings me gifts and takes me out to dinner and tries to make himself feel better. It's all guilt. It was the same way when we first met, when *I* was the other woman. I should've known better. Once a hound, always a hound."

She took another big swallow. A little of the drink sloshed out and she steadied the glass, then slowly licked the spill off the back of her hand. Her eyes were on Solomon, watching his reaction. He could feel himself blush.

"But Grace, if you've known all along about this behavior, why have you waited until now to file for divorce? What's changed?"

"Africa, that's what. He's been spending a lot of time over there, and you know he's doing the same things he always does. Whores. You know how many people over there have AIDS?"

Solomon gave her a nod, conceding the point.

"How about if I speak to Dom about this?" he said. "He could talk to Michael, make him straighten up."

She shook her head boozily, and said, "It's too late, Solomon. I've set it in motion. I've got an attorney and she wants nothing more than to kick the Sheffield family's collective ass."

"I'm sure that's not necessary, Grace. If there's no chance of reconciliation—"

"There's not," she snapped.

"Then I'm sure we could work out a settlement. Dom has always liked you, and he can be very generous."

She shook her golden head. "Not good enough. I want to hurt Michael, humiliate him. Exactly the way he's made me suffer."

"But—"

"I'm not settling for pocket change, either. I know what kind of settlement they'd offer. I want more than that. I want it all."

"You can't win, Grace. The Sheffields have more lawyers than you can ever hire. They'll outnumber you. They'll drag it through the courts so slowly, you'll be old and gray before you ever see a dime."

"Let 'em try it. I trust my lawyer. She's a spitfire. She wants to go after the whole family, not just Michael."

Solomon didn't like the sound of that.

"This lawyer, what's her name?"

Grace narrowed her eyes. "What? You're gonna try to buy her off? The way the Sheffields always do?"

"No, I—"

"Go ahead and try it. See how far you get. I tell you, this lawyer's got what it takes. She'll bring the whole family down."

Solomon sighed. This day was going right down the crapper. No chance he'd sleep in his own bed tonight. He'd be stuck in San Francisco, chasing lawyers and conferring with the Sheffield brothers and trying to salvage this situation.

"Call her," Grace said. "Her name's Lucinda Cruz. She'll kick your ass, too."

Solomon took a pad out of his pocket and wrote down the name. "Here in the city?"

Grace nodded, and drained the last of her drink. She looked down into the glass, as if it had disappointed her.

"Charles!"

"Grace, I really don't think you need another—"

"Shut up, sugar. Don't tell me what I need."

Solomon clamped his lips shut.

"Now don't go getting all frowny," she said. "We're havin' a party. You should be happy. Nothing you like better than having a bunch of work to do for Dom. My attorney's about to send the whole family scurrying around, trying to protect its many, many secrets. Ought to keep you busy for weeks to come."

Months, Solomon thought, maybe years.

Grace shouted for the butler again, to no avail.

"I'll find him," Solomon said, getting to his feet. "I've got to go anyway."

Grace looked at him through her eyelashes, smiling, flirty. "Now don't go running off, sugar. I've got *plans* for the day ahead. Big ole boy like you. We could have a good time."

She was so drunk. He wondered whether he should have the servants put her to bed. Whether she'd let them.

"I'm sorry about this, Grace," he said. "I wish there were some answer other than divorce."

"Oh, don't be sorry, Solomon. I'm a big girl. I knew what I was getting into, marrying someone like Michael. I made that age-old mistake. I thought I could change him. You can't change a man like that. You can only make him pay."

"I'll send the butler."

Solomon looked back as he went through the sunroom door. Grace still sat curled up in the chair, staring out at the fog-shrouded bridge. Her eyes had filled with tears.

He found the albino in the kitchen, sitting on a stool, his slippered feet propped on a rung. He had the Chronicle spread before him, studying the want ads. An Asian cook busied herself at the stove at the far end of the room. Solomon caught the butler's attention and jerked a thumb toward the front of the house. The little man jumped down from the stool and followed him to the foyer.

Solomon reached into his pocket and pulled out a sheaf of hundred-dollar bills. He handed five of them to the butler, who hesitated only a second before taking the money and folding it into his pocket.

"Look after her," Solomon said. "See if you can get her to go to bed, and sleep it off. And stop feeding her booze in the middle of the day."

"She insists—"

"Water 'em down, at least. Give her a fighting chance."

Charles pursed his lips and nodded.

"I'll be in touch," Solomon said. "She's talking divorce. It's about to get real weird around here."

Charles arched his thin eyebrows. "As if this household could get any stranger."

"Trust me. This is only the beginning."

CHAPTER 15

•••••••••••••••••••••

Bart Logan watched from the passenger seat of the anonymous gray Ford as Solomon Gage strode across Michael Sheffield's manicured lawn toward the waiting limo. Solomon was scowling, his eyebrows nearly touching.

"Looks like he got some bad news," Bart said to Lou Velacci, who slumped behind the wheel, filling the Ford with his cigarette breath.

"Maybe he was hittin' on the wife," Velacci said. "She looks like the type who'd turn a man down and make it hurt."

Bart shook his head. Velacci didn't know shit.

"Just because that's what you would do, doesn't mean Solomon would. Never cross his mind to bed one of the family members. He's too loyal. He's like a fuckin' St. Bernard."

"I thought those were the dogs rescued people in the snow," Velacci said. "With the booze."

"Never mind. Just wait until that limo pulls out, then follow them."

"You got it."

Velacci straightened in his seat. He was a fat man, and his nylon windbreaker made whooshing noises when he moved, like it was whispering. He reached for the ignition.

"Not yet, numbskull," Bart said. "Wait 'til they're under way. They'll hear the car cranking up."

"They ain't gonna hear nothing. That limo's soundproof. And they're facing the other way."

"Trust me. That son of a bitch is on full alert all the time."

As the limo pulled away, Velacci started the Ford and eased away from the curb. The limo turned a corner up ahead, looked to be heading out of Sea Cliff. The windows were darkened, but Bart could make out the silhouette of Solomon's big head through the rear window.

"Looks like he's talking on the phone," Velacci said.

"Probably calling Dom. Reporting in."

"That why you hate this guy so much? Because he's in tight with the old man?"

Bart ignored the question, too busy thinking about what Solomon might've been doing at Michael's house while Michael was out of the country, nailing down the final details on the Africa project.

Bart had hustled over to Sea Cliff after getting a call from the taciturn chauffeur he'd recently put on the payroll. He'd told the driver to report on Solomon's movements, and now he was glad he had. As soon as Bart heard Solomon had gone to Michael's house, he knew something was up.

The limo turned onto California Street, headed east. Bart tensed as Velacci ran a yellow light to keep it in sight. Somebody honked behind them.

"Think you could tail them without getting us killed?"

"Take it easy," Velacci said. "People here drive like a bunch of pansies. Waiting on the yellow and stopping for pedestrians and using their blinkers. Shit. They wouldn't last a week back home."

"Home" was New York City, and Velacci never let anybody forget it. Always talking about how things were better there, always going on about how New Yorkers embraced life and lived it to the fullest. The fat wop was a pain in the ass.

"Yeah, yeah," Bart said. "Only people in the Big Apple know how to drive. Funny how the rest of the world seems to get from place to place, in cars, when they don't know how to do it."

"I'm just sayin'. You gotta relax. Somebody honks, it don't mean you're in danger. In New York, we honk at each other, it's a simple gesture. Like waving."

"Or flipping the bird."

"Exactly."

"I'm trying to think here," Bart said. "Can you drive without yakking?"

"Sure, sure. Shit, take it easy."

Easy for Lou Velacci to say. He didn't know about Niger. Bart had shepherded this deal ever since he went to work for Sheffield Enterprises. Three years of cultivating contacts and scheming with General Goma and kissing Sheffield ass, just to get to this point, where the deal was about to go down. Bart was in for a big slice of the pie. He'd get his share, quit this fucking job and take a permanent vacation. One that didn't involve following assholes like Solomon Gage.

"They're turning," Velacci said.

"I see that."

Velacci goosed the accelerator. The Ford shot forward.

"Not so close," Bart said. "Jesus. He's going to spot us."

"You want to drive?"

"No, I want you to do it the right fucking way."

Bart sighed and leaned his head back. Closed his eyes. He ran through a mental checklist, looking for holes or leaks or hazards, anything that might jeopardize his big payday.

For the Sheffield brothers, the Africa deal was about more than money, of course. Sew up a market, and you play from a position of strength. But Bart didn't give a shit about all that. He wanted the money. Let the power brokers and influence peddlers fight it out among themselves. Bart would be on a beach somewhere, sipping a tall drink and counting his dough.

Still time for it to go wrong. Any overlooked detail could derail the whole operation. Look what happened with Abby Maynes and her big mouth. Fucking druggie. She'd nearly blown the whole deal out the water. Still could, for that matter, since she got Solomon interested.

Bart wondered what she was telling the shrinks at the rehab clinic. What if she left fingerprints all over that crack house in Oakland? Last thing they wanted right now was for cops to come asking questions. That would get Dom fired up, and he might come down to the city and make a lot of noise, as only the old man could, and ruin everything.

Just a few more days, that's all they needed. They had to keep the old man in the dark. If that meant taking somebody out, then so be it.

Killing Solomon wouldn't be easy. Jesus, look at what he did to that giant Mick Nielsen, faster than a blink. But if Solomon got in the way, Bart wouldn't hesitate to remove him.

The Ford slowed, and he opened his eyes. The limo had stopped at a red light, two cars ahead. Bart saw that they'd climbed into Pacific Heights.

"I know where he's going," he said.

"Yeah?"

"The company owns an apartment building on Sacramento Street, near Lafayette Park. We keep a place on the ground floor and rent out the rest. Dom used to live there before he moved up to Cutthroat. Solomon stays there when he's in town."

"Why's he goin' there?"

"Dom must've told him on the phone to spend the night down here."

"To do what?"

"That's the question, isn't it? We'd better keep an eye on him."

The limousine's brake lights flared up ahead.

"Stop here," Bart said. "That's the place."

He'd always admired the apartment building. Five stories of stately stone and stucco in grays and dark blues, squeezed between two more modern buildings. One apartment occupied each floor, with bay windows that looked out on the steep grassy hillside and windswept cypresses of Lafayette Park.

"Guess you called that right, boss," Velacci said, sucking up. He was like that. All brass balls and tough talk, unless he thought he'd gone too far. Then he'd kiss your ass all day long.

The Ford bumped the curb as Velacci pulled into a red zone. They watched as Solomon got out of the limo, carrying his aluminum briefcase, and went into the apartment building's lobby. The limo pulled away.

"Find a place to park," Bart said. "Someplace you can sit and watch the door."

He popped open the passenger door.

"Where you going?"

"I got things to do," Bart said. "I'll call the office. Get 'em to send me a car."

"I just sit here? Waiting on this guy?"

"You got a problem with that?"

"Not at all."

"Good. Call me if he makes a move."

Bart stepped out and checked the sidewalk. This block was strictly residential, and there was no one around. He walked to the nearest corner and turned left, putting a building between himself and Solomon Gage, in case Solomon came back outside.

Bart dialed his phone. While it rang, he thought of steps he could take to protect his investment in the Niger deal. He couldn't count on the Sheffields, those rich fucks. If it blew up, it would be no big loss to them. They'd move on, find some other money-making scheme. But Bart had everything riding on this deal. He'd make sure it went off without a hitch.

And nobody better get in his way.

CHAPTER 16

●●●●●●●●●●●●●●●●●●●●●

Solomon crossed the familiar lobby—mailboxes, a ficus tree, an elevator like a gilded cage—to an antique door with the heraldic Sheffield "S" in gold. The caretaker, Mrs. Wong, opened the apartment door before he could ring the bell. She must've seen the limo stop outside. Not much in this neighborhood got past Mrs. Wong.

"Ah, Solomon. Come in, come in."

"Thank you, Mrs. Wong."

"It's been weeks since I've seen you last. Are you in good health?"

"Sure." He smiled. Mrs. Wong. Always the mother hen.

"Would you like tea?"

He started to pass, but he knew how that would go. No tea? Was he sure? Then coffee? No? A soda? A beer? Perhaps food? A sandwich? Mrs. Wong didn't know how to take 'no' for an answer.

"Tea would be nice."

She led him through the elegant apartment to the kitchen. Mrs. Wong was seventy years old, but she could've passed for twenty years younger, her round face unlined and her hair black as night (though Solomon suspected the color came from a box). She was dressed as usual, in knit pants and a loose, smock-like blouse. This one was black, decorated with blooms and birds in shades of green and purple.

"Mrs. Wong, you look like a hothouse flower today."

She smiled and bobbed her head, and he wondered whether she'd followed his meaning. Mrs. Wong had been in this country since her teens, but she sometimes still had trouble with idiom. He'd often heard her talking to herself in Mandarin, a running kitchen commentary that sounded like somebody hitting a cymbal with a cat.

Solomon sat on a tall stool at the kitchen's central counter and watched Mrs. Wong busy herself with teapot and water and fire.

"You staying here tonight?" she asked over her shoulder.

"Looks that way. Something's come up."

Mrs. Wong arched an eyebrow, but didn't ask.

"Clothes for you in the bedroom," she said. "After the last time you were here, I had them cleaned."

"Thank you."

"My brother's laundry. Always a top-notch job."

Solomon smiled. He enjoyed these visits with Mrs. Wong. They reminded him of long-ago conversations with his own mother. The utter banality of such everyday chitchat made a pleasant departure from most of his conversations, which centered on deadlines, tense business deals and Sheffield family problems. So much to keep track of. So many secrets to keep.

Solomon recalled a quotation from Balzac he'd once read: "Behind every great fortune there is a crime." The Sheffields weren't above breaking the rules on occasion, particularly when it came to protecting their own. They had their share of crimes to conceal over the years; many committed on their behalf by Solomon himself. The Oakland shootout flashed through his mind: the crunch of Tyrone's face against his knee, the bloody spray from Jamal's head.

Mrs. Wong set a steaming cup in front of him, snapping him out of his dark thoughts.

"You okay, Solomon?"

"Lot on my mind, that's all. Business as usual."

"You always take care of the family, Solomon. You do a top-notch job."

"Just like your brother at the laundry."

"Oh, yes. But your job, I think, is much harder." She winked at him. "Different kind of dirty laundry."

Yes, he thought, not much gets past Mrs. Wong.

He changed the subject, asking about her own family, steering her away from the Sheffields' troubles. She chattered happily, though she must've sensed that Solomon had too much on his mind to follow. She promised to make a batch of potstickers for him before she went home for the day, so he could heat them up later.

"You know those are my favorite, Mrs. Wong. Thank you."

He downed the last of the green tea, and Mrs. Wong said, "No more tea for you now. You got work to do."

He thanked her for the tea, then stood and picked up his briefcase.

"Solomon?"

He turned back to find her studying him.

"You look tired," she said. "Take care of yourself."

He thanked her again, and slipped out of the kitchen, leaving her to whip up the promised stuffed dumplings. Normally, spending the night in San Francisco would mean dinner out on the corporate credit card, taking advantage of the city's hundreds of excellent restaurants, perhaps in the company of a local divorcee he sometimes dated. But tonight, he'd eat alone at a desk. Mrs. Wong was right—he had a lot of work to do.

He went to a front bedroom that long ago had been converted into an office. He could've commandeered office space at Embarcadero Center, but he had everything he needed here, and he could work without worrying about snoopers. He took off his jacket and hung it on an antique coat rack. Opened his briefcase and took out his laptop and set it up on a Queen Anne desk that faced a window overlooking the park.

The four-square-block park was a grassy hilltop criss-crossed by paths and topped by a grove of exotic trees. Two boys, maybe four years old, chased and rolled around in the grass. He could hear their laughter through the thick, beveled glass. A woman stood uphill, hugging a cardigan tight around herself. Watching, making sure the kids didn't venture too close to the street. Solomon sometimes wondered what it would be like to be a parent, to be entrusted with a young life. Other times, he felt he had all he could handle, babying the Sheffields.

He focused on the computer. His fingers rapped the keyboard as he searched the websites of area newspapers and TV stations, looking for anything on the Oakland shooting. All he found was a two-paragraph article in The Oakland Tribune, which identified the dead man as twenty-year-old Jamal Booker and said police believed the shooting was "drug-related." Solomon felt certain investigators would make no connection to the Sheffields, that they wouldn't even look very hard for Jamal's killer.

Next, he did an online search for "Niger." Grace said the decorative masks came from there, so it was a place to start.

Solomon had never visited Africa in his wide-ranging travels for Dom. Like most Americans, he only thought of Africa when it was in the news—terrible drought or starving babies or civil war or genocide in Rwanda or Darfur. Never good news out of the Dark Continent.

Most of the articles and websites he found were devoted to desertification, the Sahara's slow southward expansion gobbling up the rangelands that provided much of the nation's meager economy. Niger was among the poorest countries in the world, gripped by famine and drought. Population: 14 million. Gross domestic product: $10 billion. Average annual income per person: $900.

Jesus.

The landlocked republic gained its independence from France in 1960. French remained the official language, the monetary unit was the franc and French companies still operated there. Solomon noted that the flag was red, white and green, like the sash on the man he'd seen at corporate headquarters. But a quick search through an online encyclopedia confirmed that red and green were the predominant colors in many African flags.

He scanned through histories of Niger, finding the usual coups and assassinations. Things had been a little more stable in the past decade, under an elected president. Solomon did the math and saw that the country was due for another election. He wondered if another revolt was in the works.

More interesting to him were articles that talked about the nation's uranium mines and a refinery for producing yellowcake from the raw ore. At the beginning of the war that overthrew Saddam Hussein, the White House had accused the Iraqis of trying to buy yellowcake from Niger as a step toward producing a nuclear weapon, and had used that as a justification for war. The yellowcake information supposedly came from British intelligence, but the allegations later were found to be a hoax perpetuated by an informant, and the resulting scandal rocked Washington.

Could Michael's trips to Africa have something to do with uranium? As head of Sheffield Extraction Industries, he would be looking for mining opportunities. Companies were exploring for gold in one section of Niger and oil in another, but those ventures seemed highly speculative, long shots at best. Michael fancied himself a gambler and wildcatter, but Solomon couldn't see him expanding into Africa unless it was for a sure thing. Especially since Dom seemed dead-set against investing there.

Solomon read through the research again, taking his time. The market for uranium had boomed during the 1960s and 1970s, and Niger's economy had boomed along with it. Then came a price slump, and the country's economy tumbled into ruin. Uranium ore bottomed out at seven dollars a pound in 2001, just in time for Niger to get hit by another drought.

While the drought showed no sign of letting up, the country's economy showed hints of a rebound. Nuclear power was in vogue again, with fifty new power plants planned in a dozen countries. Uranium ore was up to fifty-two dollars a pound. Not much of that money reached the starving masses, but it made other nations more willing to lend money to Niger.

A French-led consortium still ran two giant mines, and the yellowcake refinery had been renovated in anticipation of higher production. Sounded like the French had the industry sewn up, which made Solomon question his theory that Michael was interested in uranium. Hell, for all he knew, Michael traveled to Africa in search of nothing more than decorative masks and willing whores.

Solomon looked up from the computer screen and was surprised to find that night had fallen outside. He'd been at it for hours. He stretched and twisted, working a kink out of his back.

One more search, then he'd take a break. He punched the name of Grace's attorney into the computer, and found dozens of articles that mentioned Lucinda Cruz, mostly in big-name divorce cases. She'd also won a couple of class-action suits that grabbed headlines, including one against a chemical company that resulted in a multimillion-dollar payoff to the plaintiffs. Cruz clearly was an excellent lawyer who knew how to play the game with the media as well as win in court. Wealthy enough that she couldn't be bought. And it looked as if she might carry a grudge against corporate America.

He found a profile of her published in the San Francisco Chronicle a couple of years earlier, shortly after she'd won the lawsuit against the chemical company. The article painted her as a crusader who'd grown up in poverty in Miami's Little Havana, gone to school at Berkeley on a scholarship, earned her law degree with honors at Hastings. A woman who'd made a success of herself while remembering her roots, one who went to bat for the little guy, the battered wife, the neglected child.

A photograph accompanied the profile, and Solomon leaned forward, his nose nearly touching the screen. He'd expected a battle-axe, but Cruz was around his age, with petite features, honey-colored skin and tightly curled black hair parted in the middle. She was smiling, but there was a predatory glint in her chocolate-drop eyes, the kind of confidence you hate to see in an opponent.

Solomon looked her up in the phone book and called her office, but an answering service picked up. He left no message. He glanced at his watch. It was later than he'd thought.

His stomach growled. He stood and listened to the quiet apartment. He could hear Mrs. Wong's potstickers calling.

CHAPTER 17

•••••••••••••••••••

Victor Amadou slouched behind the wheel of the little Japanese car. He wasn't a large man by American standards, though he was broad-shouldered and in good shape for a man in his late forties, but he didn't see how anyone could be comfortable in the small car. He'd tried adjusting the seat every way possible, but he still felt cramped and restless.

He probably should call it a night. He'd been in the little car for hours now, playing a hunch, watching for the big white man whose head was shaved smooth as a bullet.

Victor was desperate to make the visit to San Francisco pay off. He'd accompanied the ambassador on the cross-country flight without complaint, but he'd feared all along that the mission would fail. Ambassador Mirabeau, that pompous idiot, thought he could talk sense to the Sheffields, get them to voluntarily retreat from their interference in Nigerien affairs. But Victor knew diplomacy didn't work on men like the Sheffields. They understood only one thing—power—and it had been a long time since Niger's government could act from a position of power. These days, the ambassador went to bigger governments with hat in hand, begging for food for a starving nation, willing to hand over natural resources in exchange for enough hard currency to get through the famine. But what the Sheffields were doing, that was far beyond—

A light switched off in the downstairs room of the apartment building where the man had been working. Victor sat up straighter, watching the entrance. Maybe he would come out now. Or maybe he was going to bed. Exactly what Victor should be doing.

Victor hadn't intended to follow the man when he set out from the rundown consulate in the borrowed car. He'd only planned to drive past Michael Sheffield's huge home, make sure Sheffield was not in San Francisco, as his fat brother had claimed during the meeting with the ambassador. Instead, he'd spotted the beefy bald man that he'd seen at corporate headquarters, leaving the mansion and climbing into a waiting limousine.

Victor recognized something in the balanced way the man carried himself. In another setting, he would've guessed military or mercenary, some kind of trained killer. He'd known many such men over the years. Soldiers of fortune. Security specialists like himself, who protected diplomats and businessmen and bagmen from the predators who treated Africa like a bloody playground.

His decision to follow the man was validated somehow by the fact that another car tailed the limo as well. Victor had stayed well back, watching the second car jump traffic lights and change lanes to keep up with the limousine. Even on these unfamiliar streets, Victor managed to keep both vehicles in sight. Near as he could tell, no one noticed him.

One of the men in the trailing car had disappeared, but the other still sat behind the wheel of the large Ford, watching this apartment building. A fat white man with slicked-back black hair, dressed in a dark blue windbreaker. Since it got dark, Victor had kept track of him by the orange glow of his ever-present cigarette. A mistake to smoke while on surveillance, especially at night. That glow would make a fine target if someone decided he didn't want to be watched anymore.

Victor wondered whether the man with the shaved head even knew he was being followed. He hadn't acted like it, hadn't taken precautions. Victor never went anywhere in a straight line himself. He always doubled back, checking for tails, watching over his shoulder. Already, he'd lived past the average life expectancy of men in his home country. He intended to live as long as possible, and that meant constant wariness.

Earlier, he'd phoned the consulate with the license plate number of the Ford, and was surprised to learn it was registered to Sheffield Enterprises. A company car, which meant the company was keeping watch on one of its own. Strange.

The big man didn't emerge from the building. Victor had hoped he could lead him to Dominick Sheffield, could get him an audience with the patriarch, so he could tell him about the elections in Niger. If he could get the Sheffields to keep their hands off, the voters might take care of the rest. But it was late now, and he was losing hope.

Victor sighed. He was wasting his time here, watching and wondering. And time was too scarce to squander.

CHAPTER 18

••••••••••••••••••

Solomon Gage snapped awake Tuesday to the trill of his cell phone on the bedside table. He blinked twice, remembering where he was and why. The San Francisco apartment. Grace and Michael. Mick Nielsen. Dom.

He glanced at the glowing clock. It said 7:38 a.m., long past when Solomon normally rose. He'd worn himself out last night, prowling the Internet, trying to make sense of Michael Sheffield's travels to Africa.

He flipped open the silver phone before it finished ringing again.

"Yes?"

"Is this Solomon?" A woman's voice, shrill, upset.

"Yes. Dorothy?" Dom's daughter. Abby's mother. Calling from Los Angeles.

"Oh, Solomon, what's happened?"

"I don't know what you mean. I just woke up."

"Abby! Why is she out of rehab already?"

Solomon sat up. The covers fell away from his naked chest. The air in the room felt cool against his skin, but heat rose within him.

"She's out?"

"Didn't you know that? What the hell is going on up there?"

"Easy, Dorothy. Tell me what happened."

"I got a call a few minutes ago from a doctor at Willow Glade. He said Abby checked out last night. They were supposed to call me before letting her go, but somebody screwed up and—"

"When did she leave?"

"Around dinnertime. She could be anywhere by now, Solomon. She could be doing anything."

He had a pretty good idea what Abby Maynes was doing, but how had she managed to bust out of rehab? He'd specifically told the hospital to call him and to call Dorothy before releasing Abby. How did she even get a ride? Willow Glade was isolated, out in the country—

"You didn't know about this?" Dorothy's voice was veering toward panic.

"I'm as surprised as you are."

"Oh, my God!"

"What? What's wrong?"

"If you didn't know about it, then something's really wrong. Something's happened to my baby."

"I don't understand."

"They said it was you, Solomon! They said you were the one who picked her up!"

He said nothing for a moment, absorbing that. Surely the rehabilitation clinic would've required some sort of identification before handing over the granddaughter of Dominick Sheffield—

Dorothy burst into tears. "Oh, my God," she warbled. "What's happened?"

"I'll find out, Dorothy."

"I'll catch a plane," she said. "I'll come there right away."

"Just sit tight. I'll call you as soon as—"

But it was too late. She'd hung up.

Solomon leaped out of bed, hitting the speed dial on his phone while he hurried to the closet for fresh clothes.

"Sheffield Enterprises," chirped an early-bird receptionist.

"This is Solomon Gage. I need a car and driver. Right now."

CHAPTER 19

•••••••••••••••••••

Luckily for Solomon, Carl Jones was the one who showed up sleepy-eyed outside the apartment twenty minutes later. If anyone understood the urgency of the situation, it was the driver who'd toured the dingy backstreets of Oakland in search of Abby Maynes.

The ride was a Lincoln Town Car, and Carl put its big engine to use as they zoomed over the Bay Bridge. The elevated freeways above Oakland were crowded, but most commuters were headed the opposite direction, and Carl made good time.

Solomon stared out the window, lost in his anxious thoughts. He wasn't completely surprised Abby found a way to escape rehab. Other Sheffield offspring had pulled similar stunts over the years. That was why he placed the restrictions on her release. But someone had impersonated him to get Abby out of Willow Glade, and that gave him the creeps. While Carl navigated through the hills, Solomon called his bank and credit card companies on the East Coast, making sure the impersonator hadn't robbed him of more than his identity.

By the time he determined his accounts were safe, the Lincoln was climbing the long driveway to Willow Glade. The stately white building oozed calm and quiet, but on the inside, the clinic had gone into crisis mode. The director had been summoned, and he met Solomon at the door. He introduced himself as George Mifflin and gave Solomon a sweaty handshake.

"I don't know how this could've happened," he said as they marched down a hall to his office. "We have strict protocols in place for patient releases. Clearly, someone made a mistake."

"Clearly," Solomon said.

Mifflin gulped. He was a scrawny, awkward man, all angles and elbows and knees. His hands were like dancing spiders as he outlined all he knew about what happened the night before, which was damned little.

"I assure you," Mifflin concluded, "if we find any sort of, um, *collusion* here, heads will roll."

The threat would've carried more weight if his voice hadn't cracked as he said it.

Solomon sighed. He was accustomed to this reaction; nobody wanted to upset the Sheffields. But such a flustered response required more patience than Solomon possessed at the moment. He leaned forward and rested his forearms on the front edge of Mifflin's desk.

"Do you have any idea where Abby was taken?"

"No, I talked to the night nurse and—"

"Is she here now?"

"The nurse? Why, yes. I mean, she'd already gone home. Her shift was over. But I figured you might need to talk to her, so I called and asked her to hurry back. She got here just a few minutes before you did—"

"Then what are you waiting for? Every minute that passes gives Abby that much more of a head start."

"Right. Of course." Mifflin pushed an intercom button on his desk. "Maggie? Send in Nurse Forester. Please."

The nurse was a stout black woman, maybe fifty years old, with plump cheeks and kind eyes. She still wore her white uniform and thick-soled shoes. She wasn't one of the nurses Solomon met when he checked Abby into Willow Glade.

He stood and shook her hand. She introduced herself as Norma Forester. Her eyes widened when he said his name. He gestured her into a nearby chair, then turned his chair so he faced her.

"Tell me exactly what happened," he said.

She nervously glanced at Mifflin, who nodded vigorously to show her it was okay.

"A man showed up here last night a little before eight," she began. "He said there'd been a death in the family, and Miss Maynes was needed immediately. I told him it wasn't a good idea, pulling her out of rehab so soon. She was still in detox. But he said it was an emergency."

"This man," Solomon nudged, "what was his name?"

"He said his name was Solomon Gage. I guess he was lying?"

"You're sure you heard him correctly?"

"Absolutely. I made him show me some ID. That's standard procedure here when a patient—"

"He had ID with that name?"

She nodded. "California driver's license. His picture. Your name."

Solomon could feel the muscles clenching in his jaws. He rotated his head on his neck and took a deep breath. He knew he unsettled people when he looked angry. Mifflin and the nurse leaned back in their chairs, giving him room. He tried smiling at them, but feared the effort produced a frightening rictus.

"What did this man look like?"

Nurse Forester swallowed and said, "White, heavy-set, not nearly as tall as you. He had a thick mustache, came all the way out past the corners of his mouth. He wore a baseball cap, so I didn't see his hair. Got the feeling he was bald. You know, how you can just tell?"

Solomon ran the description through his mental files, but didn't come up with anyone. Michael Sheffield was bald and wore a mustache, but he could hardly be described as "heavyset." Unlike his fat-ass brother, Michael was in good shape for his age. Besides, Michael wasn't even in the States.

Silence filled the office. Mifflin finally cleared his throat and said, "Does that ring any bells?"

Solomon shook his head.

"Anyone else meet this man?" he asked.

"I don't think so," she said. "I was at the front desk, so he came straight to me. He waited there while I fetched her."

Mifflin sputtered through another apology, saying the clinic's safeguards should've prevented Abby's release. When Solomon didn't respond, Mifflin turned his attention to the nurse.

"You violated our protocols," he snapped. "You can expect to be disciplined. I'll talk to the medical staff first, but don't be surprised if you're looking for another job."

Nurse Forester looked stricken.

"Don't blame her," Solomon said. "How was she to know the man was a fake? She'd never met me before. And he showed her ID."

Mifflin rested his bony elbows on the desk, his hands clasped together near his chin. A praying mantis.

"We had specific instructions on Miss Maynes' chart that her mother was to be notified," he said. "A patient getting checked out in the middle of the night—"

Solomon stood suddenly, making Mifflin's hands flutter.

"I want you to understand how seriously we take our responsibilities here at Willow Glade. If there's any way we can make it up to you, to the family—"

"Only one way you can help now," Solomon said. "Would anyone else here have any idea where Abby went?"

They both shook their heads.

"I've got to find her."

He turned and walked out.

CHAPTER 20

••••••••••••••••••••

Christopher Sheffield sat in the back of the black limousine, watching through tinted windows as his brother came down the steps of a Gulfstream jet outside Sheffield Aviation. The wind was blowing in off the bay, and Michael's fringe of graying hair danced around his bald head. Every time Chris saw Michael, he worried about his own thinning hair. He'd read that baldness was inherited from the mother's side of the family, which explained why Dom still had a full head of silver hair at his age while you could see your reflection in Michael's scalp. Chris already used Rogaine, but he was pretty sure his hair had packed its bags and was ready to go.

Michael walked briskly toward the car, one hand carrying a black briefcase, the other smoothing his lush mustache. It wasn't lost on Chris that Michael grew the mustache after he lost his hair. Some kind of compensation.

Goddamn, he was mad at Michael. This whole situation was typical of his brother: Big dreams, big ideas, but too little follow-through and too few results. A chance it all would blow up in their faces.

Wind gusted into the car as the driver opened the back door for Michael, who fell into the seat beside Chris.

"Hello, brother. Didn't expect to see you here. Let's have a drink. I've been flying for twenty hours and I'm beat."

Michael opened the wooden cabinet that held the limo's minibar, but Chris reached across with his foot and kicked the door shut.

"Fuck that. I came out here because we need to talk. Right now."

The limo's engine turned over, and the driver steered the long car around the aviation building, headed for the frontage road along Highway 101. Chris pushed a switch to make sure the soundproof glass was closed, so the driver couldn't hear.

"Abby's still missing," Chris said. "For all we know, she's blabbing our secrets all over town."

"She doesn't know enough about Niger to reveal anything."

"She knew enough to get Solomon interested."

"It's only five more days," Michael said. "No way Solomon will sort it out by then."

"You'd better hope not. If Dad finds out—"

"Relax, Chris. It'll be fine."

"You think so? You let a goddamn junkie in on our biggest deal ever, and now you say it'll all be fine?"

"You wanted me to hire her, as I recall."

"I never meant for you to involve her in this. You can't trust a druggie, even if she is family."

"Too late now. Yelling at me won't accomplish anything. If Abby's run off, she won't be talking to anyone who matters. Think they're real interested in uranium down at the local crack house?"

"Solomon's looking for her," Chris said.

"Maybe he won't find her."

"He did last time."

"I'm telling you, it'll be fine."

Chris took a deep breath and let it out slowly.

"Maybe you're right," he said. "I hope so. But Abby may be the least of your problems."

Michael stared out the window as Candlestick Park slid past on the right. Chris waited, but his brother wouldn't look at him.

"Grace is on the warpath," Chris said. "That attorney she hired, Lucinda Cruz? She hates big corporations. She's going after all our records. How long before she turns up Niger, too?"

"Won't happen," Michael said. "We'll tie her up in court. By the time she figures anything out—"

"No, goddamnit, you're not getting it. Even if everything goes perfectly over there, we're not off the hook. We need to keep Dad in the dark. If it comes out in court, even years from now, he'll never forgive us."

"He's not going to be around forever," Michael said.

"You want to bank on that? You want to count on Dad kicking the bucket before he finds out?"

"No, but—"

"Reminds me of when we were kids. You always got us in trouble, thinking you could slide everything past our parents, right under their fucking noses. I'd end up taking the blame to save your sorry ass."

"This isn't kid stuff."

"You got that right," Chris said. "I'm not taking the fall for you this time, Michael. Dad starts cutting people out of his will, I'm not going down with you. I'll be there handing him a pen."

"All right, all right. I get it. What do you want me to do?"

"Fix things with Grace."

"Are you kidding me? She's ready to nail my balls to the wall."

"If that's what it takes—"

"Come on, Chris. You can't really expect me to save my marriage overnight, just to keep a nosy lawyer out of our business."

"That's exactly what I expect. Buy us some time."

"Grace might not even talk to me."

"Find some way to shut her down."

"But how? If she wants a divorce, how can I talk her out of it?"

"Maybe talking won't be enough. Do whatever it takes, Michael. Whatever it takes."

Michael stared out the window, absently stroking his mustache. His brows crouched low over his eyes. Chris couldn't tell if he was angry or just concentrating on how to solve the problem. But he was sure of one thing: For once, his brother was focused.

CHAPTER 21

∙∙∙∙∙∙∙∙∙∙∙∙∙∙∙∙∙∙∙∙∙

Jean-Pierre Chatillon wasn't happy with the surveillance. The rented pickup truck, its silver body coated in dust and grime, didn't fit among the sleek urban vehicles that crowded the streets around Embarcadero Center.

He and Robert Mboku sat at the curb in the truck, on Drumm Street, facing the main entrance to Embarcadero Center Four. High above them, the Sheffields had their corporate offices. But down at street level, it was stores and signs and milling crowds. Jean-Pierre bought food and coffee at a brightly lit place down the block called "Carl's Jr." The food stank up the truck. The coffee made Robert edgy, and that made Jean-Pierre nervous.

Still no sign of Michael Sheffield. Jean-Pierre and Robert had repeatedly checked his San Francisco home, even made that trip to his father's lodge up north, but nowhere had they spotted the man whose photograph had been supplied by their bosses. Here, outside Sheffield's busy office building, was no good for an ambush, but perhaps they could at least pick up his trail. Of course, there was no way to know whether he'd use this entrance. The skyscraper complex had dozens of doors. Jean-Pierre had thought about sending Robert around to the other side to keep watch over there, but Robert stood out worse than the pickup truck. He wore a bright red shirt and brand-new Levi's that were four inches too long. Jean-Pierre had tried to explain that he could buy jeans that were the proper length, but Robert had simply cuffed the pants halfway up his calves. To Robert, who for years had worn the same fatigues day in and day out, a pair of American jeans, no matter how long, were a gift you didn't question.

With his blue-black skin and nappy hair and bad teeth, Robert looked so foreign, so *African*, among the plump, healthy Americans. He gawked at everything, too, staring up at the sky-scrapers and down at the paved streets and at every passing pedes-trian. This trip was full of firsts for Robert: first plane ride, first time outside Africa, first time he'd seen such tall buildings.

Jean-Pierre spent a lot of time pondering Robert Mboku, who'd come to him after years as a boy soldier in the West African civil wars. He often thought Robert would make a good case study for a psychiatrist researching the effect of random violence on the human mind. Robert was in his early twenties now and child-like in his awe of the modern world, but quick and vicious when it was time to kill.

As near as Jean-Pierre could tell, the only life the orphan could remember began when he was seven years old. He'd joined Charles Taylor's guerilla army in Liberia, and proved himself be-fore he was even big enough to lug around a rifle. He survived the tribal fighting that spilled across the region, then drifted eastward after Taylor was overthrown. Was he following Taylor into exile in Nigeria? Fleeing the massacres that followed the revolt? Who could say?

He'd known Robert was special the first time he saw him. Driving on a dusty street on the outskirts of Niamey, the capital of Niger, Jean-Pierre had stopped in traffic near an open-air bazaar. He'd noticed Robert sitting at a table outside a primitive cafe, chewing on a piece of charred chicken. He was dressed in an olive drab uniform, his clothes soiled and torn, his feet bare and dusty.

The traffic jam was caused by two men fighting in the street. Maybe they were fighting over a prime market space or a woman, Jean-Pierre was never sure. All he knew was that they screamed and swung fists in the middle of the street, and a crowd gathered, and traffic came to a halt.

Robert scowled at the commotion. He got up from the table and pushed through the crowd, a machete dangling from his hand. Jean-Pierre watched as Robert shoved the two men and shouted. They pushed back, still intent on fighting with each other, and Robert's machete flashed and both men fell bleeding to death in the street. The crowd scattered. And Robert walked back to his table, sat down and resumed gnawing his chicken. As near as Jean-Pierre could tell, the two murders meant no more to Robert than swatting a flea.

Jean-Pierre knew immediately he could use such remorseless talent. He threw open the door of his Land Rover and shouted to Robert, inviting him into the vehicle. That was four years ago, and they'd been partners ever since. They were a perfect team, making Jean-Pierre a rich man.

Robert, of course, knew little about the money. He was like a dog that had been trained to kill. As long as he got food and sleep and the occasional kind word, he was happy. Well, not *happy* exactly. That word didn't suit him. But he seemed satisfied.

Jean-Pierre had survived thirty years of wars and coups and terror in Africa, and was perfectly capable of fighting his own battles, but he'd always kept a few black youths under his wing, skillful young men willing to take risks. Now, just the one soldier seemed plenty.

The past two years, Jean-Pierre and Robert had found steady work with the French consortium that ran the uranium mines in Niger, menacing suppliers and keeping the miners in line. This new assignment was different, and Jean-Pierre recognized how much was riding on it. His bosses had sent him to the States, the first time Jean-Pierre had been off the African continent in decades, and they'd arranged passports and visas so he could bring Robert with him. They even had weapons waiting, including a brand-new machete for Robert. The weapons were delivered by a swarthy Algerian who lived across the bay. The arms merchant, Hakim, had also given Jean-Pierre a list of mercenaries, local talent he could trust to be discreet, but Jean-Pierre didn't think he'd need them. Bloody work to be done here in lovely California, yes, but no one better suited for it than Robert.

Jean-Pierre would've preferred to catch their prey on a lonely African highway, make him disappear in the veldt. But he'd been told that assassinating Michael Sheffield in Niger would cause too much political fallout. Jean-Pierre didn't care about the politics. All he needed was an assignment: Find Michael Sheffield and anyone else who seemed to know about his business in Niger. Eliminate them. Then get the hell out, away from this foggy, crowded city and back home to the dust and sun and bloodshed that was Africa.

Jean-Pierre's thoughts were interrupted when Robert touched his arm. He jerked as if from an electric shock. Normally, the only time Robert touched other people was when he was killing them. Jean-Pierre turned to find Robert staring intently through the windshield.

"*Regardez.*"

Jean-Pierre's eyes went to where Robert pointed. A long black limo had pulled up in front of the office building, as close as it could get to the concrete plaza that separated the lobby from the street.

A man climbed out of the back seat before the black-uniformed driver could make it around to open his door. He was tall and trim, with a bald head and a thick mustache. Jean-Pierre compared the man to the tattered photo he'd carried with him from Niger. Michael Sheffield. No question.

"That's him," Jean-Pierre said in French. "Who is with him?"

Another man crawled out the back door, a fat man whose face flushed from the effort. Despite the layer of lard on his body, he strongly resembled Sheffield.

"The fat one from the lodge," Robert said. "The Warthog. His brother?"

"Probably."

"Do we kill them both? Now?"

"Look around," Jean-Pierre said. "Too many witnesses. Let's see where they go."

The brothers, if that's what they were, conferred for a moment, their suits rippled by the breeze off the bay. The fat one hurried toward the building's entrance and Michael Sheffield climbed back into the limousine.

"We follow him," Robert said.

"He's probably going home."

"We'll follow him there."

"That's right."

"And we'll kill him."

"Perhaps. We can afford to take our time. We still have a few days. As long as he's dead before the election, it will be fine."

Robert shook his head. "Let's do it sooner. I want to go home."

Jean-Pierre started the truck and pulled out into the traffic. "You don't like it here, Robert?"

"Too much noise. Too many people. Too many police. Let's do the job now, so we can go home."

"Soon, Robert, soon. For now, we watch him. We watch for an opportunity."

Robert plucked the machete from the floorboard and set it across his lap. The razor-sharp edge of the blade caught the sun and flashed into Jean-Pierre's eyes. He blinked it away, and focused on the limo.

CHAPTER 22

•••••••••••••••••••

This time around, Solomon and Carl started with the rotten neighborhood where they'd found Abby Maynes three days earlier. It still took hours to find a street dealer who recognized her photograph.

He was a skinny black kid, maybe seventeen years old, dressed in Oakland Raiders gear, including a cap squashed down sideways on his head. He barely glanced at the photo, but Solomon saw recognition flash in his eyes.

"You know her."

"Don't know her, 'zactly. I seen her today, though."

"Where?"

"Why should I tell you, muthafucka?"

Sneering, the kid handed the photo back to Solomon, who still sat in the back seat of the Lincoln. Rather than taking the photo, Solomon grabbed the kid's thin wrist and yanked hard. The dealer fell forward, and his head whacked against the roof of the car. His hat went flying.

"Ow! Hey!"

Solomon kept pulling on the arm until he had the kid halfway into the Lincoln, through the open window up to his waist. His head was in Solomon's lap. His shirt rode up, and Solomon found a gun stuffed in his waistband, as he'd expected. He took the gun and hefted it in his hand. A .32-caliber Raven semi-auto. Small but deadly.

The kid howled and squirmed until Solomon stuck the barrel of the gun in his ear. Then he got very still.

"I don't have time for a lot of jawing back and forth," Solomon said. "You know where this woman is, you tell me right now, or I'll splatter your brains all over the floorboard."

The punk's mouth opened and closed a few times, like he was trying to find some air to breathe. Solomon twisted his wrist, grinding the gun into his ear.

"Okay, okay. Don't shoot. She's close by. Turn right on Portnoy."

Solomon looked up, met Carl's eyes in the rear-view. "Go."

"With his legs hanging out the window?"

"It's not far."

Carl gave a curt nod and threw the Lincoln into gear. The tires squealed as the car lurched away from the curb.

"Hey," the kid said. "Hey, man."

His expensive sneakers kicked as he tried to writhe the rest of the way into the Lincoln. Solomon held him in place.

"Hey. I'm tryin' to help you out, man."

"Shut up."

Carl spun the wheel when they reached Portnoy. The narrow street was lined by old junkers and rundown two-story houses shedding dried paint like dandruff.

"Which house?"

"Third one," the kid said into Solomon's lap. "On the right. The pink one."

Carl whipped the Lincoln over to an empty spot at the curb and stood on the brakes. The kid's bony hips bounced against the car's frame.

"Ow! C'mon, man!"

Solomon grabbed his head and twisted it around so the kid was looking up at him.

"Who's in there with her?"

"I dunno, man."

Solomon shoved the kid out the window. He collapsed into a pile on the sidewalk, then scooted backward on his ass to keep from getting whacked as Solomon threw open the car door.

Didn't really matter who was inside that house. Solomon was going in, and it was too late for stealth. You come screaming into a neighborhood in a fast car, a pair of kicking legs dangling from the back window, most everybody on the block would know you arrived.

He pointed the gun at the kid and said, "Run."

Homeboy didn't have to be told twice. He scrambled to his feet, and took off down the sidewalk, back the way they'd come.

Solomon stalked toward the pink house. Behind him, Carl called, "Hey," but Solomon didn't pause. He trusted Carl now. He knew the car would be there when he came back. If he came back. He switched the kid's gun to his left hand and pulled his own .45 from its shoulder holster.

The pink house had a small wooden porch jutting from its center, which made it look as if it were sticking out its tongue, saying "aaah." Solomon leaped up the two steps and slammed his size-twelve foot against the door, just beside the doorknob. The rotten jamb splintered. Another kick, and the door slammed back out of the way.

He went inside, pointing the guns ahead of him. He was in a narrow foyer, with doors leading off it in three directions and a set of rickety-looking stairs going up. Two of the doors were open and he could see into dusty rooms furnished with gut-sprung sofas and milk-crate tables. The house stank of cigarettes and urine and rotting garbage.

"Abby!" he shouted. "Abby Maynes!"

No answer.

The third door was opened by a young black woman. She had sleepy junkie eyes and a bony frame and once-straightened hair matted to her head. Her lips were dried and cracked, and her skin looked ashy.

"You lookin' for that white girl?" she asked, her voice so matter-of-fact, Solomon wondered whether she'd even noticed the pistols aimed her way.

"Where is she?"

The woman pointed at the stairs. "She up there."

"Who else is up there?"

"Nobody. They all gone now."

She turned and shuffled away, moving like an eighty-year-old rather than someone not much past eighteen.

Solomon sprinted up the stairs. In a bedroom, he found Abby Maynes. She was curled in a fetal position on a mattress on the floor. She wore only a soiled T-shirt and yellow panties. She was so skinny, her hipbone looked like a plow jutting up under her sallow skin. Her hands were tucked under her chin, and her hair was loose over her face. She reminded Solomon of the unconscious girl he'd seen at the seedy hotel. Used up and discarded.

He moved quickly down the hallway, checking the other bedrooms and a filthy bathroom, leading with the two guns. Nobody.

Solomon went back to the room where Abby lay unconscious. He holstered his gun and stuck the dealer's pistol in his pocket. He felt her neck for a pulse. Fluttery, but there. He checked the insides of her arms, and found welts left by hypodermic needles.

"Aw, hell, Abby."

He got his hands under her, and lifted her like a baby in his arms. She weighed maybe ninety pounds. A bag of bones.

Solomon checked the foyer from the top of the stairs. Still empty. He hurried down the steps, carrying Abby in his arms. Her head lolled on her neck, tipped back in the crook of his elbow. A stink rose from her mouth, and he tried not to breathe it in as he reached the open front door.

Nobody on the little porch or on the sidewalks nearby. A radio played somewhere down the block, the thump of rap music.

Carl saw him coming and jumped out of the Lincoln and hurried around to help with the door.

As he got the door open, the stillness was shattered by gunfire off to Solomon's left. The window of the open car door shattered and glass sprayed the sidewalk.

Carl said, "Unnh!" and spun halfway around, blood blossoming on the lapel of his black suit. Another bullet whistled past Solomon's face.

Everything seemed to slow. The Lincoln suddenly seemed far away, those last two steps to the open door an impossible distance to cover amid the bullets that whizzed past like wasps.

A bullet tore across Solomon's chest, just below his collarbone, and zinged away down the street.

Carl was spinning, falling, and another bullet went through his upraised left hand, making a sound like someone snapping a green branch off a tree. He moaned and fell backward onto the sidewalk.

Another bullet pinged off the car, then Abby's head exploded in a cloud of red spray. Hot blood spattered Solomon's face and neck and shirt.

He lunged forward, still clutching Abby, throwing them both into the back seat of the car. The back window shattered, spraying glass everywhere. Flying shards stung Solomon's head.

The shooting stopped. Tires squealed down the block, and Solomon raised up and looked through the gaping hole in the back window. He got a glimpse of a black car roaring away. An anony-mous American four-door sedan, maybe a Ford, but he couldn't be sure.

He'd pulled the Colt from his shoulder holster without even realizing it, but it was too late. The shooter was gone.

And so was Abby Maynes. The bullet hit her in the top of the head and exploded out under her jaw, tearing away her throat, leaving a bloody maw where there had been smooth young skin only a minute earlier, when he'd felt there for her pulse.

Her eyes were wide, staring at the ceiling of the Lincoln, as if the shot had awakened her as it destroyed her brain. The car seat's plush upholstery soaked up the blood like a sponge, sucking Abby dry.

Nothing Solomon could do for her. He slid backward out of the car, onto his knees on the sidewalk. Gun still in hand, he checked the street for another shooter. He couldn't see anyone, couldn't hear anything except the gunshots echoing in his head.

He crawled to Carl, who writhed on the sidewalk, his face screwed up tight against the pain. The chest wound was pumping blood. Solomon holstered his gun and pulled out his cell phone. He dialed 911 with one hand while he pressed on the hot geyser with the other. Carl gasped against the pressure.

"Hold on, Carl," Solomon said. "Help's coming."

The phone rang in his ear. A woman dispatcher came on the line.

"Man's been shot," he said. "Need an ambulance. Portnoy Street in Oakland."

He looked across the street, saw rusty numbers next to the door of a house. He read them into the phone, then flipped it closed before she could ask more questions. He set the phone aside and used both hands to put pressure on Carl's chest wound.

"Hang on," he said. "You're going to be okay."

Carl's eyes rolled back in his head.

Solomon's hands were sticky with blood. Sweat stung his eyes. A searing pain streaked across his own chest, and he wondered whether he was bleeding to death, too. But he couldn't take his hands off Carl long enough to check.

Up the street, a couple of baggy-pants teens leaned cautiously off porches to check on the noise. Another neighbor, an old man, hurried toward Solomon.

Sirens wailed in the distance.

CHAPTER 23

●●●●●●●●●●●●●●●●●●●

Police arrived before the ambulance did, but Solomon ignored their commands to step away from Carl and show his hands. He leaned over the driver, keeping the pressure on the wound. The bleeding had slowed, but he wasn't sure that was good news. Maybe Carl didn't have any blood pressure left. The red puddle surrounding them had grown, warm and sticky where it soaked into the knees of Solomon's pants. He felt glued to the sidewalk.

The uniformed cops crowded close, their guns drawn, pointed at him. One shouted about the dead girl in the Lincoln, another shouted into a radio. Chaos.

An ambulance screeched to a stop nose-to-nose with the Lincoln. Two paramedics leaped out, their hands full of gear, and shoved Solomon out of the way. They went to work on Carl.

Solomon struggled to his feet, his dripping hands held out from his sides. The cops backed up a step when they saw how large he was. He focused on the oldest one, who had sergeant's bars on his sleeve.

"My name's Solomon Gage. I've got a gun in a shoulder holster under my left arm and another one in the pocket of my jacket."

The sergeant, who had grizzled hair and an acne-scarred face as hard as pitted sandstone, said, "That's fine. You hold real still and we'll relieve you of the weapons."

At the sergeant's signal, a young black officer carefully approached and took the guns. The .45 had blood on it, and the officer held it between forefinger and thumb, out away from his body. He backed away and set the guns on the trunk of the Lincoln.

"Bag those," the sergeant.

"Those guns haven't been fired," Solomon said. "I never got the chance. I was carrying the girl out of that pink house when somebody down the street started shooting. The girl and the driver were hit before I could get her into the car."

"Looks like you caught one, too," the sergeant said.

Solomon looked down at his chest. The bullet had gouged a four-inch-long furrow across the front of his jacket. He touched his chest and was rewarded with a stab of burning pain.

"Just grazed me."

"We'll get you checked out," the sergeant said. "Another ambulance will be here any minute."

Solomon told the cops the shots had come from a black car at the end of the block, that the car had sped away to the north, that he thought it was a Ford Crown Victoria. The sergeant relayed the information through a radio mike clipped to his shirt, and requested an APB for the car. A dozen cops were milling around now, and he told a couple to haul ass that direction and see if they could spot the car. They obeyed, rushing away with bubble lights and siren going.

"What the hell were you doing in this neighborhood?" the sergeant asked. "With a driver, no less."

"Looking for the girl," Solomon said. "She was hooked on drugs. We had her in a rehab clinic, but she took off last night. I tracked her down, was going to take her to a hospital. But somebody shot at us."

The sergeant squinted at him. "You know who it was?"

Solomon thought about the skinny drug dealer who'd directed them to the pink house. Solomon had taken his gun off him, but maybe he'd had another handy or maybe he rounded up some friends to get even. A wave of guilt washed over him. Had he caused all this by impulsively roughing up that kid?

As another siren wailed nearby, a different possibility reared up in his mind. Maybe somebody followed the Lincoln here and waited until he brought Abby out before opening up on them. Maybe he'd brought the shooter to this neighborhood.

Deciding his ruined suit couldn't get any worse, he wiped his hands on his jacket, getting off as much of the blood as he could. His hands still were sticky and red. He pointed at his phone, which sat on the sidewalk a few feet from where the paramedics were lifting Carl onto a gurney.

"That's my cell. May I please call my boss?"

The sergeant scowled. "Who's your boss?"

"Dominick Sheffield."

"The tycoon? *That* Sheffield?"

Tycoon. Such an old-fashioned word. Solomon nodded. "That's his granddaughter."

The sergeant cursed and looked at the sky, as if checking for a sudden shitstorm.

"Yeah," he said. "Go ahead and call him."

As Solomon bent for the phone, he heard one of the cops mutter, "Dominick Sheffield? God help us."

Solomon pushed the speed dial for Dom, thinking: God help us all.

CHAPTER 24

• • • • • • • • • • • • • • • • • • • •

Dominick Sheffield sat in his favorite chair in his study at Cutthroat Lodge, a fat biography of Andrew Carnegie open in his lap. He'd forgotten about the book as soon as Fiona hurried into the room with a cordless phone.

Solomon told him about Abby, and the news stabbed Dom in the heart. He didn't say much during Solomon's terse recounting of the shooting in Oakland. He could hear sirens in the background, roaring engines, yelling. Sounded like mayhem. Solomon needed to get off the phone.

Before he let him go, Dom asked, "Are you hurt?"

"A bullet grazed me. I'm fine."

"Let them take you to a hospital. Do you need a lawyer?"

"I don't see how they can charge me with anything. I didn't get a shot off."

"Too bad. I wish you'd killed the sons of bitches."

Solomon said, "Me, too."

"How about the driver? Will he live?"

"I think so. He lost a lot of blood, but he was still breathing when they put him in the ambulance."

"Which hospital?"

He heard Solomon ask the police. Then he came back on and said, "Oakland General."

"Have them take you there, too. I'll get Chris' people to come help you. I'll get one of our doctors over there. And a lawyer, just in case."

Solomon said, "I could use some clean clothes."

"We'll handle it. You just take care of yourself."

"Yes, sir."

Dom punched a button to disconnect, then dialed his daughter's number in L.A. He hated to be the one to give her the news, and felt ashamed at the relief he felt when her voicemail picked up. He hung up without leaving a message and dialed Chris.

"Dad? What's up?"

Dom told him what had happened, keeping it brief, talking right over Chris' gasps of surprise. When he was done, Chris said, "What a fucking mess."

"Solomon's doing his best to keep it contained, but see if you can help. Send some of your people over to Oakland General. A flack. A lawyer. Dr. Graham. Call Mrs. Wong and get Solomon some fresh clothes from the apartment."

Chris grunted, and Dom felt sure he was writing down the instructions.

"I tried to call Dorothy, but I couldn't raise her."

"I talked to her an hour ago," Chris said. "She's on her way up here on her boyfriend's jet. She'll go nuts when she hears what happened."

Dom winced. Bad enough that poor Abby was dead in such a public, bloody way. They didn't need Dorothy's hysterics making everything worse.

"Have someone meet her at the airport," he said. "Take her straight to the San Francisco apartment. Get Dr. Graham to make that his first stop. She'll need sedating."

"Right."

"And we'll need to get in touch with the driver's family, express our concerns, assure them we'll cover the medical bills."

"He's got insurance," Chris said.

"Make them happy. We don't want his relatives running to the press."

"Okay."

"Solomon said the police know that Abby was family."

"How do they know that?"

"He told them."

"Great," Chris said flatly.

"We don't have time for second-guessing," Dom said. "I'm sure Solomon's handling it the best he can. Go help him."

"Okay, okay. I'm on it. Are you headed down here?"

"I don't know. Can you handle it?"

"Of course. But Dorothy will need you. She'll fall apart."

Dom thought about that for a second. Chris was right.

"I'll pack a bag and get down there as soon as I can. When you're done making these arrangements, meet me at the apartment. Tell Solomon to meet us there, too, once he's finished at the hospital."

"I don't know, Dad. Shouldn't it just be family?"

"We need all the information we can get, Chris. Solomon has it. Get him there as quickly as you can."

"Yes, sir."

Dom disconnected and set the phone on a table beside his reading chair. His eyes felt hot and sadness welled up within his chest.

A memory flashed: Abby's first visit to Cutthroat. She'd been ten years old, still a tomboy. He'd lost track of her in the forest and had begun to worry, when he found her knee deep in his trout stream, sopping wet, chasing frogs. Her hair in pigtails. A big smile on her face. Dom closed his eyes. Let that be the way he remembered poor sweet Abby. Not as a messed-up young woman who'd lost her way.

The fucking drugs. They were responsible for her death, as much as the bullet that struck her. She never would've been in that lousy neighborhood if it hadn't been for the drugs. They'd derailed Abby during college, crippled her young career. And now they'd killed her.

Dom ran his hands over his face and massaged his forehead, where a headache was building like a thunderstorm.

What is it about the children of the rich? Why are they so spoiled, so weak? Why do they so easily succumb to vice? Look at Chris, with his gluttony and his greed. Michael, with his infidelity. Dorothy, with her series of broken relationships and her fast-lane lifestyle in Los Angeles. Only his other daughter, Elizabeth, seemed to have a normal life, and she'd had to move to England to get it. Stuck out in the Cotswolds with her aristocrat husband, riding horses and tending her garden and raising her four kids far away from anyone who might recognize her as a Sheffield.

A man works hard all his life to provide for his family. The money turns around and destroys those he loves. Lions of industry producing generations of slinking scavengers, waiting on men like Dom to die so they can pick over their riches.

Wealth steals ambition. Why should the children strive when they can simply wait on an inheritance? Even his sons, officers in multimillion-dollar corporations, never show any initiative. They sit on their asses, waiting for Dom to tell them what to do. He couldn't count on them to figure things out on their own.

So different from Solomon. Sometimes, Dom felt Solomon could read his mind. When he gave him assignments, he didn't have to explain in detail, and he could rely on him to follow through.

Was it Solomon's upbringing that made the difference? He and his mother had lived on the razor's edge of poverty before Rose came to work for Dom. After Rose was killed in the auto accident, the boy had seemed grimly prepared to go right back there. Already more mature, at fourteen, than Chris was today.

Maybe it was in the genes. Rose had been a hard worker, the most competent employee Dom had ever encountered. Loyal, strong and loving. He'd been so lonely, so bereft, after his wife died of cancer. Rose floated into his life and took care of him, made him whole again.

His kids were grown by then, but they still were broken up over Estelle's death, and he and Rose kept their relationship a secret. They talked about marriage, but it never got past talk before she was stolen away by that damned car wreck.

Dom was left to ponder what might have been. If they'd had children together, would they have turned out like Solomon? Or would they have been ruined by money?

He wiped tears from his eyes.

Goddamnit. Why couldn't his sons have grown up to be strong men? Why couldn't Abby have found the strength to avoid drugs?

And why the hell had someone killed her?

CHAPTER 25

•••••••••••••••••••••

The graze on Solomon's chest was shallow, more like a burn than a gash, and the emergency room doctors cleaned it and taped gauze over it. They gave him codeine for the pain, but he swallowed only half the dose. He wanted his wits about him.

By the time he'd finished washing up, a driver arrived with fresh clothes, so Solomon was clean, dressed and calm by the time the cops drove him to police headquarters for questioning. The building was on Seventh Street downtown, hard against the elevated lanes of Interstate 880. Inside, the floors were tile and the corridor walls were covered in creamy paint and wood veneer. The interview room was close and warm.

The lead investigator was named O'Malley. He was a middle-aged guy with salt-and-pepper hair and a chin like a shovel. He asked most of the questions, though other detectives came and went during the three hours Solomon was stuck in the interview room.

O'Malley kept saying the situation smelled wrong, kept returning to Abby's escape from Willow Glade. Solomon didn't blame him. That was the biggest question in his mind as well. But he couldn't provide the answer. Not yet anyway.

Solomon answered the questions truthfully, though he was deliberately vague about the circumstances that led to checking Abby into rehab. He worried the detectives might stumble onto a connection to the shootout with Jamal and Tyrone and Jorge.

When they finally let him go, O'Malley followed Solomon onto the sidewalk outside headquarters. A limo was waiting, and the detective leaned over and looked inside. Gave a little whistle of appreciation. "Living the good life, eh? Must be nice."

"It is. Most of the time."

The sun set as Solomon rode westward across the Bay Bridge. He stared at the San Francisco skyline, the buildings a jagged silhouette against an orange sky. The lights glowing in hundreds of windows reminded him of how many people lived and worked here, crowded together on this fist of land. The thought made him long for the quiet forests at Cutthroat Lodge.

The limo driver was the same silent guy who'd taken him to Sea Cliff the day before. He hadn't gotten any more talkative. Solomon thanked him as he got out of the limo in front of the Lafayette Park apartment building. Got a nod.

Solomon saw his reflection in the lobby door as he trudged up the steps. He looked a little pale, but otherwise okay. Better than he felt. The bandage bulged under his shirt. He still wore his shoulder holster, though it was empty.

The police had kept his gun and the one he'd taken off the kid, and that worried him. There was a very slim chance that ballistics experts might match his Colt to the bullet he'd put in Jorge the Frog-Eyed Mexican. He'd cleaned the gun at his cabin, so the detectives shouldn't have any reason to run ballistics tests on it, but you never could tell.

He'd told the cops how he'd taken the Raven off the homeboy, but he couldn't prove it. Carl, in intensive care, couldn't vouch for him. Solomon couldn't provide an identity for the dealer, and it was unlikely the gun had been registered legally. Who knows how many crimes might've been committed with that pistol?

Mrs. Wong answered the doorbell. She'd clearly been crying.

"Ah, Solomon! You are all right?"

"Yes, ma'am. I'm fine."

She hugged him tight. Her head came up to his chest and it pressed against the bandage over his wound. He clenched his teeth. She stepped back and looked up at him and said, "So sad about Miss Abby."

"Yes."

"Her mother is sleeping now. The doctor gave her pills. I made herb tea, but she needed the pills. She was screaming."

Mrs. Wong steered him toward the kitchen, but they never made it that far. Michael and Chris Sheffield emerged from the sitting room, and Chris said, "*There* you are. We were beginning to wonder."

"The police had a lot of questions."

Both brothers carried highball glasses. Chris was glassy-eyed and his tie was askew. Michael still looked sober, but he always seemed more composed than his slob of a brother. Michael's scalp looked freshly tanned. Evidence of a hot African sun?

"Where's Dom?" Solomon asked.

Chris jerked a thumb toward the rear of the apartment. "Asleep. He was with Dorothy, helping her calm down, and both of them drifted off. The doc gave Dorothy pills to knock her out, but Dad was just pooped, I think."

That didn't sound like Dom, but Solomon let it go. He was pretty pooped himself.

"Come tell us about it," Michael said, turning back to the sitting room. Solomon sighed and followed.

Mrs. Wong still stood nearby, her hands clutched before her. She chirped, "Solomon? Have you eaten?"

He shook his head.

"I will make you something. And bring some tea." She started to turn away, then hesitated, offering, as an afterthought: "Would you gentlemen like anything?"

Both brothers shook their heads, and Mrs. Wong hurried away.

"You see that?" Chris said to Michael. "The way she treated Solomon? He's everybody's favorite."

Michael ignored his brother, crossing to an antique liquor cabinet that stood open against the far wall. He hefted a cut-crystal decanter and freshened his drink.

"A drink, Solomon?"

"I'll wait on the tea."

"I'll take another," Chris said and held out his glass so Michael could top it off. Then the brothers sat together on a plump leather sofa. Solomon eased himself into a wingback chair across from them.

"Take it from the top," Chris said. "I want to hear every detail."

Solomon had gone over it a dozen times with the police. He was tired of hearing his own voice. But he cleared his throat and told it again.

The brothers sat silently, except for when Solomon described the bullet striking Abby, and Michael said, "Jesus."

Mrs. Wong tiptoed into the room with a tray, and set it on a table beside Solomon. She backed out without a word. Solomon poured himself a cup of hot tea, but didn't touch the sandwich and potato chips she'd arranged on a plate. He'd get to them once he was done answering questions.

"Jesus," Michael said again. "What a goat-fuck. How the hell did you get blindsided like that?"

Solomon nearly choked on the tea.

"Nobody was around when I went into the house," he said. "I came out, carrying Abby in my arms, and still saw no one. I didn't check every car down the block. I was focused on getting her to a hospital."

"Didn't you think that drug dealer would come back?" Chris said. "That's got to be who fired those shots. You pissed him off, so he came after you."

"I don't think so," Solomon said. "He was just a kid, and he ran off scared. I had his gun."

"Plenty of guns in that neighborhood."

"No doubt. But I was only inside the house a couple of minutes. Doesn't seem like enough time for him to make the decision, go get another gun—"

"Seems possible to me," Michael interrupted. "Maybe his car was parked down the street. Maybe he had another gun there. Why not?"

Solomon shrugged and sipped his tea. He was too tired to argue.

"What's the other option?" Michael insisted. "Somebody followed you all over Oakland, waiting for you to find Abby, then opened fire? That doesn't make any sense."

Solomon had thought about it for hours and, no, it didn't make sense. Neither had any of the theories the cops floated. None of it made any fucking sense.

"I keep coming back to the original problem," he said. "Somebody got Abby out of rehab last night. Somebody took her to that rough neighborhood. It's like they *wanted* her out there, overdosing herself."

The brothers looked at each other, then back at him. "We've been wondering about that, too," Chris said. "Especially since it was your name on the release forms. Explain that."

Solomon stiffened, which made his bandage pull and sting.

"I talked to the night nurse who let her go. She said the man had ID in my name. A bald guy with a big mustache."

Michael's hand went to his own mustache. Chris shot him a look, and he blushed and dropped his hand to his lap. Both brothers took slugs from their drinks as Solomon resumed.

"Whoever it was must've given Abby money for drugs. She was practically comatose when I found her."

Chris cursed under his breath and sucked down more bourbon.

"I keep thinking," Solomon said, "that whoever got her out of rehab was keeping an eye on that house. When he saw me carry her out, he started shooting."

"Sounds to me," Chris said, "like you're looking for anything that will take the blame off you. Trying to cover up your own screw-up."

Solomon's teeth ground together, but he said nothing.

"The fact remains," the fat man continued, "that Abby was alive until you took her into your 'care.' Now she's dead. The whole family's in turmoil now. Sometimes, I wonder if that's not the way you prefer it. Dad runs to you every time there's an emergency. Maybe you thrive on emergencies. Maybe you create them."

Solomon was on his feet without meaning to stand, his fists balled beside his thighs. Chris' eyes widened, but a smarmy smile spread across his face.

"Temper, temper," he said. "I don't think you can afford any more trouble right now."

It took an effort, but Solomon unclenched his hands. "Will that be all?"

"I think so," Michael said. "We've heard everything we need to hear."

Solomon turned to leave. He needed to get out of the apartment. Out into the cool night air. He could come back after Chris and Michael went home.

"Dad puts too much faith in you, Solomon," Chris said behind him. "He thinks you can do no wrong. But we know better."

Solomon stopped in the doorway. "Feel free to tell him what you know."

"Oh, we will," Chris said. "Not that it'll do any good. Everyone knows you're his favorite, Solomon. But Dad won't be around forever. Once Michael and I are in charge, you'll be looking for another job. Count on it."

Solomon gave them a curt nod and walked away. Trying to reach a safe distance before his emotions exploded.

CHAPTER 26

●●●●●●●●●●●●●●●●●●●

Robert Mboku watched as the big man ducked out the doorway of the apartment building. An ornate lamp illuminated the little porch, and Robert could see clearly the man's scowling face.

"That's the bodyguard I saw at the lodge," Robert said to Jean-Pierre, who sat behind the wheel of the silver pickup.

The bodyguard stalked away on the sidewalk, turned a corner, headed downhill.

"He looks angry," Jean-Pierre said. "Dealing with the Sheffields must not be easy."

They'd followed Michael Sheffield here earlier, had seen his fat brother and their father arrive as well. Robert had urged Jean-Pierre to storm the apartment, catch all the rich bastards in the same place, but Jean-Pierre had said they must wait for a better opportunity.

The waiting and watching was wearing on them both, though Robert thought he handled it better than the Frenchman. He kept his mind blank and his eyes open. He paid no attention to how much time passed, or how little.

But he understood Jean-Pierre's impatience. They couldn't go home until the job was done, and the Sheffields were not easy targets. Not in this bustling city. With their chauffeured cars and their busy offices, the Sheffields seemed to never be alone.

Jean-Pierre had a plan, and he'd spent most of the day on his cell phone, lining up men and weapons and vehicles. He looked weary, the bags under his eyes even more pronounced than usual. He smoked one of his strong, stubby cigarettes, and the truck's window was rolled down so the smoke could drift away on the night breeze. Robert wrapped his arms around his chest and rocked slightly. He did not like this city, its chills and strange fog.

Jean-Pierre flicked his cigarette butt out the window, and it hit the pavement in a small explosion of orange sparks.

"Perhaps we can make use of this bodyguard," he said. "Perhaps he could get the Sheffields in the target zone for us. Or at least look the other way when the time comes. Then we wouldn't have to kill him, too. I think that man, he would not be so easy to kill."

Robert nodded. He feared no man, but why make the job more difficult?

The apartment building's door opened and two men stepped out onto the stoop.

"It's them," Jean-Pierre said.

Michael Sheffield's bald head glinted under the porch light. The Warthog's round face was bright red. Both men wore dark suits and white shirts and neckties. Robert's hand automatically went to his machete.

"Wait," Jean-Pierre said. "Not here. Not yet."

As if by magic, a long black car angled to the curb in front of the Sheffields and they opened the back door and climbed inside.

"We follow them some more?" Robert asked.

"I don't think so," Jean-Pierre said. "It's late. We need rest. Tomorrow, we'll check out the bodyguard."

Robert sighed as the limousine pulled away.

"Not much longer," Jean-Pierre said. He smiled at Robert. "Their time is coming."

CHAPTER 27

•••••••••••••••••••••

Laguna Street cascades steeply from the heights around Lafayette Park, flattening out only at cross streets, where cars often come flying blind into the intersections. Every day in San Francisco potentially an exciting day on the set of "Bullitt."

The downhill grade forced Solomon to go slow. He leaned back against the pull of gravity, trying to keep from running away with himself. By the time he reached Union Street, his thighs burned from the strain. He stopped at a corner, lifting one knee and then the other. The stretching helped his legs, but the fire ignited by the Sheffield brothers still burned in his brain.

Tuesday night, and most of the Union Street bars and restaurants were merely full, rather than overflowing. Impatient locals and gawping tourists dodged each other on the sidewalks. Solomon, standing still, was an oversized island in the stream.

He went west on Union, looking into bars and coffee shops, searching for a quiet spot where he could sit and simmer down.

He found a narrow Irish tavern squeezed between two trendy bistros. No uproarious drunks inside, and a few empty stools toward the back. He squeezed through the crowd near the door and settled onto a stool and caught the bartender's eye. Solomon wanted something strong and quick, but he knew better. Not on an empty stomach. Not in this mood. He'd be dangerous. He asked for a Harp ale, and the bartender served it up speedily.

Solomon took such a long draught, the bubbles brought tears to his eyes. Aah. Better.

He blinked away the tears and checked out the saloon. Mostly middle-aged white guys lining the bar, their attention on a baseball game braying from ceiling-mounted TVs. A few couples, their heads together, talking over the hubbub. Near the front door sat a pouty brunette, looking right at him. She wore a tight white dress with a plunging neckline, and it said something about his state of rage that he'd blindly walked right past her. A stocky young man wearing a ratty suede jacket and a knit cap leaned close to her. They were in their mid-twenties, and clearly had suffered a communications breakdown. The girl dressed up, expecting a fancy evening out, not beers in an Irish pub. No wonder she was looking around. Calculating odds, as was his habit, Solomon figured Mr. Knit Cap was a hundred percent guaranteed to sleep alone tonight. Fifty-fifty on whether she'd see him again.

Knit Cap followed the girl's gaze and locked onto Solomon with a scowl. Solomon looked away. He couldn't face a macho showdown tonight. He was still too stirred up over the Sheffield boys blaming everything on him. As always.

Half a lifetime of their spite flashed through his mind. The Sheffield boys were grown by the time his mother went to work for Dom, but they'd always seen Solomon as a threat. Perhaps because Dom had clearly cared so much for Rose. After she died and Dom kept Solomon in the fold, his sons had a new target for their resentment. That bitterness was a lot to live with, and Solomon found it increasingly difficult to keep his anger tamped down, to do what was expected, to say "yes, sir."

He mostly tried not to think about his mother and Dom and what might've occurred between them. He and the old man never talked about it. But Solomon knew Dom's strong feelings for his mother were the initial reason the Sheffield doors had opened to him. Since then, he'd earned his keep, maybe even the right to be counted as one of the family. But Chris and Michael would never let that happen. The spoiled fucks.

He slugged more ale and ordered another, hoping the cold brew could cool him off inside.

Solomon glanced over and found the dark-eyed woman still looking his way. Knit Cap had a storm brewing on his face. Solomon averted his eyes. Drank more beer. In a bar mirror, he watched Knit Cap get off his stool. The girl grabbed his arm, but he jerked free—didn't look as if he had to try very hard—and stalked toward Solomon.

Aw, hell. Not tonight, kid.

The stool to Solomon's right was empty, and Knit Cap stepped into the space. He stood too close, waiting for Solomon's attention. Solomon stared straight ahead.

"What's wrong with you?" the kid said. "Why you making eyes at my date?"

Solomon sighed, but said nothing. Maybe the kid would get bored and go away.

"I'm talking to you, asshole."

The girl smiled smugly. She'd gotten what she wanted. She'd make a memorable night of it yet.

"Hey." The kid poked Solomon's shoulder with a finger. "I'm talking to you."

Solomon turned to him and kept his voice low as he said, "You're about to make a mistake here."

Knit Cap's jaw jutted. "You're the one making the mistake. Eyeballing my girl."

"Listen to me," Solomon muttered. "I'm in a bad mood. Force me to take it out on you, and you'll end up crippled. Understand?"

The kid puffed out his chest, but Solomon saw misgiving in his eyes.

"Think about the future. You don't want to look back and think: That's the day my life went to shit. I could've left that man in the bar alone. But I had to push it. Even after he warned me."

Knit Cap suffered a blinking fit. His lower lip quivered. Solomon needed to give him a way out.

"Okay," he said, louder. "I hear you. I was leaving anyway."

He drained the mug and stood up. The kid gave him room. Their eyes met, and Knit Cap got smarter. He went back to his date, who still perched on her high stool, smug as a cat over the fracas she'd caused. She watched Solomon as he walked past to the door, still trying to milk the situation. But her boyfriend stayed busy with his beer.

Solomon gulped the chill night air and let his shoulders sag, trying to release the tension. He needed to get off this busy street, away from people, before he vented his anger on someone else. Surely it was safe to go back to the Lafayette Park apartment by now. Chris and Michael no doubt had gone home. Dom was asleep. Solomon could use some rest himself.

He walked to the corner and looked up at the eight blocks of steep hillside he'd descended to reach Union Street. It would take half an hour to hike back, and he might need climbing gear. He speed-dialed his phone and asked the night security team to send him a car for the ride up the hill.

An indulgence. In some small ways, he was as spoiled as the Sheffield boys. The little aggravations in life were erased by Dom's money. Working for him meant comfort and luxury and influence.

Solomon certainly would miss it when it was gone.

• • • • • • • • • • • • • • • • • • • •

CHAPTER 28

Wednesday morning, Dominick Sheffield sat in the dining room at the San Francisco apartment, the windows open to a cool breeze. Traffic whooshed by as regular as ocean waves, and once in a while he could hear the distant clang-clang of the California Street cable car.

Mrs. Wong had stayed in the apartment all night, tending to his family rather than going home to her own. She kept urging Dom to eat something, but he only wanted black coffee. His eyes felt scratchy and fatigue weighed on his body like an overcoat. The loss of his granddaughter was a throbbing ache in his chest.

He sighed, and it was as if the sound summoned Solomon Gage. The big man appeared in the doorway, dressed for the day, his smooth head dotted with what looked like shaving nicks. His blue eyes were bloodshot.

"Good morning," Dom said. "You get any sleep?"

Solomon shrugged his thick shoulders, as if sleep wasn't worth comment. "How's Dorothy?"

"Better, I think. Dr. Graham put her on sedatives, and she managed to sleep through the night. Ted's on his way here this morning, to take her back to L.A."

Dom didn't think much of Dorothy's latest beau. Ted Hendrix had that slick, fast-money attitude so common in Southern California, where everything was temporary. The fact that Ted was coming to San Francisco to look after her showed he was at least trying to do the right thing.

"Think she'd be better off staying here?" Solomon asked, and Dom got that familiar feeling that Solomon was reading his mind.

"Naturally, I'd like to keep her close by. But she wants to go home, and there's really no compelling reason for her to stay. Dorothy can stage the funeral near her friends. Might make it easier for her."

"Yes, sir."

Solomon's jacket spread open as he sat at the table, and Dom saw that he'd replaced the pistol the police had confiscated. He started to ask where he'd gotten the replacement, but thought better of it. Some things he didn't need to know.

He pointed instead at the bulge under Solomon's shirt.

"That where they winged you?"

"It's nothing. They didn't even stitch it up. I put a fresh bandage on it this morning."

"You don't want it to get infected."

"Yes, sir."

"The cuts on your head?"

"Flying glass. It's nothing. Really."

Something else was bothering Solomon, but he apparently wasn't inclined to talk about it. Instead, he said, "I'd thought I'd go over to Oakland today. See if I can get a lead on who shot Abby."

Dom shook his head. "Leave the murder investigation to the police. It's better that they handle it. If they catch you poking around, they might make noise."

"I didn't intend to let them catch me," Solomon said.

"We've got other problems this morning," Dom said. "I just got off the phone with Frank Price. Grace's lawyer filed a motion seeking financial information on all our holdings. She wants a complete audit of our books by an outside accounting firm. I don't want a bunch of outsiders prying into our business."

"Can't our lawyers—"

"I've got Price's firm on it already," Dom said. "But I'm not confident they can beat the request. If we fight, it looks like we have something to hide. If we don't, the details of every business deal in the past thirty years could go public."

"Can't the court require the auditors to keep it confidential?"

"Sure. But Lucinda Cruz would leak it. She wants the world to know how much we're worth, and how we got our money. And I don't need to tell you that there's proprietary information involved."

Solomon's brow furrowed, the only sign that his brain whirred inside that clean-shaven dome.

"I'm going back to Cutthroat as soon as Dorothy heads home," Dom said. "I need you to be my eyes and ears on this divorce, Solomon. I told Price you'd come see him today. Talk to Grace again, see if you can get her to back off. And see what you can find out about this Cruz woman. Maybe there's something we can use against her, something to make her sit down and shut up."

"I checked her out yesterday," Solomon said. "She looks clean."

"There's bound to be something we can use," Dom said. "There always is."

"Yes, sir. Do you need me to help with Abby? Get her body from the cops, all that?"

"I've put other people on that already. You concentrate on Grace and her lawyer. This divorce filing threatens the whole family. You know how I want such threats handled."

"Eliminate them by any means."

"Damned straight."

CHAPTER 29

••••••••••••••••••••

Victor Amadou knocked on the door of the suite at the stately St. Francis Hotel, and waited a full minute before Ambassador Claude Mirabeau bothered to open up. The ambassador turned away without a word, and Victor followed him inside.

The suite was spacious, much grander than the room where Victor tossed and turned all night. Brocade wallpaper and brass lamps and antique furniture made the room feel old-fashioned. A king-sized bed still bore the imprint of the ambassador's long body. The tall window looked out at blue sky and skyscrapers and the perfect palm trees of Union Square.

Mirabeau sat at a round table near the window, sunlight streaming in through gauzy curtains. The remains of a huge breakfast covered the table—platters and carafes, picked-over fruit and bread crusts—and the scents made Victor's stomach growl. He'd taken very poor coffee in his room, but hadn't ordered room-service food himself. The ambassador caught him looking.

"Have you eaten?" he asked in French.

"No," Victor said. "I'll get something later."

"Always watching the budget. You're a good man that way."

Victor felt that Mirabeau was baiting him, but he said simply, "*Merci.*"

The ambassador gave him a sour smile. Mirabeau was very dark, with a high forehead and the perpetual expression of a man who'd swallowed a bug. He belonged to the same tribe as President Boudreaux, and looked very much like him. Victor had heard rumors the men were distant cousins, and liked to believe that was the only reason the ambassador got such an important post. It certainly wasn't on the basis of his intelligence or his diplomatic skills.

"Sit," Mirabeau said. "Tell me what you've learned."

Victor sat across the littered table from the ambassador, who sipped at coffee in a delicate cup. He didn't offer any to his security man.

"It's not much, I'm afraid," Victor said. "As near as I can determine, Michael Sheffield was indeed out of town when we visited his office. His father also is out of town, apparently lives in a rural area some distance north of the city. I am trying to get a precise location."

The ambassador frowned. "We need to find them. We need to sit down with them, face to face."

Victor fought the temptation to roll his eyes. "Do you really think you can talk them out of their scheme?"

Ambassador Mirabeau rocked back in his chair and frowned. His long fingers fiddled with his cufflinks.

"Don't be so quick to dismiss diplomacy," he said. "Talking can solve many problems. Not all of us are men of action such as yourself."

Another shot at Victor's pride. He'd worked security for the embassy in Washington, D.C., for ten years now, had been instrumental in protecting it against myriad threats, but Mirabeau treated him like a servant. The ambassador felt he didn't need Victor's protection. He believed the popularity of President Boudreaux—and, by extension, Boudreaux's appointees—was so solid that no one would dare make an attempt on his life. Which only proved that he was a fool.

"I'm onto another man," Victor said. "Solomon Gage. He apparently works closely with Sheffield *pere*, and perhaps he can introduce us to him."

Mirabeau nodded approvingly. "You've talked to this man?"

"Not yet. I learned his identity last night from someone at the consulate. We saw him at Sheffield Enterprises. A very large man with a shaved head?"

The ambassador shook his head to show he did not recall. Victor was not surprised. Mirabeau was oblivious to most everything but the sound of his own voice.

"I got a cable this morning," Mirabeau said. "The president isn't happy with our lack of progress. We need to get this settled. Already, uncertainty over Goma is having its effect back home."

"How so?"

"New polls." The ambassador waved a dismissive hand. "Laurent has closed the gap."

Jacques Laurent was President Boudreaux's opponent in the coming election. A reformer. Victor secretly thought a healthy dose of reform was exactly what his country needed, but Boudreaux's people tried to paint Laurent as a Communist and an opportunist and a rabble-rouser.

Victor tried to mirror the ambassador's frown, despite the little leap he felt inside.

"This business with Goma is a mere distraction," Mirabeau said, "but if we can get the Sheffields to withdraw their support, it will become a triumph. The president can go on television and radio, tell the nation how we outflanked Goma, how we outsmarted the Americans. I don't need to tell you how valuable that would be."

Victor nodded, not trusting himself to speak.

"If we can't solve the problem here," the ambassador said, "there's a very good chance Goma could succeed. We don't need a military coup, like in the old days. That would be very bad for Niger."

That was one thing upon which they completely agreed. Victor stood and said, "I will do my best."

"Of course," the ambassador said. "And be quick about it, eh? The fate of President Boudreaux's government is in your hands."

Victor nodded and turned away, thinking that Boudreaux's government could shrivel up and die for all he cared. But stopping Goma was important for the people of Niger. And for them, he would give his all.

CHAPTER 30

●●●●●●●●●●●●●●●●●●●●●

Solomon heard shrieking as soon as the butler opened the heavy wooden door of the Sea Cliff mansion. Grace's voice, louder and an octave higher than usual. The words were indistinct, but the tone said it all.

Charles seemed embarrassed by the noise. His skin glowed bright pink against his white hair and black clothes.

"I take it the man of the house has come home," Solomon said.

"They've been at it for an hour."

"Like this?"

"It seems to be escalating."

Solomon stepped into the foyer, and Charles made no move to stop him. The argument continued upstairs.

"Have you been up?"

Charles shook his head. "I don't get combat pay. Do you?"

"You might say that."

Michael Sheffield's voice suddenly drowned out Grace's: "You bitch!" Then came a smack, the unmistakable sound of flesh striking flesh.

Solomon growled, "Goddamnit," and bounded up the carpeted stairs.

Grace screamed, and there was another smack behind a door at the end of a corridor. Solomon sprinted down the hall and shoved open the door. Michael, dressed in a blue suit, complete with necktie and cufflinks, was near a four-poster bed, grappling with his wife.

Michael froze, his right hand raised to strike again. His left clutched a wad of Grace's nightgown, a slinky, floor-length number the same pale yellow as her hair. Grace's hands were near her face to ward off the blows. Her lip was split and the blood was bright red against her fair skin.

"What the hell?" Michael shouted at Solomon. "What are you doing here?"

"Let her go."

"Fuck you. This is none of your business."

Grace said, "Solomon." The word came out muddled by the blood that stained her teeth.

He crossed the room in three strides, and was upon Michael before he could slug Grace again. Michael turned loose of her, tried to dodge away, but Solomon grabbed his collar and spun him around.

"You fucking—"

Michael didn't get to finish. Solomon sank a fist deep into his stomach. Michael doubled over, and vomit spewed from his mouth. Coffee and orange juice, by the look of it. Solomon sidestepped the mess and reached for Grace. She flinched at the contact.

"Easy," he murmured. "It's okay."

She relaxed against him, allowed him to wrap his arms around her. Beyond her, the bed was a tangle of emerald-green satin sheets. He steered her toward it. "Lie down. I'll get you an icepack."

She wept in great shuddering sobs, and curled up on the bed. Solomon pulled a sheet up to her quaking chin.

Behind him, Michael coughed and spat. Solomon turned to find him straightening up, drool on his chin. His face was red. His eyes were aflame.

"You son of a bitch. Who do you think you are, barging in here?"

Solomon stood perfectly balanced, his arms loose by his sides. He knew Michael's temper, that the punch to the gut wouldn't be enough to stop him. But Solomon would not let him take another crack at Grace.

"Get the fuck out of my house," Michael demanded.

"No."

"Get out now, or I'll call the cops. You fucker. Coming in here, all holier than thou, no idea what's going on. Do you know what she said? What she did?"

"Doesn't matter. You don't get to hit her. That's not allowed."

"'Allowed?' The hell are you talking about? This is my house. I'll by God do whatever—"

Trying to catch Solomon off-guard, Michael swung a looping punch at his chin. Solomon leaned back a few inches, and the fist whistled harmlessly past. He hooked Michael in the side, not hard enough to break the ribs, but enough to force the air out of him.

Inside his own head, Solomon was saying, "Stop. Stop now." But he couldn't stop. Michael deserved more. He hit him again, a short uppercut to the jaw, enough behind it to make Michael's teeth clack together. Sounded like someone cracking a walnut.

Michael toppled over backward, his eyes rolling back in his head. Solomon grabbed his sleeve, yanked up just in time to keep his head from crashing against the floor. He let him down easy, then stepped back.

Solomon touched the throbbing bullet wound on his chest, but his hand came away dry. The bandage had stayed put.

Grace stared at him. Blood leaked from her mouth, but she tried to smile.

"My hero," she said thickly.

He shook his head. Nothing she could say would salvage this situation. He'd hit a Sheffield and there would be hell to pay.

He looked around at the cream-colored wallpaper, the luxurious furnishings, the crystal chandelier and the lump of blue business suit lying unconscious on the floor. A light glowed in the adjacent bathroom, bouncing off white ceramic. Solomon went in there, grabbed a thick towel off a rack and soaked it with cold water in the sink. He wrung out the towel, twisting it harder than he needed to, as if it were Michael's neck, and carried it to Grace.

"Thank you, sugar." She dabbed at the blood.

Michael groaned and stirred. Solomon stepped around him and went back into the bathroom. Came out with another white towel and spread it over the puddle of puke.

The fallen man rose up on his elbows and shook his head, blinking, trying to focus. Solomon waited until he was sure he was hearing properly, then said, "I've got a car and driver outside. You take them. Go to your office. Go tell Dom. I don't care. But get out of here."

Michael struggled to a sitting position. "You can't order me out of my own home."

"Wrong. That's exactly what I'm doing. Get up and go. Now."

Michael slowly clambered to his feet, glaring. Solomon didn't want to hit him again, but he would if Michael lunged at him. This time, he wouldn't pull his punches.

Michael straightened to his full height, tugged at his jacket, shot his cuffs. Once he had himself under control, he said, "This is the end for you, Solomon. I'll have your job. I'll nail your fucking hide to the wall."

"Fine. Do that. But go now."

Michael stalked out of the bedroom. Solomon stood still, listening, until the heavy door slammed downstairs.

Grace sat up, still pressing the white towel against her blood-ied mouth. The towel looked as if it had sprouted measles.

Solomon sat on the edge of the bed and lifted the towel away long enough to get a better look at her lip.

"It's swelling, but it's not too bad. You won't need stitches."

"Says Dr. Solomon."

"You want a real doctor? I can have one here in minutes."

She shook her head.

"Your cheek's swelling," he said. "You'll have a black eye."

Someone tapped ever so gently at the bedroom door, and Solomon turned to find the butler peeking in. "Everything okay?"

"It is now. Mrs. Sheffield could use an icepack. Would you bring one, please?"

"Right away." Charles scurried off.

Solomon asked Grace, "How'd Michael like the new butler?"

"We didn't get around to talking about Charles. Other things had Michael's attention."

"Like the divorce."

She nodded. "Guess the whole family's stirred up."

"It came at a bad time. Everyone's upset about Abby. You heard?"

She nodded again.

"Your attorney's pushing harder than she needs to. The family would give you a healthy settlement. Dom can be a fair man."

"That's not good enough," she said. "Especially not after what just happened."

"How did things go so wrong?" he asked. "What happened?"

"It doesn't matter, sugar. Michael was looking for an excuse. I've embarrassed him. It was only a matter of time before he blew up."

Solomon hesitated, but he had to ask: "Did you try to set him off?"

"I wasn't trying to get him to bust me in the mouth, if that's what you mean."

"No, I—"

"I didn't need to provoke him, Solomon. I've got plenty on Michael without this."

He nodded. Michael's history as a whorehound was all the edge she needed in court. But he'd handed her a lot more ammunition this morning, and Solomon was a witness. Shit.

Charles tapped on the door and hurried in with the icepack. He stood wringing his hands until Grace told him that would be all. The butler raised his eyebrows at Solomon, a silent question. Solomon nodded, and Charles left, closing the door behind him.

"Great first week on the new job for Charles," she said. "He's probably wondering how long he'll keep it, now that I'm divorcing Michael."

"We're all wondering what will happen next." Solomon stood. "Can I get you anything else?"

"No, you've done plenty. Thanks for helping me."

He turned to leave, but she wasn't finished.

"You know Michael's not going to drop this, right? No matter what Dom says. Michael will come after you. He'll never forget you slugged him."

"I know."

CHAPTER 31

●●●●●●●●●●●●●●●●●●●●

Christopher Sheffield was on the phone when his brother burst into his office, his face burning with rage.

"What the fuck?" Chris said. On the other end of the line, one of the company attorneys said, "What? I didn't catch that, Mr. Sheffield."

"I'll call you back." He hung up as Michael skidded to a halt in front of his desk.

"Look!" Michael pointed at his jaw. "Can you see that?"

Chris could see a knot growing there.

"Grace?" he asked.

"Hell, no. Grace didn't do this. It was Solomon!"

"Solomon hit you? Where?"

"Right here!" Michael pointed at his jaw. "Couple of shots to the body, too!"

Chris took a deep breath, as if he could calm down for the both of them. "Where were you when this happened?"

"At the house. Grace and I were arguing, and Solomon showed up and blindsided me. Hit me in the stomach. Made me puke. When I tried to fight back, he knocked me out. I've never been unconscious before, never. But he did it to me."

"Why?" Chris interjected.

"What?"

"Why did he hit you? Solomon wouldn't tee off on you just because you and Grace were getting loud."

"It doesn't matter! He came into my house, right into my own bedroom! And he hit me. By God, we should—"

"It does matter," Chris said. "Tell me exactly what happened."

"We were arguing, like I said. I was trying to get her to pull her claws in. This divorce is bad business—"

"Then what?"

"She refused, naturally. The bitch. And she started yelling at me, and pretty soon we're shouting into each other's faces. She called me names, screaming about whores and shit like that, so I cuffed her one."

"You struck her?"

"You know how she is, Chris. The mouth on that woman, I swear to God—"

"How many times did you hit her?"

"Just once! Okay, maybe twice. She wouldn't shut the fuck up. Then Solomon comes running into the room. I don't even know where he came from. What was he doing there?"

"Dad sent him."

"Are you shitting me? Why?"

"To talk to Grace. Try to get her off our backs. Same thing you were doing."

"But why did he hit me? Fuck, he should've hit *her*."

"Don't be stupid, Mike."

"Hey—"

"Whacking her? Are you crazy? If I'd been there, I would've hit you myself."

"Be that as it may," Michael said tightly. "I don't have to sit still and take a beating from the hired help."

"On that we agree," Chris said. "This might finally be a way for us to get rid of Solomon. Once Dad knows about—"

"Whoa. Let's think about this for a minute. I mean, if Dad hears I slapped Grace around—"

"Solomon's probably on the phone with him right now. It's up to us to spin it the right way. We can say she attacked you. That Solomon misread the situation."

"Bottom line is the fucker hit me. Three times. That's assault and battery. I could put the cops on him."

"No cops," Chris said quickly. "You want to be on the front page tomorrow? 'Sheffield Scion Charged With Domestic Abuse?'"

"Come on, Chris. Nobody would believe—"

"Did you leave a mark on her?"

Michael clammed up.

"That's what I thought," Chris said. "Her fucking lawyer's probably taking her picture right now, so she can hand it to the Chronicle. What the hell were you thinking?"

Michael stared at the floor.

Chris pushed a button on his intercom. The buzz was answered by Bart Logan, who said, "Yes, sir?"

"Get in here, Bart."

Michael fell into a chair across the desk from Chris. "Bart? What do we need him for?"

"He's had people tailing Solomon. I was hoping Solomon would screw up in some way. Maybe this is it. Maybe Bart can give us more information."

"How much more do we need? I'm telling you, the man hit me."

"What's he done since? Is he still there, tending to Grace? Is he trying to catch Dad before he goes back to Cutthroat? Maybe Bart's people can alibi you. Anybody else see him hit you?"

"Just Grace."

"Maybe we can produce another witness. Finally persuade Dad to get rid of Solomon."

Michael prodded at his tender jaw. "Couldn't we have Bart or somebody bump him off? Be easier to kill the son of a bitch. Get him out of our lives once and for all."

Chris shook his head. Sometimes his brother still acted like he was thirteen.

Logan barreled through the door. "What's up, boss?"

"We think we've finally got a way to get rid of Solomon Gage."

Logan beamed. "Sweet. How can I help?"

CHAPTER 32

•••••••••••••••••••

While waiting for a car outside the Sea Cliff mansion, Solomon dialed Dom's cell phone. Got a recorded message that said the number was unavailable. Dom probably airborne already, on his way back to Cutthroat. Solomon didn't leave a message. He'd hear from the old man soon enough.

In the meantime, he had work to do. He told the driver to take him across town to the Financial District, where the law firm of Price, White and Siemer had its offices in an old brick building that had been gutted and modernized, with earthquake-protection girders arranged in big "X's" in the windows. The firm handled much of the outside legal work for Sheffield Enterprises and would represent Michael in the divorce.

The receptionist was expecting him. She was a young Asian woman, with a face as beautiful as the moon and a red silk dress that showed off her slim legs. She smiled at Solomon and led him to a conference room where Franklin D. Price awaited. Price was a stout man, about seventy, with thinning white hair and a florid face. He sat at the head of a long table.

Solomon shook his hand and sat to his left. The leather chair sighed under his weight. Price slid an inch-thick deck of paper across to him.

"The divorce filing," he said. "As you'll see, they leave no stone unturned. I knew Lucinda Cruz was thorough, but *damn*. We'll be shoveling financial reports for six months."

"Mr. Sheffield doesn't want that," Solomon said.

"We may have no choice. She makes a good case for full disclosure. The way the corporations are set up, with Michael sitting on the boards, one can argue that his wife has the right to examine every—"

Solomon held up a hand to stop him. "Save it for court."

Price's face flushed. Clearly not a man accustomed to being told to shut up.

"Something you should know," Solomon said. "There was a domestic dispute at Michael's home this morning. Mrs. Sheffield was injured."

Price's mouth dropped open. As the news sank in, his face closed into a frown.

"He hit her?"

"Couple of times. I put a stop to it, but I arrived a few minutes late."

Price shook his head mournfully. "That will only make things worse. Where's Michael now?"

"I sent him away. He probably went to the office."

"I'll have someone call over there. We'll need a statement from him."

Solomon nodded.

Price reached out and stabbed the paperwork with a thick finger. "This is going to get bigger. And soon."

"I know."

"I'd better get to work."

Price pushed back his chair and stood. Solomon remained seated, and thanked him for the documents.

"It's public record. No reason not to show it to you, or anyone else Dom sends over. You're not an attorney yourself, right?"

"Right."

"Well, you might have trouble making heads or tails of some of this. It's boilerplate, you know, legalese."

"I'll manage."

Price gave him a curt nod and left the room, looking worried. Solomon heard him say: "Get Michael Sheffield on the phone."

The door closed with a click, shutting out the sounds from the outer offices. Only the hum of the air conditioning to keep Solomon company. He slid the court filing closer, slipped off an oversized red rubber band that held it together, and began to page through the motions.

It was tough sledding. The document was filled with allegations and citations and frustrations. Paragraph after paragraph set out the names and addresses of various Sheffield holdings all over the world and demanded full financial information about each. If all the requests were granted, Solomon imagined, the resulting stack of paper would reach the ceiling.

He came across this: "Also to be disclosed: any documents, financial reports, accountings, incorporation papers and/or legal filings regarding business dealings by Sheffield Extraction Industries or any other subsidiary of Sheffield Enterprises on the continent of Africa."

There it was again. Michael clearly had something cooking in Africa, and Grace had told her attorney about it. But how had Michael kept it secret? Dom had people throughout the family businesses, lawyers and accountants and MBAs who were paid to monitor things for him. But the old man claimed to know nothing about any business in Africa.

Solomon needed that information. No chance that Michael would talk to him now. But maybe Chris—

He dialed headquarters and reached a secretary who said Chris was in a meeting and had left orders not to be disturbed. She asked if this was an emergency. Solomon couldn't honestly say it was, though it felt urgent to him. He thanked her and flipped the phone shut. Damn.

He thought about the African delegation—if that's what it had been—he'd seen at Chris' office. Was that connected to whatever Michael was up to?

Solomon stacked the paperwork and replaced the rubber band. He carried the documents to the outer office.

The receptionist smiled at him from behind her desk. Her lipstick was the same shade as her red dress, and looked as if she'd just freshened it up.

"Can I get a copy of these?" he asked her.

"Mr. Price said that copy is yours to keep."

She beamed, and he wished he could work up a smile in return, but he had too much on his mind. He thanked her and tucked the documents under his arm. The one day he had papers to carry, and he'd left his briefcase back at the Lafayette Park apartment.

Outside, the wind had kicked up, blowing litter and grit through the concrete canyons of the Financial District. The sun was shining, though, and it was warm where sunbeams squeezed between skyscrapers. Solomon decided to walk the five blocks to Embarcadero Center. He needed the time to think.

His phone rang. He fished it out of his pocket and flipped it open. The readout made him wince. It said, "Dominick Sheffield."

CHAPTER 33

● ● ● ● ● ● ● ● ● ● ● ● ● ● ● ● ● ● ●

Dom bubbled with rage as Solomon matter-of-factly told him about the fight at Michael's house. Lots there to make him angry. Michael no doubt had made their position with the court much worse by striking Grace. Dom could practically hear her attorney licking her chops. But what he said was: "You punched my son?"

"Yes, sir."

"What possessed you to do that?"

"He'd hit Grace at least twice. When I arrived, he had his hand up to hit her again."

"Did he stop when he saw it was you?"

"He started cursing at me. I had to pull him off her."

"Then you hit him."

A long pause. "Yes, sir. Once. I didn't punch him again until he took a swing at me."

"You think that makes it all right?"

"No, sir. I wish none of it had happened. I just reacted, the way I've been trained."

"Nothing in your training allows you to hit a member of my family. We're all your employers, Solomon. You think people in regular jobs can hit the boss whenever they're unhappy?"

"This isn't a regular job, sir."

Dom took a deep breath, blew it out through his nose. He'd been pacing his study at the lodge, and he paused at the window, looking out at the redwoods that towered between the lodge and the airstrip.

"I tried to show as much restraint as possible," Solomon said.

Dom snorted into the phone.

"I pulled my punches, sir."

Dom knew that must be true. If Solomon had really let loose on him, Michael would be in a hospital.

"I suppose," Dom said, "there was no talking to Grace after that."

"I tried. But she seemed more resolved than ever."

"Goddamn, what did we ever do to her? I always liked that girl, always treated her well. Now she turns on us?"

"I don't think it's the whole family she's after," Solomon said. "Just Michael. But she's willing to take the rest of us down along with him. Especially now."

Dom noted that "us." Solomon sometimes spoke as if he were one of the family. Dom usually let it go, but he didn't feel charitable at the moment. Before he could pursue it, though, Solomon said, "I thought I'd go see Lucinda Cruz next."

Dom hesitated. Maybe they should leave this to the lawyers now. But Solomon always produced results, and Dom was sick to death of lawyers.

"Go ahead. At least get a reading on her, so you can tell me exactly what we're up against."

"Yes, sir."

"But Solomon?"

"Yes, sir?"

"See if you can manage to do it without punching her lights out."

A cheap shot, but Dom couldn't help himself. He cut the connection.

CHAPTER 34

●●●●●●●●●●●●●●●●●●●●●

Solomon stalked across a small plaza near the Drumm Street entrance to Embarcadero Center Four. A few shoppers sprawled on benches next to bright flowerbeds, yakking on phones and smoking, but he didn't register them. He felt hot, inside and out, and sweat beaded on his forehead. He had his head down, scowling at the concrete, the court document tucked under his arm, and he didn't notice the giant redhead until the man was nearly upon him.

When he did look up, his eyes met Mick Nielsen's and the fired dockworker froze eight feet away. Nielsen wore gray work clothes and black boots, and a jack handle dangled from his right hand.

"You son of a bitch," Nielsen growled. "I told you I'd get even."

He cocked the lug wrench to his shoulder, ready to crease Solomon's skull.

Solomon didn't give him the chance. He drew his .45 from the shoulder rig so quickly, it was if it appeared in his hand. Presto. He pointed it at Nielsen's face.

Nielsen's mouth opened, but no sound came out. Solomon closed the gap between them, and pressed the muzzle against the man's forehead.

Someone screamed nearby. Solomon was suddenly aware of the sound of feet slapping concrete and people shouting about a man with a gun. Damn.

"You weren't supposed to show your face around here again."

"I—"

Solomon jabbed the gun into his face.

"Drop that tire iron."

The weapon clanged to the sidewalk.

Solomon risked a glance around, saw stragglers running away, looking back over their shoulders at him. A few shouted into phones.

"Lot of witnesses," he said to Nielsen. "They'd testify that you attacked me with that tire iron. That I shot you in self-defense."

"But I—"

"Shut up."

Solomon heard a siren in the distance. He gave Nielsen a final shove with the gun barrel, and stepped back. The muzzle left a deep, round dent between his eyebrows.

"Don't ever come back here," Solomon said.

Nielsen nodded vigorously. He backed away slowly.

Impatient, Solomon jabbed the air with the gun. "Run!"

Nielsen turned and sprinted across the street to where a red Chevy pickup was parked at the curb. He jumped behind the wheel and cranked the engine.

Solomon holstered the pistol, feeling very exposed. Most of the lunchtime loiterers had vanished. A couple peeked out at him from behind concrete columns. The siren was very close now. He didn't want to take time to explain himself to the police. He had things to do.

Clutching the court filing under his arm like a football, he ran past the gawkers and into the building. He scrambled down two escalators to an underground parking garage. He knew the garage had another exit on the far side of Embarcadero Center. He could pop up there and cut through the Hyatt.

As he ran, thoughts flitted through his head: What's the matter with me? My temper keeps getting the best of me. Sure, I've encountered plenty of adversity the past few days, but I'm making mistakes, reacting, letting my emotions take over. I need to get myself under control.

His clapping shoes echoed around the concrete parking garage. He settled into a steady gait, the same pace he used when he ran among the evergreens at Cutthroat. His legs felt fine, but the motion pulled at the tape on the bandage on his chest.

Too bad he had to leave Embarcadero Center in such a hurry. He wanted to talk to Michael and Chris. He had some hard questions for them, concerning Africa.

But that would have to wait.

CHAPTER 35

•••••••••••••••••••••

Lucinda Cruz's office was in an old storefront on Geary Boulevard, in the western part of San Francisco known as The Avenues. Only a mile from Sea Cliff, but a much more modest address.

The stucco of the Art Deco building was rounded at the corners and etched with horizontal bands that made it look streamlined. The law office was wedged between a vitamin store and a travel agency with posters of exotic locales in the windows. Lucinda Cruz kept her windows covered by deep-green curtains that made Solomon think of the satin sheets on Grace Sheffield's marriage bed.

He didn't have an appointment, and a middle-aged receptionist made sure he had a nice long wait, plenty of time to absorb her perfume, which filled the outer office like a miasma of wistfulness. Solomon sat unmoving on a straight-backed chair, his hands on his knees, his eyes straight ahead, staring at a black-and-white photo of the Golden Gate Bridge on the opposite wall. He tried to find some inner calm to balance out the fact that so far today he'd punched out one man, pulled a gun on another and been chewed out by his boss. Not a good day.

The receptionist seemed unnerved by the silent visitor. She kept clearing her throat and humming under her breath and swiveling in her chair. Finally, a buzzer sounded on her desk. She sounded relieved as she said, "You can go in now."

The inner office wasn't much bigger than the reception area, and it was lined with jam-packed bookshelves on three sides, with only a tiny, frosted window in one wall to let in light. The carpet was thin and worn, but the desk and other furniture were sleek and teak and right off the Ikea showroom floor.

Solomon absorbed this at a glance, which was all he got before his gaze locked on the woman behind the desk. The newspaper photograph hadn't done her justice. Her features were perfect and her skin was the color of cinnamon and her body was voluptuous in all the right places.

Lucinda Cruz stood and reached across her cluttered desk to shake his hand. She wore a narrow black skirt with a silky sky-blue blouse. A jacket that matched the skirt draped over the back of her chair. Her hand was warm in his, and he must've held on too long, because she smiled at him, her teeth brilliantly white against her dark skin.

Solomon felt his cheeks warm. He unhanded her and fell into the chair she indicated. He still had the thick court document in his hand, and there was no place to set it down, so he balanced it on his knee.

"That looks familiar," she said.

"My summer reading."

"How do you like it?"

"Plot's a little thin, but I can't wait to see how it turns out."

"Same here." Merriment danced in her dark eyes. "I assume your coming here is a new twist in the story?"

"You know who I am?"

"Oh, yes. My client thinks very highly of Mr. Solomon Gage. She talks about you like you're her new romance."

"She's a married woman."

"Not for long."

Solomon grinned. "She's not my type."

"You don't like beautiful, wealthy women?"

"Wealthy?"

Lucinda Cruz glanced at the stack of papers resting on his knee. "She's about to get richer."

"Maybe. But it'll take years."

"Think so?"

"The Sheffields own a lot of attorneys," he said. "They won't just roll over for you."

"That makes it more interesting."

"For you, maybe. But what about Grace? She up to a prolonged court battle? A bitter divorce? Media attention?"

Lucinda Cruz's smile vanished. "Grace has more strength than you realize. And what happened this morning makes her case stronger. My investigator's over at the house right now, interviewing her, taking photos. He tells me her entire cheek is one big bruise."

"Ouch."

"I understand you were a witness. You can expect to be called to testify."

"I didn't actually see him hit her."

"You stopped him from doing it again. For that much, Grace is grateful."

"Couldn't the two of you show your gratitude by leaving me out of it? You could cost me my job."

Lucinda Cruz smiled. "Not a chance. I imagine your job's in trouble anyway. If anything will get you fired, it's beating up Michael Sheffield."

What could he say? She was right.

"To me," she resumed, "today's incident is just the latest in a pattern of abuse."

"He's hit her before?"

"He's exerted pressure in other ways. The Sheffield men think they can run the lives of everyone around them. They think they can push people around. I'm going to prove they can't."

"Sounds like you have a chip on your shoulder."

"Exactly what my opponents always say."

"Is that what I am? Your opponent?"

"You work for the Sheffields. That puts us on opposing teams."

"Even though I'm the one who slugged Michael?"

"One punch doesn't change a lifetime."

"It was three punches."

Lucinda steepled her fingers in front of her chin. She studied him, looking happy as hell, and Solomon couldn't tell what she was thinking. Damn, she was gorgeous.

"You won't win," he said. "The family can buy its way out of difficulty."

"They can't buy the court."

Solomon wanted to tell her: I wouldn't be so sure of that. Dom had paid off judges before. But that would be revealing too much. Instead, he said, "All these requests for financial disclosure? It ticks them off."

She tucked her chin, as if trying to hide another smile behind her hands.

"They'd give Grace a big settlement to make this go away. But if you push it, she could end up with nothing."

"Doesn't sound like you have much confidence in my abilities, Mr. Gage."

"Nothing against you. But I know the family's lawyers. You're outnumbered and outgunned."

"Just the way I like it."

"Is it the best thing for your client?"

"Let me worry about that. I'll take good care of my client. I always do."

"Make sure you're not letting your ambitions get in the way. You've got something against corporate America, fine. But don't let that agenda hurt Grace's chances—"

A hard glint came into her eyes. "Thank you for your concern, Mr. Gage. But I don't need a lecture on ethics."

He held up his hands placatingly. "No offense. It's easy to get carried away, taking on the rich."

"Just like it's easy to get carried away defending them. How can you live with yourself, doing the dirty work for Dominick Sheffield?"

"I never said it was dirty."

She raised her eyebrows. "I've heard stories."

"From Grace? She doesn't know as much as she pretends. If she's talking about me or about family business, she's telling you what you want to hear. Grace has a flair for the dramatic."

Lucinda Cruz didn't reply.

"Here's what I see happening," he said. "Our attorneys will put Grace on the stand. They'll get her talking in circles, sounding crazy. They'll make her out to be a psycho."

"Thanks for the warning," she said dryly. "I'll make sure she doesn't get put in that position."

"Might be impossible to stop it."

"We'll see. In the meantime, we'll get full disclosure about Michael's financial holdings, so we can carve out Grace's fair share. Those millions could buy a lot of time on a therapist's couch."

"You won't win," he insisted.

She raked her hands through the black ringlets that framed her face. Sighed. For a second, she looked tired. Then her eyes met his and she smiled again.

"I'm already winning," she said.

"How do you figure?"

"The Sheffields are worried. Otherwise, they wouldn't have sent you here."

"They didn't—"

"When Michael Sheffield beat up his wife this morning, he handed us the court's sympathies. We'll win."

They sat staring at each other. Solomon felt a strong attraction, nearly a physical force, drawing him toward the beautiful woman behind the desk. It was all he could do to sit still.

"I'm sorry, Mr. Gage," she said. "You seem like a nice man, and I appreciate what you did this morning. But you play for the wrong team."

She looked at her gold wristwatch, then pushed back her chair and rose to her feet. "I've got an appointment across town."

Solomon stood, too. He felt compelled to say something that would make him look good in her eyes. But he couldn't think of anything that wouldn't seem awkward and manipulative.

"Tell the Sheffields we'll see them in court," she said.

He nodded and turned to leave.

"Mr. Gage?"

He stopped with his hand on the doorknob.

"None of this is your fault."

"I know."

"But you look beaten down," she said. "The weight of the world on your shoulders."

"Not the whole world. Just the Sheffield family, sitting up there, relying on me to take care of them."

"Not an easy job."

"You have no idea."

CHAPTER 36

•••••••••••••••••••

Lou Velacci took a last drag off his cigarette and tossed the butt out the car window just as Solomon Gage hulked out onto the sidewalk in front of the lawyer's office. Gage looked up and down the street, and Lou slid lower in the seat.

Gage took a few steps along the sidewalk, coming his way, and for one gulping moment Lou thought he'd been spotted. Then Gage threw his hand into the air, hailing a passing Yellow Cab. Lou reached for the keys to crank up the Ford—

"Hey!"

Lou jerked in surprise, then swiveled his head to look out the passenger window. A punk was on the sidewalk, leaning over, peering into the car. Lou wasn't sure whether it was a man or a woman. The freak was maybe twenty years old, dressed in black, and the clothes were ripped and holey and studded with safety pins and rivets and other shit, an airport security nightmare. The young face was hairless, and the eyes were ringed in thick black mascara, so Lou thought maybe it was female, but the voice sounded male. The topper was the hair, dyed jet black and yanked skyward into so many spikes, it looked like one of those whatayacallem, those things that live in ocean—

"Hey," the kid said. "I'm talking to you."

Sea urchins.

"What?" Lou said flatly.

"You threw your cigarette out the window."

"Yeah? So?"

"So the world's not your ashtray. I live in this neighborhood, asshole."

Lou narrowed his eyes at the punk. It didn't matter whether it was a boy or a girl. Lou wanted to kick its skinny ass up and down the sidewalk.

"Too bad for your fuckin' neighbors," he said. "Asshole."

"Fuck you," the freak said.

Lou sighed, exasperated. Up ahead, Solomon Gage climbed into the cab.

"You're lucky I'm in a hurry," Lou said.

He shifted the Ford into gear and checked his mirrors, looking for a break in the traffic on busy Geary Boulevard.

"Asshole," the kid shouted again, flipping Lou the bird. The nail of the upraised finger was painted black.

The kid marched off down the sidewalk in what looked like combat boots, never looking back.

"This fuckin' town," Lou grumbled.

Steaming, he yanked the Ford out into traffic. Horns blared behind him. He goosed the gas, closed the gap between his car and the cab.

God, he was tired of following Gage around this stupid fucking town with its stupid fucking hills and its one-way streets and its slow-moving buses and trolleys. Lou longed for Manhattan, where the streets made sense and people fucking knew how to drive and you could at least buy a bagel from a street vendor while you waited to tail somebody. With this gig, Lou was afraid to get out of the car long enough to grab a bite. Felt like his ass was welded to the seat of the Ford.

Had to admit, though, it wasn't complete boredom like a lot of tail jobs. This guy Gage was an interesting motherfucker. Seemed like he just ran around town looking for trouble.

Lou enjoyed Gage's little dustup with the big redhead outside Embarcadero Center. Goddamned idiot, strutting down the sidewalk with a jack handle in his hand, thinking he could walk up and clobber Solomon fucking Gage. If Lou wanted to take out Gage, he wouldn't make such a big production. He'd slip up behind him. The bald-headed asshole would never know what hit him. Only way to snuff a big guy like that.

But no, the redhead had marched up to him, mouthing off. Bam, Gage stuck that gun in his face and backed him down. Made Lou laugh out loud.

Then Gage ran around Embarcadero Center like a crazy person, getting away before the cops showed up. Lou, circling, was lucky to spot him getting into a cab two blocks away. Now here they were, across town, outside some lawyer's office. Lou wasn't sure how this Lucinda Cruz fit into the picture, but she sure as hell wasn't one of the Sheffields' lawyers, working out of that shitty office.

Bart Logan had sounded interested when Lou called and told him Gage had gone to see her. Logan didn't explain the significance of the visit, of course; he'd never take a minute to tell Lou what the hell was going on.

The cab turned right twice, making the block, and Lou hung back a little. Never could tell when a cabbie might notice, might say to his fare, "Hey, you got a friend back there? Somebody following you?"

Lou didn't want Solomon Gage bailing out of the cab to stick that gun in *his* face.

His hand drifted to his fat belly, where he carried a .38 in his belt under his nylon windbreaker. If Gage wanted to play cowboy, he'd get a big surprise. One thing was for damned sure: If he ever did have to go up against that musclehead, Lou Velacci wouldn't rely on no fucking jack handle.

CHAPTER 37

●●●●●●●●●●●●●●●●●●●

Lucinda Cruz was at the state courts building, a granite bunker on McAllister near City Hall, when the doors opened Thursday morning. She had to pull some strings, but by 11 a.m., she had a hearing before the Honorable Pauline S. Coburn, a Superior Court judge known to be sympathetic to abused wives.

Grace Sheffield's face was purple and puffy, and one eye was swollen shut. Her busted lip was swollen, too. As instructed by Lucinda, she wore no makeup, so the injuries stood in sharp contrast against her creamy skin and pale hair. Grace wore a simple dress in navy blue, buttoned to her throat, and the outfit looked mournful and demure. Perfect in every way.

Lucinda was dressed in her usual suit and silk blouse, and only she knew she wore skimpy underwear beneath the lawyerly exterior. She'd like to tell herself she didn't know what had gotten into her, wearing lacy underthings into court, but she knew exactly what she'd been thinking when she reached into her dresser drawer. She'd been thinking about Solomon Gage.

Not that she expected him to see her lingerie. Oh, Lord, no. But she'd awakened with him on her mind, must've dreamed about him. How else to explain the sexy way she felt that morning?

Lucinda never had a shortage of men asking her out. Lawyers and court employees and businessmen and cops and assorted bullshitters. White men, black men, Asians, Hispanics, all lured by her slim good looks, her golden skin and her bright smile. Hell, even some of the shitheel husbands she faced down in divorces had the nerve to ask her out, sometimes right in court.

Lucinda could afford to be choosy. She'd kissed enough frogs to know she wanted the complete prince package. She wanted an athletic man who took pride in his body but who was no strutting peacock, who was ambitious but not consumed with his career. A man who made her feel safe. A man with brains, grit and a sense of humor.

Solomon Gage seemed to fit the bill, though he'd been pretty much all business the day before. She'd seen the way he looked at her, the hunger in his eyes. She'd felt the attraction, too, and the feeling lingered long after she'd gone home to her apartment on Russian Hill.

Too bad he worked for the Sheffields.

No sooner had she thought of the Sheffields than one came into the courtroom. Michael Sheffield looked angry as hell, which was ideal for Lucinda's needs. Old Franklin Price leaned close to him, whispering, warning him to stay calm. Three of Price's fresh-faced associates, who'd do the grunt work in the divorce case, followed. One, a pale, doughy guy who looked like he'd bought his blue suit at Sears, blushed furiously when he saw Lucinda watching them. He couldn't keep his eyes off her, stealing glances as they arranged themselves around the long table reserved for defendants.

Grace sat next to Lucinda, careful not to look in her hus-band's direction, as instructed. Grace had the makings of a perfect client.

A pudgy bailiff called for everyone to rise, and there was the usual rustle as people got to their feet for the judge's entrance. Only a few people were scattered around the spacious gallery—lawyers and clients waiting their turns, and a handful of jaded spectators. Lucinda had thought about alerting the media, but had decided against it. Plenty of time later, if she needed the help.

Judge Coburn was a tall, thin woman with iron-gray hair and the stern face of an elementary school teacher. She folded into the chair behind the bench, and told everyone to be seated.

In some courts, attorneys stood and formally introduced themselves at the beginning of each proceeding. Judge Coburn kept things as informal as possible. She ran her court in a brisk manner, and woe to the attorney who couldn't keep up. Screw up before Coburn, and she'd have you in chambers so quickly, you wouldn't know what hit you.

The judge shuffled through papers on the bench, then looked up at the attorneys.

"A motion for a temporary restraining order," she said. It wasn't a question, but Lucinda stood and answered, "Yes, your honor."

The judge's gray eyes drifted to Grace, and she frowned.

"As you can see, your honor, my client has been injured at the hands of her husband," Lucinda said. "We're asking the court to order Michael Sheffield to keep away from her."

The judge held up a hand for "stop," and Lucinda obeyed. Judge Coburn sifted through the paperwork again.

Franklin Price had said nothing, and Michael Sheffield glared at him, a look that said, "What are we paying you for?" Price got the message. The plump attorney got to his feet and said, "Your honor, if I may—"

The judge cut him off. "Not yet, Mr. Price."

Price plopped back into his chair. Gave Sheffield a helpless shrug. It was all Lucinda could do to keep a straight face.

"Were there witnesses to this assault?" the judge asked.

"Yes, your honor, and we'd be happy to call them, if that's required," Lucinda said.

"Have you filed a police report?"

"No, ma'am. My client wishes to stay out of the newspapers, if possible. She feels a civil action is the best course for now."

Judge Coburn scowled at Lucinda, who gave her back impassive.

"It's not the job of this court to give advice, but I have to say, if I'd been brutalized in this way, I'd want the police involved."

"Yes, your honor."

In her peripheral vision, Lucinda saw Grace reach up with a handkerchief and dab away a single tear. Perfect.

"Mr. Price," the judge said, and the Sheffield lawyer stood.

Lucinda sat. She heard a door close behind her, someone else entering the courtroom, but she didn't take her eyes off the judge.

"Mr. Price, does your client claim mitigating circumstances?"

"Your honor, this is a simple domestic dispute. Things may have gotten out of hand, but—"

"Mr. Price," the judge cut in. "Did you look at the plaintiff's face?"

"Yes, your honor. This is a tragic misunder—"

"Does your client plan to contest the divorce?"

"Absolutely, your honor. Ms. Cruz is overreaching in her motions to—"

"That's not the issue before the court," the judge snapped. "I was simply wondering whether this is the first salvo in what will be a long court battle."

"I'm afraid so, your honor."

"Thank you, Mr. Price."

He slumped into his chair, defeated without firing a shot. Michael Sheffield looked as if he could chew through the tabletop.

"My concern today is to see that violence doesn't occur again while the divorce proceeds," Judge Coburn said. "Therefore, the temporary restraining order is granted, effective immediately. Mr. Sheffield, you're not to come within one hundred feet of Mrs. Sheffield at any time. Is that understood?"

Michael Sheffield started to say something, but Price gave him an elbow, and Sheffield got the message to stand up. After he was on his feet, he said, "Your honor, if I may, there's no reason to—"

"Make that one hundred *yards*," the judge said.

"But we live in the same house! How am I supposed to—"

"Not anymore, you don't. You are ordered forthwith to relocate until the divorce court resolves who will retain ownership of the house."

"Wait a minute! I paid for that goddamned—"

Franklin Price yanked on Sheffield's sleeve to silence him, but it was too late. Judge Coburn's face darkened.

"Another outburst, Mr. Sheffield, and I'll have you thrown in jail for contempt."

Michael Sheffield got himself under control and nodded. Except for the click-click of the court reporter's transcription machine, the courtroom fell silent.

Lucinda felt Grace give her a little nudge under the table, but she didn't dare look at her client. Everything was going their way.

"Mr. Price," the judge said, and Price leapt back to his feet, looking like he wanted to slug his client. "Instruct your client to have his clothes and other personal items removed from the house. Perhaps send one of your bushy-tailed assistants to take care of it."

All three of Price's associates turned red, but they sat very still, hands in laps. They were well-trained. Unlike the man they represented.

"Yes, your honor," Price said.

"Mr. Sheffield," the judge said. "There is no motion before this court to require you to undergo counseling or anger management training, so I'll not address that issue. But you clearly have a problem. You might want to seek help."

Michael Sheffield said nothing, his face a volcano ready to erupt.

"If you violate the terms of the restraining order, you will go straight to jail. Is that clear?"

Sheffield managed a nod.

"Ms. Cruz?"

Lucinda stood.

"You'll finish up the amended paperwork with the court clerk?"

"Yes, your honor."

"I assume you've taken photographs of your client's face, for use in the future?"

"Yes, your honor."

"The motion is granted as amended. Court will recess for lunch. Next case at 1:30 sharp."

The judge banged her gavel a little harder than necessary. She shot Michael Sheffield one last withering look, then swept out of court in a whisper of black robes.

Sheffield glared at Lucinda and Grace, but Price grabbed his arm and one of the associates got hold of his other arm, and they hustled him out of the courtroom.

Lucinda turned to Grace, found her smiling past the bruises and swollen lips.

"That was beautiful."

Lucinda winked. "You ain't seen nothing yet."

CHAPTER 38

••••••••••••••••••••

Outside the courthouse, Solomon peeked around a bus shelter, watching Lucinda Cruz load Grace into a cab. The sidewalks were crowded with people headed to lunch, and his eyes shifted among them before returning to Lucinda's curvy form.

He'd already made sure Michael and his lawyers had left. Solomon caught only part of the hearing, but he'd seen Michael's display of temper. He wanted to make sure Michael didn't accost Grace outside the courtroom. This was ugly enough without a public catfight.

Lucinda turned his way, looking at her wristwatch as the taxi pulled away, and Solomon's heart skipped a beat. She'd been on his mind since the meeting in her office. He had a dozen things to do for Dom, but he kept daydreaming about Lucinda Cruz.

Now, here he was, hiding and watching her—stalking her, when you got right down to it—and he had to wonder whether he'd lost his mind. It was as if he were watching himself from a distance, his own movements beyond his control. How else to explain what he was doing now, right this minute? Hurrying along the sidewalk to catch up with her.

"Ms. Cruz?"

She jumped a little as he appeared beside her, head and shoulders taller, looming over her. Too impulsive. Could he make a worse impression?

But a bright smile dawned on her face, and he smiled, too.

"Mr. Gage," she said. "You following me?"

"Waiting for you. I knew you'd come out soon."

"How did you know that?"

"I caught the end of the hearing."

"What did you think?"

"Our side didn't stand a chance."

She'd stopped walking and turned to face him. The sunshine made her squint.

"You're lucky I didn't spot you in court. I might've called you to testify."

"That's why I slipped in late and sat in the back. But you didn't need me."

"All the testimony I needed was on Grace Sheffield's face," she said.

"Michael didn't help himself, blowing up like that. The judge is right: He's got an anger management problem."

"Is that what you call it?" she said, a twinkle in her eyes. "I'd call him an asshole."

"No argument from me. I'm the one who slugged him, remember?"

He dropped his voice when he said it, and she took a step closer. Solomon felt as if sparks were flying between them.

"It's nice to see you again," he said.

"Did the Sheffields send you to flirt with me?"

"Am I flirting?"

"Aren't you?"

He laughed. "Hard to tell. I think I'm out of practice. Nobody sent me. In fact, if they spotted me here talking to you, I'd probably be in trouble."

"So why take that risk?"

"I thought I'd ask you to lunch."

Her eyebrows arched. "Business or pleasure?"

"Strictly pleasure. If we talk business, it might end up in court. I'm already on your witness list."

"That's right," she said. "Which means it would be unprofessional for me to join you on a lunch date. Probably unethical as well."

"Same for me. Against all my training. Against all good sense. But I'll promise not to talk about the Sheffields or your court case."

She said nothing, thinking it over.

He said, "Please?"

"I must be crazy," she said.

"Me, too."

"There's a place on Larkin a couple of blocks from here," she said. "You like Cuban food?"

"Sounds good."

Still, she didn't move. "It's just lunch?"

"Right."

"We go Dutch?"

"Whatever you say."

"What are we standing around for?" she said. "Let's eat."

They walked side by side, the sun warming their backs, their shadows stretched out on the sidewalk before them. Both carried briefcases in their outside hands—Solomon's brushed-aluminum case and Lucinda's a fat leather model. Their empty hands brushed once as he stepped around an oncoming pedestrian, and it felt like an electric charge between them. He glanced over, saw she was smiling, her eyes straight ahead.

The café, La Floridita, had a green awning out front over a large plate-glass window, and its white walls were decorated with stenciled palm trees. Inside, it was jammed, but a slick-haired waiter recognized Lucinda and signaled to her. Another couple had finished at a small table and the waiter spoke rapid-fire Spanish to a busboy, who hustled to clear it.

Solomon, standing behind Lucinda, leaned forward to mutter into her ear. "That where you want to sit? Right in the front window?"

"Doesn't look as if we have much choice. Besides, if somebody's looking, they'd see us no matter where we sat."

"Right." He checked the sunny, busy street. Nobody appeared to be watching, but hell, who could tell?

The waiter pulled back Lucinda's chair with a flourish and they sat, Solomon barely fitting between the arms of the bentwood chair. The waiter, in accented English, recited the day's specials, but Solomon wasn't listening. He was watching Lucinda's face, in profile as she gave the waiter her full attention, and admiring her high cheekbones and the sleek angle of her jawline.

She told the waiter she'd have the fish special, and Solomon said, "Same for me," though it could've been piranha for all the attention he'd paid. The waiter hurried off to the kitchen.

Lucinda set her purse and briefcase on the floor, and said, "Okay, Mr. Gage, we're at lunch, like you wanted. Now what?"

"Please call me Solomon."

"That's kind of a mouthful. What do your friends call you?"

He paused. "They call me Solomon. Not that I have that many friends."

"You're not the friendly sort?"

"I work all the time. And I live out in the country, so I don't meet that many people."

"Up at Cutthroat Lodge?"

"You've been doing your homework."

right. But I shouldn't have said that. It violates our pact to not talk about the Sheffields."

"It's beautiful up there, I can say that much. There's a lake and a trout stream and redwoods. Clear water and clean air."

"Sounds wonderful."

"One of the best perks of my job. But it is kind of isolated."

"Not great for your dating life," she said.

"I get into cities a lot, especially San Francisco. Sometimes go out on dates. But Cutthroat's been home since I was twelve."

"Twelve? That's recruiting 'em kinda young."

"I wasn't working there then. My mother was. She was Dominick Sheffield's executive assistant."

"She doesn't work for him anymore?"

He shook his head. "She got killed in a car wreck a couple of years later—"

"I'm sorry."

"I was fourteen, and Dom took me in, put me through school, trained me to be his assistant. So, I've lived there ever since, except when I was away at college, and I've worked for him since I was old enough to have a job."

"No wonder you're so loyal."

"Yeah," he said glumly. Wasn't he violating that loyalty by being here? What would Dom think?

The worries must've shown on his face because Lucinda said, "Not too late to call this off."

"No, no. It's fine."

She unfolded her napkin, not looking at him. "What do you do for fun? Up there in the boonies?"

"Fish. Swim in the lake. Run in the woods."

"Looks like you lift weights, too."

"A little."

"And that's your idea of fun?"

"Well, like I said, it's pretty isolated."

"Mister, you don't know what fun is. Sounds to me like you've grown up under Dominick Sheffield's command, and you've never taken any time for yourself. What about nightclubs? Dining out? Movies? Parties?"

He shrugged. "I don't have a lot of time—"

"You have to *make* time. Otherwise, all you do is work until you're on your deathbed, saying, 'Where did my life go?'"

Solomon nodded. In recent weeks, he'd thought a lot about the way he spent his time. They hadn't been happy thoughts.

"When was the last time," she asked, "you took a vacation?"

He didn't want to answer, wasn't sure he even knew the answer. He was rescued by the waiter, who arrived with a tray loaded with plates and saucers and glasses of iced tea. He set the dishes on the table, chattering at Lucinda in Spanish. Solomon spoke a little Spanish, but this was the *rapido* Cuban version, and he couldn't keep up. Lucinda smiled at the waiter and cut her eyes at Solomon, as if they'd enjoyed a little joke at his expense. Funny, he didn't mind a bit.

The food smelled wonderful. A charbroiled slab of fish covered most of Solomon's plate, along with fried plantains and a side of black beans.

Once the waiter hustled away, Solomon said, "You're a regular here?"

"It's close to the courthouse," she said. "And a little taste of home. But I couldn't eat here all the time. My waistline wouldn't permit it."

"So," he said. "'Home' is Miami?"

"Isn't that where all Cubans come from?"

"Not from Cuba?"

"Well, yes, but I was too young to remember much of Cuba. We were Marielitos. Came over in the boatlift in 1980. I was only four years old. My father was a doctor in Cuba, and he was pretty vocal in his disdain for the regime. Fidel was happy to kick him out."

Lucinda paused to take a bite of her fish. She closed her eyes, barely chewing, letting it melt in her mouth. It appeared to give her so much pleasure, Solomon got a rush watching her. He'd like to make her that happy, given the chance.

"Things were different once we got to Florida. My father wasn't licensed to practice medicine here, of course, and Fidel kept our money. So Dad worked as a medical technician, and my mom cleaned other people's houses."

"And they put you through college."

"They helped, but mostly I did it myself, working part-time jobs and getting scholarships. I came out here to go to school. Liked San Francisco so much, I decided to stay."

"This city does that to people."

She smiled. "Not you, though. You can't wait to run back up to the woods."

"I'd happily spend more time in the city, given the right reason."

She smiled at him, and they stared at each other for a long, loaded moment. Then they broke eye contact, both suddenly interested in their food. Solomon tried to eat slowly. He wanted the meal to last forever.

When the conversation resumed, they chatted about the city and food and music. Nothing too personal. Nothing too revealing. And, for damned sure, nothing about the Sheffields.

The waiter offered dessert, but Lucinda looked at her watch and said she needed to get back to the courthouse. As agreed, they split the check. Solomon left extra for a hefty tip. Since this was

Lucinda's favorite café, he wanted to be remembered here. He wanted to come back. Often.

Sunshine filled the street. Solomon slipped dark glasses out of an inside pocket and onto his face.

Lucinda said, "Now you look like a bodyguard."

"Yeah?"

"Big scary man."

"Should I take off the sunglasses?"

"No, it's okay," she said. "You don't scare me."

They walked together, carrying their briefcases. Solomon felt an urgent need to say something that would guarantee he'd see her again, but he couldn't think what. He felt dazed and sluggish, an overfed lump of muscle wearing sunglasses.

At the courthouse entrance, a line of people waited at a metal detector. Guards opened briefcases and wielded beeping wands. Solomon didn't want to run that gantlet again, and couldn't justify it anyway. He had no more business in the courthouse. He needed to get back to the Lafayette Park apartment, where he'd left his gun and his laptop, and get to work.

Lucinda turned to face him, standing close. He felt clumsy, sticking out a big paw for her to shake.

"Thanks for the company," she said.

"I had a wonderful time. Can we do it again?"

She smiled. "I'd like that."

Lucinda raised up on her toes, leaned into him, kissed him lightly on the lips. Before he could kiss her back, she stepped away, moving into line, holding the handle of her briefcase in both hands.

"So long, Solomon Gage. See you around."

He gave her an awkward little wave, then turned away to hide the stupid grin on his face.

CHAPTER 39

●●●●●●●●●●●●●●●●●●●●

Bart Logan sat on the plush sofa in Christopher Sheffield's office, watching Michael pace and rant. It was all Bart could do to sit still. He'd like to jump up and knock Michael's goddamned head off. Stupid motherfucker, blowing up in court, slapping his wife around, endangering everything.

The absolute worst time for Grace's divorce craziness. Reporters had gotten wind of it, and the phones were ringing off the hook downstairs in Sheffield Enterprises' media relations office. Fucking buzzards, circling the carcass of Michael's marriage.

Too goddamned many distractions. Bart and the Sheffield brothers needed to focus now, pull together the last threads of the Africa project. The Nigerien election was on Sunday, only three days away. They couldn't afford this crap right now. Not baying reporters or snooping attorneys or Grace showing up in court looking like bruised fruit—

"And that fucking lawyer!" Michael shouted. "You should've seen her! She knew exactly what she was doing, shopping around for the right judge, some *woman* who'd give Grace anything she wanted. Woman judge, woman lawyer, woman plaintiff. See a pattern here? You think they don't have it in for me? For us?"

Chris sat behind his desk, a fat, silent Buddha, stuffing one chocolate after another into his mouth. He seemed completely tuned out. At least he had snacks to keep him busy. Bart's problem was he kept *listening* to the stupid son of a bitch.

"Hey," he cut in. He couldn't fucking stand it anymore. "Hey!"

Michael wheeled on him.

"How about if we get back to business?" Bart said. "You're not changing anything, yelling and stomping around."

"Listen here, you—"

"Hey," Bart said again. "Don't even try to take it out on me. You might bitch-slap your wife, but I won't sit still for it."

Michael doubled his hands into fists, his breath coming hard. Bart glanced at Chris, whose face had spread into a grin.

"We've got work to do," Bart said. "The fucking clock is ticking."

Bart's reasonable tone seemed to work. Michael's breath steadied and he slumped into a chair.

"You're right," he said. "I need to get hold of myself. Remember what's important here."

"That's right." Bart kept his voice low. "You've worked too hard to let this thing fall apart now."

But he was thinking: *I've* worked too hard to let you shitheads drop the ball this late in the game.

Chris put away his sweets and wiped his mouth with a handkerchief. "What's the latest on that ship?"

"It docked in Porto Novo during the night," Bart said, "and they're loading the goods onto trucks. But they've still got to drive to General Goma's place. That's the whole length of Benin, then a hundred miles into the interior of Niger. It'll take all day."

"Any way to speed that up?" Chris asked.

Michael shook his head. "We'll be lucky if the trucks get through in a single day. That's pushing it on those roads. Once they make it to the border, I've got safe passage arranged. Goma's ready with his men. As soon as the weapons arrive, they'll pass them out and get moving."

"So we're talking what," Chris said. "Thirty-six hours from now? Forty-eight?"

"Cutting it damned close," Bart said.

"We knew it would be dicey," Michael said. "And it didn't help, that ship getting held up in Dakar for days. But it'll be all right. It's not the end of the world if Goma has to wait until after the election."

"Our position is much, much better if Goma acts before the vote is counted," Bart said.

The brothers exchanged a look, then both turned back to Bart, expecting him to have all the answers.

He sighed. "There's another problem. My sources tell me the load on that ship is light. Some of the weapons disappeared along the way. When Goma gets the shipment, he'll notice he's missing stuff. He'll be pissed."

"*He'll* be pissed?" Michael shouted. "*I'm* pissed. We paid for that shipment."

Bart held up his hands, trying to slow Michael before he became a runaway train.

"This shit happens," he said. "That's Africa for you. Somewhere up the coast, a junior Che Guevera's polishing his nice new rifle and planning a revolution."

"But—"

"Take it easy. The weapons will be sufficient. Goma's got half of Niger's army in his pocket. The other half's not going to stand and fight."

"Maybe Michael should get on the phone," Chris suggested, "and warn Goma about the missing stuff."

"Good idea. If he's calm enough to be diplomatic. But I wouldn't use the phones around here."

Michael stiffened. "Why the hell not?"

"You never know when somebody might be listening."

"You think our phones are tapped? Don't we pay your people to prevent that? How could our competition get access—"

"It's not our competitors I'm worried about," Bart said. "It's your dad. He's got ears everywhere. I wouldn't put it past him to tap our lines, especially if he thinks we're up to something."

"Why would he think that?" Michael demanded.

"Lucinda Cruz mentioned Africa in her court filing," Bart said. "Solomon Gage has been sniffing around."

"Fucking Solomon," Chris muttered.

"He's the biggest threat," Bart said. "We can stall in court and we can tell the reporters to go fuck themselves. But Solomon's got access, and he's got ideas. He'll run right to Dom if he gets wind of—"

Bart's cell phone chirped. He pulled it out of his pocket and checked the readout: "Lou Velacci."

"I need to take this." He stood and turned his back on the brothers.

Bart answered the phone and heard Lou say, "Boss? I've got great fucking news."

CHAPTER 40

●●●●●●●●●●●●●●●●●●●●●

General Erasmus Goma stood on the hood of a Land Rover, the heels of his knee-high boots leaving horse-hoof dents in the metal. From behind mirrored sunglasses, he surveyed his ragged troops. A thousand men were spread over acres of arid rangeland, squatting among their pup tents and cooking fires. They seemed listless and bored.

Goma, too, was tired of waiting, but timing was of the essence here. A false step, and he and all these men could vanish before their little war even got started. President Boudreaux's people were watching Goma's "training maneuvers," announced so close to the election. Boudreaux's opponent, Laurent, had his own operatives. Everybody spying on everyone else, the tension mounting, the stakes ever higher.

The whole country held its breath, expecting violence to break out before the vote. Boudreaux promised fair and open elections, as United Nations poll monitors poured into the country and his own people sharpened their knives. Laurent's restless young supporters seemed ready to take to the streets. And here was Goma, with his little force of men, braced to make history.

A phone warbled inside the Land Rover, and his driver answered it.

"General!"

"*Oui*, Reynard."

"A call for you."

Goma looked into the distance. "I do not wish to talk on the phone."

"But, sir, it is Mr. Sheffield."

Goma sighed. If Michael Sheffield was so interested in the coup he was funding, he should've stayed and watched it himself. Goma was weary of giving him updates. But he leaped down from the hood and took the phone.

"General Goma?" The connection was scratchy.

"You called at a good time," Goma rumbled in his heavily accented English. "I was about to give my men a rousing speech. Perhaps you have news I can give them?"

"Yes, sir. But I'm afraid it's good news and bad. The arms have been loaded onto trucks in Porto Novo, and they're headed your way. But some items turned up missing during shipment."

"Missing? How missing?"

"Stolen, I suppose. These things happen. But Bart has assured me there's still plenty in that shipment for your purposes. With the weapons your men already have—"

"Bullshit." Goma's favorite word in English. "That is bullshit. We had an agreement. My men need superior firepower."

"If they're taking control of the whole country, but that's not exactly what we're after. It's a pinpoint plan you've got, General. Hit the capital. Quick in, quick out, and it's over. You don't need to blow up the whole countryside."

"Don't tell me what I need," Goma said. "No more bullshit. When will the weapons arrive?"

"They're right on schedule. I just wanted to warn you that a few things were missing and—"

"Enough. I'll check the shipment. If it is sufficient, you will get your revolution."

Goma tossed the phone to a startled Reynard, who caught it against his stomach. The general pulled a flask from his hip pocket, unscrewed the top and took a slug of Chivas Regal.

Damned Americans. He should've known better than to throw in with them. They were dreamers and talkers and backslappers. Inefficient. Ineffective.

Goma was a practical man in a land of scarcity. He believed you took what you wanted without apology. If you can't succeed through scheming and manipulating, then you take more extreme measures. Whoever has the biggest army wins.

The general let his gaze roam the encampment. The sullen men watched him, waiting for a signal, some indication that he knew what he was doing, that they'd signed on with the right team.

But Goma didn't feel like giving a speech anymore. He pocketed the flask, gave his men a half-hearted salute and went around to the other side of the Land Rover. He climbed into the passenger seat and slammed the door.

"Take me home, Reynard."

CHAPTER 41

•••••••••••••••••••••

Solomon worked at the Lafayette Park apartment through the afternoon, but his mind kept drifting to Lucinda Cruz and their lunch in the sunny café window and the electric feel of her full lips.

He read through the divorce filing again, but that didn't get him anywhere. Michael was a heel, no question, and Grace was right to dump him. If only Lucinda hadn't made her discovery motions so wide-ranging, if only she'd accept something less than full financial disclosure, Dom might go for that. But Lucinda wouldn't settle for less, especially now that Michael had used Grace for a punching bag.

After hours of this, Solomon had nothing to show for it but a headache. Mrs. Wong brought him some tea, and told him she'd leave food for him in the refrigerator. Then she went home, and the apartment was even quieter. He hadn't noticed her humming and puttering around the place until she was gone.

He sorted through papers in his briefcase until he found a business card he'd been given by the lead investigator at the Oakland Police Department. The dogged Irishman. Peter J. O'Malley.

Solomon dialed the number. He had to go through a switchboard and two other detectives before somebody located O'Malley, who came on the line barking his name.

Solomon asked whether there was anything new in the shooting death of Abby Maynes, and O'Malley went cagey.

"You asking for yourself or for Dominick Sheffield?"

"I'll be talking to him. I'd be happy to report whatever progress you've made."

O'Malley sighed. "I'd make more progress if I didn't spend all my time on the phone with you people. Not to mention the reporters. Once they found out the victim was a Sheffield, they went nuts."

"You've gotten calls from others at Sheffield Enterprises?"

"Your boss called at one point to make sure we understood that this murder was a bigger deal than the other one hundred we'll investigate this year. A Michael Sheffield called, and one of your attorneys called twice. Your security guy, Bart Logan, called three times. All of them offering help and wanting updates and urging us to go faster. You're tying us up when we could be investigating."

"I'm sorry," Solomon said. "I didn't know. I'll put the word out for everyone to leave you alone."

"You could do that?"

"One call to Dom."

"Great," O'Malley said. "I mean, we get it: It's a terrible thing, that girl getting killed. And her family's a big deal. But it looks like a drug killing. Somebody got pissed off and started shooting. That's what happens in that neighborhood. Might've had nothing to do with the Sheffields."

That didn't ring true to Solomon. Unless the shooter was the young drug dealer he'd roughed up, in which case Abby's death was his own damned fault. He asked O'Malley if they'd had any luck tracking down the dealer.

"You're kidding, right? That description you gave could be any one of five hundred street dealers. I mean, we're beating the bushes, trying to turn him up. He'll blab to somebody and that somebody will tell somebody else and eventually we'll hear about it. But it takes time."

"I understand," Solomon said. "Again, my apologies for bothering you."

"I didn't mean to snap at you. It's been a long day, you know?"

Solomon thanked the detective, pledged to get the Sheffields off his neck and flipped the phone closed.

Interesting that Michael called the police department. One would think he had plenty on his mind already. Of course, Abby had worked with him at Sheffield Extraction Industries. Maybe they were closer than Solomon knew.

He remembered what she said when he'd plucked her out of that flophouse. How she was important to "Uncle Mike." How she knew a lot about the mysterious "Africa deal."

Solomon wondered again whether Michael could've had something to do with Abby's death. The nurse had said the impostor was a bald man with a thick mustache, which described Michael. But she'd also described him as "heavy-set" and he'd been wearing a cap, so even the baldness was a guess on her part.

One way to make certain. He called Willow Glade and asked if Nurse Norma Forester was on duty, and the operator said she'd page her. Solomon tapped his feet against the marble floor impatiently. It was past six in the evening, but Nurse Forester was on the night shift and—

"This is Nurse Forester."

"Solomon Gage calling. Remember me?"

"How could I forget that name?"

"Yes, ma'am. I guess you've heard what happened to Abby Maynes."

"I'm so sorry. She seemed like such a nice girl. Troubled, but—"

"Yes, ma'am. I'm still curious about who took her away from rehab. I wonder if I could show you a picture of someone. I could e-mail it to you."

As he talked, he punched buttons on his laptop, calling up a corporate photo of Michael Sheffield.

The nurse gave Solomon an e-mail address, and he typed it in and sent the photo to her. She told him she'd call him back as soon as she got a chance.

His stomach growled. He felt too keyed up to eat, but his stomach clearly had other ideas. He carried his phone to the kitchen, and was bent over, looking in the fridge, when it rang.

"Solomon Gage."

"This is Nurse Forester. I got that photo."

"That was fast."

"I opened it right away. I'm as anxious as you are to find whoever was responsible."

Solomon doubted that was the case. He said, "So?"

"It's not him."

"You're sure?"

"Absolutely. The man who pretended to be you was stockier, and he had a bigger chin."

Solomon tried not to let disappointment leak into his voice. "Okay, thank you very much."

"I'm sorry," she said.

"Mostly, I was trying to rule him out. You've been very helpful."

She asked him to keep in touch and once again expressed her condolences before Solomon could get her off the line.

Damn. He was right back where he started. Without a clue.

And his appetite was gone, too.

CHAPTER 42

•••••••••••••••••••

Dominick took a helicopter to San Francisco on Friday, then rode impatiently as a limousine carried him through morning traffic to the apartment overlooking Lafayette Park. He wore a black business suit rather than his usual outdoor gear, and the heels of his dress oxfords clacked on the marble floor as he brushed past Mrs. Wong without a word.

He found Solomon Gage in the kitchen, drinking coffee, a newspaper spread out on the table before him. He was dressed for the day, his gray suit jacket on the back of his chair. The usual black turtleneck stretched tight across his broad shoulders, bunching slightly around the black webbing of the shoulder holster. His eyes widened when he looked up and saw Dom's scowling face.

"Good morning, sir. I didn't expect to see you—"

"I'll bet you didn't," Dom snapped. "Here. Explain this to me."

Dom tossed a large manila envelope onto the table, and crossed his arms over his chest, holding himself together. Solomon picked up the envelope and looked it over. Both sides were blank.

"Just open the goddamned thing."

Solomon lifted the flap and let the color photographs slide out. They landed face up, in the same order Bart Logan showed them to Dom the night before.

Solomon blushed as he peered at the top photo, which showed him and Lucinda Cruz, walking down a sunny sidewalk together, big grins on their faces.

The second photo showed them sitting in a café, right in the goddamned window. Leaning across the table toward each other. The woman laughing about something.

The third showed the couple on the sidewalk in front of the gray courthouse. Lucinda Cruz up on tiptoe to plant a kiss on Solomon's mouth.

"What the hell is that?"

Solomon shrugged. "We had lunch."

"And?"

"That's all."

Dom pointed at the photo of the kiss. "So that's dessert?"

Solomon's jutting jaw reminded Dom of when he was a teenager, those sullen years after Rose died, when the kid was determined to make it on his own. Dom practically forced his help and guidance on the boy, made him see that he had a future with the Sheffields. Dom felt himself softening, and that made him mad. He came here to tell Solomon off, not to go for a jaunt down Memory Lane.

"I've seen some botched-up jobs," he snarled, "but never anything quite like the past few days. I send you after my granddaughter, and she ends up with her brains splattered all over the street. You punch out Michael. I give you one chore to do: Derail this divorce proceeding. And what do you do? You take Grace's lawyer on a *date*."

"It wasn't like that—"

Dom held up a hand, stopping him.

"My sons tried to tell me you'd gone off the rails, but I refused to believe them. And now this."

Solomon dropped his gaze to the photographs spread out before him. When he looked back at Dom, there was anger in his eyes.

"They had me tailed," he said.

"Bart Logan's had people following you since that travesty in Oakland. He thinks you're culpable in Abby's death. He was looking for proof."

"Do you believe her death was my fault?"

"How the hell do I know? I wasn't there. Abby's dead. The driver's still in intensive care. Nobody—but you—can tell us what happened on that street. But I was willing to give you the benefit of the doubt. Now I'm not so sure."

Solomon stabbed the photographs with a finger. "It was just lunch. We ate. We talked. Not about business. Not about the family. We simply chatted, the way normal people do."

"Next you'll be telling me that's not a kiss right there. What, she was checking your temperature with her lips?"

The color rose in Solomon's cheeks.

"You've overreacting, sir. All this, over a *kiss*?"

Dom took a deep breath, trying for calm.

"The woman's an attorney," he said. "She was using you, and you fell for it. I'm disappointed, Solomon. You're better than this. You don't chase after skirts when you're supposed to be taking care of business."

Solomon didn't blink. His blue eyes filled with ice.

"Am I fired?"

Dom raked a hand back through his hair. "You've always been the one man I've trusted. Without trust, we've got nothing."

"I've done nothing to violate your trust."

"I pray that's true," Dom said. "I don't want to get rid of you. I need you. But not right now. What I need at the moment is for you to go away. Call it a leave of absence. Call it a vacation. But get out of my sight."

Solomon didn't say another word. He stood, plucked his jacket off the back of the chair and slipped it on. Then he strode past and out of the kitchen.

Dom stood with his head bowed, listening to the big man's feet echoing off the floor. Then the rattle of the front door latch. Solomon slammed the door, which seemed out of character for a man so habitually polite.

Dom wondered if he'd ever see him again.

CHAPTER 43

●●●●●●●●●●●●●●●●●●

Still steaming, Solomon paid off the turbaned driver and climbed out of the Yellow Cab under the skywalk linking the mezzanine floors at Embarcadero Center. Smokers and slackers loitered around the office tower's entrance. Solomon wondered whether any recognized him as the man who'd pulled a gun on Mick Nielsen near here. He hid behind his sunglasses as he stalked into the lobby.

He got off the elevator on the thirtieth floor, where three receptionists were busy under the big Sheffield Enterprises logo. A beefy, gray-uniformed guard sat near the entrance to the executive offices, and Solomon recognized him as Davis, the surly one who'd left his feet in the way a few days ago. Solomon thinking: Davis better not make the same mistake today.

As soon as he spotted him coming off the elevator, Davis leaped to his feet and said, "Hold it." His hand drifted to the butt of the pistol he wore on his belt.

"I'm here to see Bart Logan."

"Not today," Davis said. "Mr. Logan thought you might stop by. He said to tell you he's busy."

Solomon felt heat rise within him. "All right, you've told me. Now get out of my way."

"No, sir." The guard's holster had a leather strap to hold his black Glock in place, and he unsnapped it. It sounded unusually loud in the reception area. The chattering receptionists had fallen silent.

"You're willing to shoot me to keep me from going through that door?"

"If that's what it takes."

Solomon nodded, thinking it over. "We always reward such loyalty here at Sheffield Enterprises."

The guard stared at him.

"In fact, we'll pay the resulting legal fees. And your hospital bills."

Davis pulled the pistol, but kept it pointed at the floor. His finger was outside the trigger guard.

"Nobody's going to the hospital here," he said. "Except you, if you try me."

One of the receptionists gasped. Solomon didn't turn to look. He hoped the women were getting down behind the wooden counter, in case this idiot decided to shoot.

"Turn around," Davis said. "Get on that elevator and get out of here. There's no reason for this to get out of hand."

"You're the one who pulled a gun," Solomon said.

"I'm following orders."

A walkie-talkie on the guard's belt crackled with static, and Solomon seized on the distraction.

"Get on your radio. Call Logan."

"I use that radio, it's to bring reinforcements," Davis said. "That what you want?"

"Go ahead. It won't make any difference."

"How's that?"

"You're not going to be talking."

Davis' brows clenched as he tried to puzzle out what that meant.

Solomon lunged forward, sweeping his left hand to the side, striking the wrist of the guard's gun hand before he could use the pistol. Solomon jabbed his right hand straight up, the fingers stiff, and hit Davis in the throat. He pulled back on the blow at the last second, so he wouldn't crush the guard's windpipe.

Davis gagged. He tried to raise the gun, but Solomon had hold of his wrist now. He grabbed his thumb and wrenched it backward. The Glock dropped to the floor. Solomon kicked it away.

He spun Davis around, and slammed his forehead into the wall. Davis slid to the floor, coughing and whimpering.

One of the receptionists screamed, but Solomon didn't pause. He went through the glass door and turned a corner into the long corridor that bisected the executive floor. He hustled down the hall to Bart Logan's office. He knew he didn't have much time. The receptionists would alert the rest of the security detail.

Logan sat behind his desk, a phone to his ear. The receiver tumbled from his hand when Solomon stormed in. He fumbled for the center drawer of his desk.

Solomon reached inside his jacket for the Colt.

"You want to play quick-draw? Go ahead. See if you can get your gun out of that drawer."

Logan slowly pulled his hands back, and raised them to shoulder height. "Take it easy, man."

"Don't tell me to take it easy, you fucking sneak. Having me followed, then running to Dom with those photos. Trying to undercut me."

"Hey," Logan said. "You deserved it. Smooching with that attorney? Mr. Sheffield needed to know."

"You made it look worse than it was."

"Fuck you, Solomon. Don't tell me how to do my job. I'm looking after the family's best interests. You seemed to have forgotten how to do that. Go ahead and shoot me. See if that gets you back in Dom's good graces."

Logan was all bluster. His upraised hands trembled, and beads of sweat glistened on his forehead.

Solomon would love to shoot the snake. But what would that solve? He needed to pull himself together and—

The door behind him banged open. Solomon wheeled, his hand on his still-holstered pistol. Two guards burst through the doorway and pointed guns at him, yelling "Freeze!" and "Hold it right there!" Two more ran down the hall behind them, coming this way.

Solomon let his hands drop to his sides. The biggest of the guards cautiously stepped closer, his revolver steady in both hands, pointed at Solomon's face. He pressed the muzzle to Solomon's cheekbone while the other three surrounded him. One wrenched Solomon's gun out of his holster.

They stepped away, making a perimeter around him, giving him room. All the guns were aimed at him.

"Davis is down," one of the newcomers said. "This guy hit him in the throat."

General growling and muttering among the guards. Solomon braced, expecting that one of them would get brave, but before they could any ideas, Logan said, "He'll live. If Gage wanted to really hurt him, Davis wouldn't be breathing."

Nobody moved. Logan said, "Turn around. Slowly."

Solomon did as he was told, the gun muzzles following his every movement like coal-black eyes.

Logan clapped his hands once, and cackled with laughter. "Boy, I thought you'd fucked up before, but this is even better. Charging in like this, hurting people, threatening me. This is the end for you, buddy."

He told his men to empty Solomon's pockets. Solomon stood still while they cautiously followed orders. Logan picked up his phone from the floor. He punched a button, then said, "Hey. Get down to my office. Right now."

The guards dumped Solomon's belongings—gun, wallet, phone, keys, sunglasses, corporate ID and the deck of Sheffield money from his inside jacket pocket—onto Logan's desk.

Logan pawed through the stuff, plucking out the money, the corporate ID and the keys. He took Solomon's corporate credit card out of his wallet.

"You won't be needing this stuff anymore." He dropped the items, along with Solomon's gun, into a desk drawer.

Chris Sheffield puffed through the door and pulled up short when he saw the guards pointing pistols at Solomon.

"Son of a bitch. What's going on here?"

"He roughed up one of my men," Logan said. "Threatened to shoot me. These guys got here in the nick of time. Saved my life."

Solomon said nothing. Chris wouldn't believe him anyway.

"That's it," Chris said. He fought to keep a smile off his fat face. "That's the last straw. You're fired, Solomon. You men escort him off the premises."

Solomon nodded. It was what he expected. He picked up his wallet, phone and sunglasses and put them in the appropriate pockets. He walked toward the door, the guns tracking his movements.

He paused when he reached Chris, who flinched and took a step back.

Solomon shook his head slowly, then marched off down the hall, the guards hard on his heels.

In the reception area, Davis was sitting in a chair, one of the young receptionists leaning over him, giving him a glass of water.

His face reddened at the sight of Solomon, but he didn't say anything. The receptionist glared on his behalf.

The elevator opened as they reached it, and Michael Sheffield stepped off. He said, "What the hell?"

Solomon ignored him. He went into the elevator and stood with his back against the wall. Three guards crowded inside, still aiming guns his way, and one punched the "express" button so the car wouldn't stop until it reached the ground.

He calculated how he could disarm them in these close quarters. What moves he would use, which guard would have the quickest reflexes, how much damage might be done by ricocheting bullets.

But what was the point? He was through at Sheffield Enterprises. He'd let his temper get the better of him, and he was paying the price. He was on his own now.

When they reached the lobby, he walked away without looking back.

CHAPTER 44

•••••••••••••••••••••

Solomon walked three or four blocks, west to Sansome, then south, no idea where he was headed, before he sensed someone trailing him. Foot traffic in the Financial District was in a mid-morning lull, everybody indoors trying to make a buck, and that was the only reason Solomon noticed the black man on the other side of the street, carefully keeping a full block between them. The man was bareheaded and wore a brown overcoat that flapped around his legs.

Solomon paused outside a coffee shop called Café Olé, as if reading the menu in the window. The front was mostly glass, reflecting the sunlit skyscrapers across the street. The door stood open, letting the aroma of fresh coffee out into the street, and the angle was perfect to reflect the opposite sidewalk. The black man walked right into the frame before he realized it. He hesitated, then quickly entered an office building across the way.

Solomon hadn't made out the man's face, but that hesitation told him what he needed to know. He glanced up and down the street, then hurried south, toward busy Market Street in the distance.

Now that he knew the guy was on him, it was easy to pick him up as he emerged from the building and resumed his pursuit. Solomon thinking: That son of a bitch Logan never gives up.

He made sure the tail saw him veer into a cobblestone alley between two brick buildings that looked as if they dated from the era of the 1906 quake. The narrow alley cut through the block, blank service doors facing each other along its length. A trash bin sat near the far end, and Solomon sprinted for it.

He skidded to a stop and looked back, but the man in the overcoat hadn't reached the mouth of the alley. Solomon crouched behind the reeking dumpster, his ears straining against the rumble and honk of distant traffic, trying to make out footfalls. His hand automatically slipped inside his jacket before he remembered his holster was empty.

His sudden disappearance must've made the tail nervous. The man rushed into the alley, not as careful as he should be, his heels thudding on the uneven cobbles.

Solomon tensed as the footsteps neared. When the front edge of the flapping overcoat appeared at the edge of the trash bin, he launched himself forward and tackled the man, who shouted in surprise as he fell backward onto the grimy cobblestones. They landed hard with Solomon on top. He cocked his fist back, ready to clobber the bastard.

Then he recognized him. The security guy, the one with the African delegation Solomon had seen departing Chris Sheffield's office.

The man's light-brown eyes were wide with surprise, and Solomon kept his arms pinned so he couldn't make any kind of move.

"Who the hell are you?" Solomon said, his breath coming hard. "Why are you following me?"

"I want to talk to you," the man gasped. He had a French accent. "About the Sheffields."

"You want to talk, why didn't you just stop me on the street? Why the tail?"

"I wanted to make sure the Sheffields didn't have people tracking you. They've been following you for days."

"How do you know that?"

"I've seen them."

Solomon lowered his fist, but he didn't get up. He glared at his captive, wondering how many people had been tailing him the past few days, and why the hell he hadn't noticed.

"Please," the man said. "I mean you no harm. I just want to talk."

Solomon patted him down, found a pistol in a shoulder holster. He pocketed the gun, then rolled off him and got to his feet.

The man in the overcoat rose onto his elbows. He looked up at Solomon, who loomed over him.

"My name is Victor Amadou. Thank you for not killing me."

"You're welcome," Solomon said automatically. He reached out a hand, helped the guy up.

They both took a moment to straighten their clothes and brush off the alley grit. Amadou patted his short gray hair.

"Perhaps some coffee?" he said. "Back at that shop where you spotted me? There's no reason our conversation can't be civilized."

Solomon agreed. They walked out of the alley and around the corner.

"That was very good," Amadou said. "That trick in the alley."

"You knew I'd spotted you. Why didn't you hang back?"

"I got careless. I was in a hurry. Time is running out, and we have many things to discuss."

"What kind of things?"

"First, the coffee. Perhaps a croissant."

Café Olé was furnished with a counter and a few round tables. Ornate sombreros and bullfight posters hung on the plaster walls. Only one table was occupied, by a grizzled old man reading a newspaper.

Amadou examined the pastries spread out behind glass in the counter, and shook his head in disappointment.

"These do not look fresh," he muttered to Solomon.

They ordered coffees and carried the hot paper cups to the most isolated table and sat facing each other. Amadou sniffed the coffee, took a sip and shrugged, as if to say, "It will have to do."

"So, Victor," Solomon said. "Where are you from? Niger?"

"I work for Claude Mirabeau, Niger's ambassador to the United States. Normally, we are in Washington. But we came to San Francisco to meet with the Sheffields and talk them out of interfering in our country."

Solomon simply nodded, trying not to give away how little he knew.

"We had a most unsatisfactory meeting with Christopher Sheffield before we saw you in the corridor. The one we really wanted was Michael Sheffield, but he was unavailable."

"He was in Africa," Solomon said.

"So I've heard. But if he was in our country at the time, he entered illegally. There was no record of him being there. I checked."

"How difficult to enter unnoticed?"

"Sadly, not difficult at all. Our borders are quite porous. We cannot even keep track of herds of cattle going back and forth to Nigeria, much less people, who tend to be craftier. But perhaps Michael was in a neighboring country, meeting with General Goma. That is certainly possible."

"Goma?"

"You know him?"

Solomon hated to show his cards, but he'd never heard the name and he told Amadou so.

"Ah. Perhaps you would like a little lesson in Nigerien government."

"Why not?"

Amadou smiled and took a sip of his coffee before he began.

"We are a democratic republic, yes? With presidential elections every five years. The next election is on Sunday. For the past ten years, our president has been a man named Ibrahim Boudreaux."

Solomon nodded. He remembered the strange name from his online research.

"Boudreaux does not have, shall we say, the best reputation," Amadou said. "Our country is very poor, yet he has become rich in office. This always raises, um, suspicions."

"You're saying he's a crook."

Amadou laughed, exposing bright, even teeth. "Very good. I love that word 'crook.' So American. Yes, by your standards, Boudreaux is a 'crook.' He takes money that is meant for the people. Many countries and the UN have sent money and food to Niger during the drought. Boudreaux and his people end up with much of the money and they sell the food. My people starve—"

"And Boudreaux and his buddies get rich."

"Exactly. Our country depends on agriculture, mostly cattle, but the drought has ruined the grazing. We do not have many other natural resources to exploit—"

"What about the uranium?"

Amadou's eyes lit up. "Ah. Now we are getting to it. We have the second largest uranium deposits in the world, after Australia. Two giant mines near the town of Arlit and a yellowcake refinery, run by a consortium of French businessmen."

"Let me guess: They pay off Boudreaux, too."

"You are a very astute man, Mr. Gage."

"Save it. Where do the Sheffields come in?"

Amadou held up a long finger. "A little more background. As I said, my country votes on Sunday. Boudreaux is running again, of course, and doing all he can to rig the elections in his favor. But there is a very good chance the people will vote him out of office in favor of a man named Jacques Laurent. Have you heard of Laurent? No? Laurent is a reformer, a little bit to the left, but not so much as to alarm the West. He is a college professor in the capital. He preaches responsible government and wants to put in measures that will stop the graft."

"Bad news for Boudreaux's buddies."

"And for the French, who are happy to pay Boudreaux to keep the mines open and running smoothly."

"And the Sheffields? Who do they like in this horse race?"

"'Horse race?'" Amadou laughed again. "Horse race. That's very good."

Solomon stared at him, waiting.

"The Sheffields do not like Boudreaux, of course, because he is—how do you say it?—in the pocket of the French. *Oui*? But they do not like Laurent, either, because he wants to take the uranium back, give the profits to the people."

Amadou paused, his eyebrows raised, waiting for a prompt. Solomon said, "Let me guess. This is where this guy Goma comes in."

"Very good. General Goma runs the military. He's not happy with Boudreaux and he naturally cannot stand Laurent."

"Naturally," Solomon said flatly.

"General Goma would like to run the country himself, but the people would never vote for him. He has, let us say, some bad history. People have disappeared, allegations have been made. The usual problems."

"He's a killer."

Amadou gave an elaborate shrug. "Some would say. But General Goma is very astute, too. He sees that if Laurent takes office, he will be out of a job. So he wants to derail the election."

"Or overthrow the government."

Amadou frowned. "Goma's got half the army at his ranch north of the capital, on 'maneuvers,' but we think he is preparing a coup."

Solomon tried to twist a kink out of his neck. "This sounds familiar."

"Sadly, it is a common story in Africa. We threw out the foreign imperialists forty years ago and set up our own governments. Our leaders have been robbing us ever since."

"Why don't you people put a stop to it? Vote the rascals out, put in people like Laurent."

"Exactly what I would like to see," Amadou said. "My employer, Ambassador Mirabeau, serves at the pleasure of Boudreaux, so it would not work out so well for him. But sacrifices must be made."

"Let me ask again, since we can't seem to get around to it: What do the Sheffields have to do with Goma?"

"Ah." Amadou drained the last of his coffee, made a face and set the cup aside. "We think they are backing Goma financially."

"Why would they do that?"

"The uranium, of course. If Goma takes over, he could break the contracts with the French and sign new ones. Mining is a big industry for the Sheffields, no? They could take over the mines and the refinery. Goma could say they are only running them temporarily, helping our poor, uneducated populace. But the Sheffields would take the profits, and the people still would get nothing."

Solomon thought it over. Amadou watched him silently, a smile tugging at his full lips.

"You are seeing it now, eh?"

"Have you got proof the Sheffields have been in touch with Goma?"

"Michael Sheffield was seen going to Goma's ranch. Why else would he meet with Goma?"

"That's not proof."

"No, but it's all we have at the moment. My people are trying to get more evidence."

Solomon sighed. "Couple of things wrong with this theory."

"Tell me what is wrong. Please enlighten me."

Solomon ignored his tone.

"First of all, Michael and Chris don't run Sheffield Enterprises. Their father does. And Dominick Sheffield would never get involved in overthrowing a foreign government. Don't get me wrong: The Sheffields are capable of much chicanery when it comes to business, but nothing like this. It's too big a gamble. Dom prefers a sure thing. There's no shortage of them available to a man of his wealth."

Amadou interrupted: "Forgive me, but Dominick Sheffield is an old man. His sons may be acting without his knowledge."

"Objection Number Two," Solomon said. "Dom has never done business in Africa. His sons have no experience there. How did they suddenly get involved in the internal politics of Niger?"

"A good question. We believe it's through another man in your company. A man named Bart Logan. Do you know him?"

Solomon nodded.

"Logan was involved in Africa years ago, before he went to work for Sheffield Enterprises. Smuggling in the Congo. A land fraud in Kenya. Always one step ahead of the authorities. I understand he is a wily man, this Bart Logan."

"More than I ever suspected."

"My sources tell me Logan is afraid to come to Africa himself, in case the authorities are still looking for him. But he keeps in touch. One of his friends undoubtedly put him onto Goma's 'opportunity.'"

"I'm still not convinced."

Amadou smiled. "Ah, now we will have Objection Number Three."

Solomon kept his voice low, "Your country's uranium isn't that valuable. I looked it up the other day. The market went south after Three Mile Island and Chernobyl, and it's only now beginning to recover."

Amadou nodded.

"So why the hell would the Sheffields bother?"

"The value of uranium is not merely its price," the African said. "It's leverage. Iran wants uranium to make bombs. So does North Korea, Pakistan, India, Malaysia. The Saudis are plunging billions into nuclear power plants. Whoever holds the uranium holds many strings. They can pull those strings and make industries, whole governments, jump."

Solomon shook his head. "That doesn't sound like Chris and Michael. They're more interested in money than in power. There must be another explanation."

Victor Amadou held out his hands, as if he wanted Solomon to place that explanation in his palms. "What could it be? Please, tell me."

"I don't know."

Amadou slapped his hands together and wiped the palms against each other, as if brushing off crumbs.

"I believe we are right. General Goma is getting help from the Sheffields. And Goma must be stopped before Sunday's election."

The men sat in silence for a time. Solomon's head reeled with the new information. Amadou watched him carefully, as if waiting for it all to click into place.

"Why are you telling me this?" Solomon asked finally. "Why did you track me down?"

"I saw you the other day in that corridor. And I recognized something of myself in you. I believe you are an honorable man—"

"You know nothing about me."

"Perhaps, but you know the Sheffields. I need to know what they're doing."

Solomon slowly shook his head.

"If you would help us," Amadou said, "we could pay you—"

Solomon snorted. "I thought you were a 'poor country.'"

"General Goma is a powerful man. If the Sheffield millions are behind him, there will be no way we can stop him. But if we can find a way to thwart him—"

"You've got the wrong guy," Solomon said. "I've worked for Dominick Sheffield my whole life. No way I'd turn against the family."

"Even though the sons clearly do not trust you?"

"What's that supposed to mean?"

"They are having you followed. When you left their building today, you seemed very upset. All is not well there, I presume."

It was tempting to turn on Michael and Chris and, especially, Bart Logan, but Solomon shook his head.

"What if I brought you proof?" Amadou said. "What if I showed you Michael Sheffield is involved with Goma?"

"You said you had no proof."

"Some is coming. Very soon."

"If you had proof, maybe I could show it to Dom."

"The old man. He is the key?"

"To everything," Solomon said.

CHAPTER 45

• • • • • • • • • • • • • • • • • • • •

Solomon checked the street outside Café Olé before emerging with Victor Amadou. Several vehicles were parked down the block, and a hundred windows looked down on the street; any of them could conceal surveillance. He gave Amadou a business card with his personal phone number

"My gun?"

"Right." He slipped the pistol to Amadou, who stuck it back in his holster. They walked away in opposite directions.

Solomon went all the way to Market Street before he found a taxi. He fell into the back seat, his head swimming, and told the cabbie to drive him to the Lafayette Park apartment.

No one seemed to be following him now. Maybe the Sheffields had decided he wasn't worth the bother. They probably assumed he was out of the game now, thrown out of the fold with nothing but the clothes on his back.

But Solomon had resources of his own. The shock of being orphaned at fourteen had taught him to always protect against loss. He'd squirreled away money and gear over the years. Had loyal contacts and informants. He wasn't done yet.

The cab pulled to a stop in front of the gray apartment building. Solomon paid the cabbie, making a mental note to stop by a cash machine later. Without the Sheffield money in his pocket, he was running low.

He went into the lobby and rang the bell, and the apartment door opened right away. Mrs. Wong stood inside, looking somber in a black pantsuit. She held his briefcase in both hands.

"You can't come in," she said sadly. "Chris called and told me you were no longer with the company. Is that right?"

"Afraid so."

"He said you're not allowed on company property, including this building. I'm sorry, Solomon."

"That's okay, Mrs. Wong. I expected as much."

"Mr. Sheffield said everything here belongs to the company, but I don't think he meant your clothes."

"No, those are mine."

"I thought so. I folded them for you. Put them in your brief-case. Is that okay?"

"Yes, ma'am. I appreciate it."

Mrs. Wong held the five-inch-thick case flat. When he reached for it, she pulled it back slightly.

"Maybe you should open it," she said. "Make sure every-thing's okay."

"I'm sure it's fine." He reached for it again, but she didn't want to let it go. He popped the latches and opened the metal lid.

A gray suit was folded neatly into the space, under a black shirt and some underwear.

"Very nice," he said, and tried to take it off her hands.

She held fast. Solomon lifted the clothing and looked under-neath. The flat leather bag that held his toiletries. And, cushioned in the bottom, his company-owned laptop, full of data about the Sheffields.

"Ah. You did a very thorough job of packing."

"I'm glad you like it," she said. There was a smile in her voice, but she kept her face blank. When he clicked the case closed and took it in his hands, she allowed herself a quick wink.

"Take care of yourself," she said. "I'm sure this will be straightened out soon."

"Thanks, Mrs. Wong. I hope you're right."

She closed the door, and the latch sounded very loud as it clicked shut. Solomon went out into the bright sunshine.

He needed another cab. Not much chance one would wander past the park. He could call one and wait, or he could walk downhill to busy Van Ness Avenue. He put on his sunglasses and started walking.

Mrs. Wong had acted so circumspect, slipping him his laptop and spare clothes, almost as if she thought they were being watched. As Solomon paused at Gough Street, he heard a car engine crank up behind him.

He wheeled around, and saw a gray Ford sedan wedged into a spot at the curb, between two smaller cars, half a block away. The guy behind the wheel looked like that fatass New Yorker who worked for Bart Logan. Lou Velacci.

Goddamnit. Solomon set his briefcase on the sidewalk, and sprinted toward the car.

CHAPTER 46

●●●●●●●●●●●●●●●●●●●●

Lou Velacci saw the big bruiser running toward him and said, "Oh, fuck. Get me outta here."

The Ford was trapped in its parking space. Earlier, some motherfucker in a Toyota had climbed right up Lou's ass, squeezing the little car into a too-small space. Lou had only inches between the Ford and the bumpers of the cars front and back. He whammed the Ford backward into the Toyota, got a little movement there. He shifted into drive, spinning the steering wheel, trying to get the car out of the tight space.

Holy fuck, Solomon Gage was almost on top of him. Lou reversed into the Toyota again, but saw he couldn't escape in time. He locked the Ford's doors. He turned the steering wheel again, straining to move faster, his nylon-sheathed elbows hammering his own gut.

Gage was beside his window now, his shadow blotting out the fucking sun, shouting, "Roll down your window!"

Fuck that. Gage looked mad as hell, his shaved head glowing and those dark sunglasses hiding his eyes. Looked like the fucking Terminator.

Lou wished he'd run when he had the chance. He sure as hell wished he'd covered up the Nikon with the telephoto lens sitting on the seat next to him. That camera told Solomon Gage everything he needed to know about—

Crash! Gage kicked out the window, showering Lou with glass.

"Shit!"

Gage leaned into the car and grabbed Lou by the throat.

"Shit!" Lou said again, though this time he sounded like Donald Duck. "Let go!"

He yanked the steering wheel back and forth, as if he could lift the Ford out of its space and fly off down the street, with Solomon Gage hanging out the window. Spots appeared before his eyes as Gage reached through the window with his free hand and killed the engine.

Gage ran his hand around Lou's waist and took his revolver. Lou had forgotten about the gun, too busy trying to flee.

Gage let go of his throat. Lou gasped, and sweet, precious air filled his lungs. Oh, thank Jesus.

The relief was momentary. Gage jabbed Lou in the temple with his own gun. Which hurt.

"You're Bart Logan's man," Gage said.

Lou couldn't speak. He nodded.

"He's had you following me for days."

"That's right." Lou didn't sound like a duck anymore. More like Louis Armstrong. He wondered whether Gage had done permanent damage to his voicebox.

"You took pictures of me with Lucinda Cruz."

Lou didn't want to answer that one. But hell, the camera was sitting right there—

"Take a message to Logan for me," Gage growled, and Lou felt a glimmer of hope: If Gage wants a message boy, then maybe he won't kill me after all.

"Tell Logan to stop putting tails on me. Tell him to back off. You boys don't want to piss me off further. Understand?"

"Yeah, I got you."

Gage jabbed the gun against his head.

"I mean, yes, sir," Lou croaked.

"Tell Logan that if I spot one more tail, I take everything I know about the Sheffields to the newspapers."

"Yes, sir."

"And I know it all. Everything. I'll take the whole family down."

"Okay."

Jab.

"I mean, yessir."

Gage stepped back. Sudden relief made Lou's breath catch in his throbbing throat.

"Tell him," Gage commanded. He turned and walked away, the way he'd been going before. He slipped Lou's revolver into his jacket pocket. Damn. Lou had liked that gun. But he wasn't about to ask for it back. Gage picked up his briefcase and set off down the hill.

Lou brushed broken glass out of his lap. He reached into his shirt pocket and fished out a cigarette with trembling fingers. He managed to get it lit, and took a couple of deep, nerve-settling drags, thinking: Jesus, I hate this town. I hate my job. Most of all, I hate that fucking Solomon Gage.

Another big drag of smoke down his sore gullet, then he dialed Bart Logan on his cell phone.

"Boss? You're not gonna believe what the fuck just happened."

CHAPTER 47

●●●●●●●●●●●●●●●●●●●

Robert Mboku clapped his hands and laughed aloud as the hulking bald man choked the man in the car. The Ford kept getting in the way of their surveillance, and Robert had harbored thoughts of hurting the driver himself.

"Did you see it?" he said in French to Jean-Pierre. "Boom, he kicked the window. Then he squeezed his neck. Haha."

"I saw it." Jean-Pierre wasn't amused. "Lucky he didn't see us watching. He might try to do the same to us."

Robert's laughter died on his lips. "I would like to see him try it."

He plucked his machete from the floorboard of the silver pickup and gestured with it, a slashing move, just out of sight below the dashboard.

"Put that away," Jean-Pierre said wearily, "before you cut my leg off."

"Bah, I am tired of sitting and waiting. Let's catch the big man and make him talk to us."

"You saw him put that gun in his pocket."

"He won't shoot us. He'll never see us coming. We are invisible to him. He didn't see us outside the company headquarters, waiting for Michael. He didn't see us follow him here."

Jean-Pierre shook his head. "He talked to Victor Amadou. That changes everything. He's on alert now. We have to assume the Sheffields are, too."

Robert set the tip of his machete on the floorboard and leaned the hilt against his knee. He still wore his new Levi's with the bottoms rolled up. The cuffs of his loose cotton shirt were unbuttoned and flapped around his wrists.

"So we kill Amadou. We kill the big man. We kill the fat boy in the car there. Kill the Sheffields. Kill them all, Jean-Pierre. It is the best way."

Jean-Pierre sucked on his stubby cigarette, scowling. "This is not the bush. You can't just leave bodies for the hyenas. Here, the police investigate every disappearance. And in a city, there are witnesses. Look around. People in the park. People behind the windows of these buildings. Eyes everywhere, watching everything."

Robert was not convinced.

"The big man kicked out that window, choked the driver, took his gun," he said. "No one even looked. Even now, no one is looking. You worry too much about witnesses."

Jean-Pierre shrugged and crushed out his cigarette. The ashtray was full of smelly butts. Another reason to get out of this truck, to do something, to *move*.

"The city is no good," Jean-Pierre said. "We need to get the Sheffields out to the old man's place in the forest. We can take a few men, treat it like a war zone, wipe them all out."

Robert smiled. "Give them the chop. Hang their heads from the trees."

Jean-Pierre stared at the corner where the man with the shaved head had disappeared. Robert thought Jean-Pierre looked more tired than usual. The bags under his eyes were puffy and gray. He had much on his mind.

"We need to make some noise." Robert struck his palms together once, sharply, making Jean-Pierre turn toward him. "Let them know they are not safe."

"What would that accomplish?"

"You want the Sheffields to run to Papa? Scare them."

Jean-Pierre considered that for a full minute. Then he smiled and pointed at the fat man in the Ford.

"Make it quick," he said. "And quiet. Remember how many people are nearby."

"Quiet as a snake." Robert opened the truck's door and slithered out, his new sneakers landing on the pavement without a sound. He slipped the machete up under his shirt, felt the cold blade against his chest.

Then he sauntered toward the gray Ford.

CHAPTER 48

●●●●●●●●●●●●●●●●●●●

When Solomon reached Van Ness, he found all six lanes thick with cars, bumper to bumper. A landscaped median ran down the middle of the street, and a couple of pedestrians were stranded out there, standing in the shade of a laurel tree. Cars inched forward, everybody trying to make it through the intersection before the traffic light changed. Like it made any difference.

Lunchtime traffic. All these motorists, fleeing their offices, and they end up spending their whole lunch hour sitting in traffic.

The chances of finding a vacant cab here were next to nil. He could see a bus coming, but it was still three blocks away and, the way traffic was snarled, it might be ten minutes before it got to him. Then what? Stand on a crowded bus while it was stuck in traffic?

Solomon felt he needed to land somewhere. Sit still. Think. Boot up his computer and see if he could learn any more about the Sheffield boys' bad behavior. If he took Amadou's accusations to Dom, he'd need ironclad evidence.

Other pedestrians had wandered up, massing around Solomon, waiting for the "walk" signal. The light changed, and they hustled out into the street, squeezing past the bumpers of cars stranded in the intersection. Solomon followed, lost in thought, wondering where he should go.

A cable car dinged nearby. The cables sang beneath the street. The California Street line, the east-west artery of the cable car system, runs from Van Ness all the way to Embarcadero Center. Solomon thought about catching a ride to the Hyatt near Sheffield Enterprises headquarters, but then he spotted a place, a block down Van Ness.

It was a narrow sliver of a building, wedged between two apartment towers. A small sign over the entrance said, "Hotel Blue." One of the boutique hotels that had sprouted all over the city, aimed at rich visitors who wanted convenience and concierges and class, wrapped in a tidy little package. Perfect.

The lobby was decorated with swooping neon, crystal vases and Italian furniture. The walls were painted swimming-pool blue.

The clerk at the front desk gave Solomon an effusive welcome, and said they did indeed have a vacancy for only four hundred bucks a night. Solomon put it on his personal credit card.

The elevator hummed up to the fourth floor. The doors opened into a narrow hallway that connected only four rooms. The hotel was five stories tall. How did they stay in business, renting twenty rooms? By charging four hundred bucks a night, that's how.

His cornflower-blue room was so narrow, Solomon could stretch out his arms and almost touch opposite walls, but it had everything he needed: bed, bath, phone, desk, coffeemaker. He set his briefcase on the desk and went to the window, looked down on Van Ness. The traffic jam hadn't improved. He could hear grumbling engines and muted honks through the plate-glass window. He hoped it would be quieter at night.

Solomon stripped off his jacket and hung it in the room's tiny closet. The .38-caliber revolver he'd taken off Velacci weighed down one pocket. He took it out and tried to fit it in his shoulder rig, but the holster was designed for a semi-auto and was too narrow. He set the pistol on the desk, and slipped the shoulder holster off, hung it in the closet, too.

He opened his briefcase, removed the clothes Mrs. Wong had packed for him and put them away. He arranged the desk, moving the pistol out of the way so he could set up his laptop. While the computer booted up, he thought about what to do first. He needed to check what Amadou had told him about Michael Sheffield and this General Goma character over in Niger. He needed to get into the Sheffield Enterprises accounting system, see if he could find payments to travel agencies or airlines. Get some dates when Michael traveled, then go from there, assembling evidence, building his case. Just like a lawyer.

His thoughts shifted to Lucinda Cruz, her efficient manner in the courtroom, the way she'd outflanked Michael's legal team, her deep brown eyes, the way her left cheek dimpled when she smiled—

Solomon caught himself, but he was already reaching for the phone. The receptionist answered and said Ms. Cruz was in a meeting and could not be disturbed. He told her his name, and asked her to double-check. She put him on hold, and a minute later, Lucinda came on the line.

"I was wondering if I'd hear from you today," she said.

"I would've called earlier, but I was busy getting fired."

"No."

"They had someone tailing me. He took pictures of us having lunch together."

"They can't fire you for that."

"They can do whatever the hell they want. They're the Sheffields. No higher power on this Earth."

"I'm sorry. I never dreamed they—"

"It's probably temporary. I'm onto some things. Once I get them nailed down and tell Dom, I'll be reinstated."

"Why would you want that? After the way they've treated you."

Good question. He wasn't sure how to answer. Wasn't sure he knew the answer. Instead, he said, "How are things with you?"

"Lots of reporters calling, but I'm not talking to them. I refer them to the court filings."

"Which sends them howling after the Sheffields."

"Oh, my." A smile in her voice. "I guess it might at that. How terrible."

"How's Grace?"

"I told her to lie low for a day or two. Recuperate. She needs to pace herself. This kind of a divorce, so public, is emotionally draining."

"You hear anything from Michael's lawyers?"

"No, but I didn't expect to. That's okay. I've got a ton of other work to do."

"I should let you go. I just wanted to, um, let you know I was thinking about you."

"How sweet. You've been on my mind, too."

"Listen," he said. "How would you feel about lunch again? Or dinner? If you don't mind eating with an unemployed guy—"

That made her laugh. "Guess I'll be buying."

"We can still go Dutch. At least until I run out of money."

"Call me tomorrow," she said. "We'll work something out."

"Okay, I will."

A pause. He really should hang up.

"Lucinda?"

"Yes?"

"Watch yourself. The Sheffields are on the warpath. If they were having me followed, they've probably got somebody on you, too."

"Think so?"

"You've seen how Michael can act when he's out of his head. He might make a mistake. Send somebody to hurt you."

A pause, then: "Are you trying to scare me, Solomon? Because you're doing a heck of a job."

"I'm telling you to be careful."

"I will."

He told her good-bye and flipped the phone shut. The computer purred on the desk. He typed a password and waited for the expensive machine to link to the Sheffield Enterprises mainframe. A box appeared on the screen: "Invalid password. Try again." Uh-oh. He typed it again. The same message appeared.

"Damn."

The company security people had blocked his access. Chris and Michael had thought of everything, it seemed. He wondered how long they'd been planning his dismissal, whether he'd played right into their hands, blowing up in Logan's office.

Still, there were things he could do. He started calling people, sources inside the company, people who might know about Michael and Goma and uranium. He spent a good chunk of the afternoon on the phone, chasing leads. Many of the Sheffield employees he reached were wary, and he guessed word of his dismissal had already reached them. Others simply had no idea what he was talking about.

He finally got lucky, though, reaching a market analyst at Sheffield Extraction Industries, Audrey Hamilton, a slim blonde he'd met at a party the previous Christmas. They'd flirted a little over the eggnog and she'd given Solomon her number, but he'd never followed up. She didn't seem to hold it against him. She was just as chatty as he remembered.

After they got through the social preliminaries, he asked what she knew about uranium.

"Funny you should ask," she said. "Nobody around here has *ever* been interested in the uranium market, and suddenly I've got people asking me about it all the time."

Solomon tried not to let excitement leak into his voice. "Really? All the time?"

"I've been trying to get somebody here interested ever since the market started to rebound, but nobody would listen. Then, a few months ago, Michael Sheffield suddenly goes gaga over yellowcake and wants all the data I can get."

"Is that right?"

"Of course, when Michael gets a little bit excited, everyone else goes out of their heads. Pretty soon, I've got every muckety-muck in the place asking me for copies of my analysis. Even got a call from Chris Sheffield's office."

"Must be exciting for you."

"For a while," she said. "But they asked for a lot of information, then never did anything with it."

"Are you sure?"

"Well, they never got back to *me* about it. My boss comes in a couple of weeks ago and says, forget uranium and go to work on coal. Coal! What is this, the nineteenth century? I've been stuck in Research Hell ever since."

"Maybe that's where they want you," he muttered.

"Why? I gave them exactly what they wanted!"

"You know how executives are," he said. "Short attention spans. Hang in there. Your work will pay off eventually."

"Hope you're right," she said. "I've put in six years here. I've got a lot to lose."

Yeah, he thought. Me, too.

CHAPTER 49

•••••••••••••••••••

Bart Logan checked his wristwatch as he marched down the long hallway toward his bosses' offices. Nearly five o'clock. Lucky for him that Chris and Michael Sheffield were still in the building; usually, by this time on a Friday, the big chiefs were long-gone.

He rapped twice on Chris' door, then entered. Chris sat at his desk, across the room, near the windows that looked out over the sailboat-dotted bay. Michael sprawled in a chair nearby. Both had their neckties loosened. Drinks in their hands.

"This better be good news, Bart," Chris said. "It's already been a hell of a long week."

"It's news, but not good." Bart came to a halt in front of the desk, stood at parade rest. The brothers glowered at him.

"You know Lou Velacci? That fat guy, works for me? Somebody killed him."

The Sheffields raised their eyebrows, but nobody looked grief-stricken.

"I think it was Solomon Gage," Bart said.

Ah. That got their fucking attention. Michael started, spilled a little of his drink on the carpet. Chris rocked back in his swivel chair.

"I've had Lou tailing Gage," Bart said. "He's the one who shot the photograph of him kissing that attorney. Today, I had Lou watching the Lafayette Park apartment, making sure Gage didn't come back there, try to start some trouble."

"Yeah?" Michael prompted.

"I got a call from him couple of hours ago. He said Gage had indeed returned. Only stayed a few minutes. Gage spotted Lou as he was leaving the place, ran over to him, kicked the window out of his car and choked Lou."

"Jesus Christ," Chris said. "The man's lost his mind."

"He gave Lou a message to give to me. Said we'd better back off or he'd go to the news media, tell them everything he knows about Sheffield Enterprises."

"He can't do that," Michael blurted. "He signed a confidentiality agreement—"

"Wait," Bart interrupted. "That's not all of it. He took a pistol off Lou, then disappeared."

"But this Lou," Chris said, "he was still alive when he called you."

"Not for long," Bart said. "I just got a call from the cops, saying they'd found Lou's body. He was still in the car, parked by the apartment. Somebody cut his fucking throat."

"Holy shit," Michael said.

"They traced the car, which is owned by us, and called here, got transferred to my office," Bart said.

"Did you tell them about Solomon?" Michael said.

"Damned straight. Told them that he'd come after me this morning, that he'd assaulted a guard here, threatened people, been dismissed. He's the top suspect in Lou's murder."

"But you said Solomon just choked the guy," Chris said. "Then he walked away."

"Guess he came back," Bart said. "The man hasn't been acting rationally. I told that to the police. They've put out a be-on-the-lookout for Gage."

Chris gulped the rest of his drink. He swallowed, then said, "I don't like this. Doesn't sound like Solomon to me."

"None of it does," Bart agreed. "But we don't want to take any chances. You fired Gage. If he's gone nuts, who do you think he'll try to kill next?"

The brothers exchanged a fearful look.

"We'll keep you protected," Bart said. "Put extra security on the office, at Chris' apartment. We won't let that bastard get to you."

The Sheffields nodded, but they didn't look relieved.

"And if it's not him?" Michael said. "If somebody else killed this guy, Lou?"

"Extra security makes sense either way. And as long as the cops are after Gage, maybe that'll be a help to us. Keep him out of our way. Keep him from getting to Dom."

Michael's expression brightened. "Even if he talks to Dad, we can say he's crazy, that he's a killer. No reason for Dad to believe him."

Bart nodded, felt himself grinning. The Sheffield brothers were smiling, too.

"Too bad about your guy, Lou, though," Chris said.

"Yeah, it's a tragedy," Bart agreed.

But they were all still smiling.

CHAPTER 50

Hours later, an exhausted Solomon was washing up for bed when someone knocked on the hotel room door. Shirtless, he stooped to look through the peephole, saw a man and a woman in the dim corridor. He didn't recognize them. He glanced at the revolver sitting on the desk, but decided to leave it. He opened the door.

The woman was a brunette, her hair short and feathery, framing her face. She wore black slacks and flats and a black top that wasn't much more than a T-shirt, stretched tight over athletic-looking shoulders. No jewelry. A large, portfolio-style purse hung from her shoulder by a strap. Her expression was all business.

The guy behind her was about the same age—late thirties—and he looked Mexican-American, with bronze skin and black hair. He wasn't much taller than the woman, but wider. A bodybuilder in a Brooks Brothers suit.

"Solomon Gage," the woman said. Not quite a question. She looked him up and down, pausing at the bandage on his chest.

"Yes?"

"We're with the federal government. We'd like a few minutes of your time."

He stepped out of the way and let them come in. When they saw how small the room was, the weightlifter edged past the woman and went over by the window so they wouldn't be bunched together by the foot of the bed.

"Give me a minute," Solomon said. He went to the bathroom and slipped on his black shirt. When he returned, the woman was standing by the desk, pointing at the revolver.

"Yours?" she asked.

"No. I took it off a guy today."

"Sounds dangerous."

"Not really."

She almost smiled.

"My name's Hart," she said. "That's Gallegos."

"Would that be *Agent* Hart?" Solomon asked. "Deputy? Marshal?"

"Ms. will do for now."

"Okay, Ms. Hart. What can I do for the federal government this late on a Friday night?"

"You work for Sheffield Enterprises. Correct?"

"No."

Her eyebrows lifted.

"They fired me today."

"Ah. Before that, you'd worked for them for ten years?"

"A little more."

"You're close to Dominick Sheffield?"

"I thought so. Until today."

"And you know his sons? Christopher and Michael?"

"Why are you asking? You already know the answers."

"Just trying to establish a few things," Hart said.

"Such as?"

"Such as what you were doing, meeting in a coffee shop with Victor Amadou of the Republic of Niger."

"Who says I was?"

She slipped a manicured hand into the open top of her purse and pulled out an eight-by-ten photograph. She handed it to him.

It was a grainy photo, shot from a long way off, but it clearly showed Solomon and Amadou sitting in Café Olé.

"You people are following me, too? Seems like everyone's tailing me these days. You're all so busy watching me, it's a wonder you're not walking into walls."

"Not us," she said. "We were watching Amadou. What were you doing with him?"

"Drinking coffee."

"And talking about what?"

Solomon didn't like the way this was going. He sat on the end of the bed.

"Before we get into that, maybe I should ask which branch of the federal government you represent."

"It doesn't matter."

"Might matter to me."

"We're not here to arrest you."

"Good. Because I haven't done anything."

"You ever hear of the International Anti-Bribery Act of 1998? Or the Foreign Corrupt Practices Act?"

"Can't say that I have."

"Federal laws. They make it a crime for American corporations to pay off government officials in other countries."

"Is that so?"

"Corporations can be fined millions if the government catches them paying bribes to get business overseas. Corporate officers can be sent to federal prison."

"Fascinating."

She sighed. "We have reason to believe the Sheffields are trying to buy their way into the uranium business in Niger. That they're prepared to interfere in the elections there. Any of this familiar to you?"

Solomon said, "I feel like I'm back in school."

"Victor Amadou works for Niger's ambassador to the United States. We also believe he's sympathetic to Jacques Laurent, a candidate to be the next president of Niger. You walk out the door of Sheffield Enterprises, go four or five blocks and sit down in a café with Amadou. We think there must be connections there."

"It does seem fishy, doesn't it?"

"Seems criminal," Gallegos said from the window.

"Ah," Solomon said. "I wondered when we might hear from you."

Gallegos narrowed his dark eyes.

Hart talked on. "It's important that management of the uranium in Niger stay in safe, stable hands, carefully monitored by international agencies. Terrorists would love to get their hands on yellowcake so they can build dirty bombs. I don't think you'd like to see that happen, Mr. Gage."

"No, ma'am. I wouldn't."

"That's why we're here. We need to determine the Sheffields' interests. We need to find out why the ambassador went to see Chris Sheffield. Most importantly, we need to make sure the Sheffields aren't meddling in the Nigerien election process."

Solomon said nothing, letting her stew.

"It's high stakes, Mr. Gage," she said. "Not a game for amateurs such as yourself."

"So why are you telling me about it?"

"Because you keep turning up," she said. "First, with the Sheffields. Then with Amadou. Are you the liaison?"

"No, ma'am."

"Why did you seek out Amadou?"

"I didn't. He was following me. I jumped him in an alley."

She glanced at Gallegos. Clearly, their surveillance people had missed that encounter.

"Then you just brushed yourselves off, and sat down to coffee?"

Solomon shrugged. "Sounds screwy, I know."

"What did Amadou want?"

"Same thing you do. He wanted to know about the Sheffields' interest in Niger, if any."

"What did you tell him?"

"Same thing I'm telling you. It's all news to me."

"Did you ask the Sheffields about it?"

"Didn't get the chance. They'd already fired me."

She studied him for a minute, then said, "You know more than you're letting on. Maybe you think you can sell information to the highest bidder."

"Then why haven't I tried to sell it to you? Surely, the federal government can afford to pay informants more than the government of some pissant country in Africa."

"What about the French?" she said. "They might pay handsomely for information about a threat from the Sheffields."

"I haven't been contacted by anybody from France," Solomon said. "They're probably out in the hall, waiting their turn."

Hart went over to the desk. Solomon thought her partner might take up the questioning, flex his muscles, but Gallegos stayed quiet.

"We're not offering you money," Hart said. "We're offering you an opportunity."

"To do what?"

"Your patriotic duty. It's vital to national security that we get information about what's happening in Niger. Before it's too late. Before some jackass starts spreading radioactive material all over the globe."

"I understand that, ma'am. I'd love to help you out. But I've got nothing you want."

Hart stared at her feet for a few seconds. Then she reached into her portfolio and produced another photo.

"Pretty neat, how you keep doing that," he said.

She handed him the photo. This one was sharp and the colors bright, particularly the blood. Lou Velacci, sitting behind the wheel of a car, his head thrown back and his mouth open. His fat throat was slashed all the way across, a bloody gash like a crimson smile under his chin. Blood soaked the front of his shirt all the way down his fat belly.

"You know that man?" Hart asked.

"Lou Velacci. Sheffield security."

"That's right. He's been tailing you."

Solomon said nothing.

"He was found this way by a pedestrian today, near the Sheffields' apartment building across from Lafayette Park."

He stared at the photo of the dead man.

"The body was found," Hart continued, "only minutes after you were seen leaving the building."

"Your people watched this happen?"

"No, but eyewitnesses said—"

"If you have witnesses, then you know I had nothing to do with this," he said. "I talked to this guy, even took that gun over there from him, but I didn't cut him. He was alive when I walked away."

She took the photograph from him and tucked it back in her bag.

"I believe you," she said, "but the SFPD wants to talk to you. We could hand you over to them. Let them sort it out."

"Why would you do that?"

"Score some points with the locals. Make you play ball with us. We need information, and we don't have time to screw around."

He pointed at the phone on the desk. "Call the cops. I don't have the information you want."

Hart looked over at Gallegos, who shrugged his broad shoulders.

"Look," Solomon said, "you've tried threats, you've tried coercion, you've appealed to my sense of patriotism. None of it's working because I don't know any more than you do. We're wasting each other's time."

"I think you're hiding something," she said.

Solomon raised his hands and held them out, palms up. "Search the room, if you like. You won't find anything."

She didn't move, but her eyes roamed the room.

"The cops might be interested in that pistol," she said.

"They can have it," Solomon said. "I've got others."

Hart stared at him for a while, but he gave her back nothing. Finally, she reached into her bag and produced a white business card. She handed it to Solomon. He expected an FBI seal or a CIA logo, but the card bore only the name "Patricia Hart" and three telephone numbers, two with San Francisco area codes, one in Washington, D.C. The card was on lightweight stock, felt temporary.

"If you hear anything," she said, "call me. Don't interfere. Don't play hero. Just call me."

"Don't worry about me," he said. "I don't even work for the Sheffields anymore. I'm an amateur, remember?"

She shot him a look, then she and Gallegos left without saying good-bye. Solomon shut the door behind them, and stood with his back to the door.

He'd used his personal credit card to pay for this room. The information went into a bank's computer somewhere, which was about the same as putting it on a billboard on Market Street. These days, with Homeland Security laws and National Security

Administration snooping and cameras everywhere and eye-in-the-sky spy satellites, the feds probably knew where every American on the planet was at any given moment.

Time for Solomon to get off everyone's radar screens. Time to disappear.

CHAPTER 51

•••••••••••••••••••

Saturday morning, Solomon packed his computer, spare clothes and other gear in his briefcase. He put a fresh bandage over the tender wound on his chest. He put the late Lou Velacci's gun in his pocket. Then he went down to the aqua-tinted lobby of the Hotel Blue and checked out.

He examined the street as much as the hotel's glass doors would allow. He didn't see anyone watching. Of course, he hadn't spotted any tails before, and he knew now that he'd had so many people trailing him, it was as if he'd been leading a marching band.

Out the door, he strode briskly to the south until he came to one of the corner markets that are everywhere in San Francisco. He ducked inside and took the maximum three hundred bucks out of the store's ATM, figuring it was the last time he'd use that card for a while.

The store had a rack of baseball caps near the cash register. Basic black caps with the San Francisco Giants' orange "SF" logo stitched on the front, thirty dollars apiece. Solomon couldn't possibly care less about baseball, but the cap would cover his conspicuous shaved scalp. He bought one and fitted it on his head.

He backtracked to California Street, arriving just in time to squeeze onto a departing cable car. It was jammed with locals who did their best to ignore a family of braying Midwestern tourists who were thrilled to be aboard.

The cable car operator whanged a bell as the car approached intersections, even though the traffic lights were synched to his approach. The operator, a sturdy black man with a big grin, worked the four-foot-long lever that operated the clamp that caught the cable that hummed under a groove in the pavement. The car would jerk and shudder, then smoothly roll down the center of the street. Every few blocks, the operator released the clamp and hit the brakes and used the bell to announce a stop. More people got on, few got off, the car got more crowded.

Solomon stood near the rear of the car, his eyes glued to the street behind them. He saw nothing suspicious, which troubled him. Surely everyone hadn't given up and gone home.

The cable car climbed to the top of Nob Hill, where Grace Cathedral and the giant old hotels lured some of the passengers off, including the braying tourists. Brakes shuddering, the car went down the other side toward Chinatown's crowded streets.

Solomon stepped off the cable car at the next stop and did his best to disappear into the Chinatown throng. Not easy for someone who was six-foot-four, but he kept his head down as he navigated through the tourists and shoppers.

Lucky Day Jewelers stood in the middle of a block, its barred windows wedged between a vegetable market and an import store. An elderly Chinese man with a face like a dried apricot stood behind the counter, his fingertips resting on a glass case full of jade bracelets and rings.

Solomon removed his baseball cap, but the old man showed no sign of recognizing him.

"I've got a safe deposit box in the back," Solomon said. "I need to get into it."

The proprietor nodded somberly, but still said nothing. He simply held out a hand, waiting for Solomon to show some ID.

The jewelry store had once been a tiny bank that served immigrants who were refused service at regular banks. It had a vault in the back where the old jeweler kept his finest wares, and a tiny room lined in safe deposit boxes that he rented out. The boxes were old, with ornate scrollwork on the doors. Solomon had kept a box here for years, paying annual rent so he'd have a place in the city to stash his stuff. He had similar caches—in banks and rented storage units—in several cities.

The old man stayed behind the counter while Solomon went through a heavy curtain to the back room and opened his box with a tiny key he kept hidden in his wallet. He pulled out a drawer with a hinged lid. Inside was a .45-caliber Colt Commander wrapped in an oily cloth, a box of ammunition, a thousand dollars in hundred-dollar bills, and a cell phone and charger. Solomon put the items in his briefcase, then replaced and locked the safe deposit box.

He thanked the old man on his way out, but the jeweler merely nodded. Hanging onto his words as if they were as valuable as his gems.

Solomon settled the Giants cap back on his head as he stepped outside. He felt better now, equipped and ready. He walked through the shoppers, headed downhill toward the even larger crowds around Union Square.

Safety in numbers, he told himself. Get into a big group, then find a way to vanish.

A parking garage sits under the terraces and palm trees of Union Square, and Solomon crossed the plaza to the south side and entered the garage. He went into a public restroom and stripped off his jacket and stuffed it in his briefcase. He turned his baseball cap around backward and put on his sunglasses. He looked in a scratched mirror. Not a huge change in his appearance, but perhaps enough to throw off any tails.

He walked quickly through the throngs in front of Macy's and turned onto Powell Street, where a long line of tourists waited to board cable cars that would take them north to Fisherman's Wharf.

Solomon skirted the line, then turned right at Market, glancing behind him as he went around the corner. Nobody.

A concrete plaza lay before him, thick with homeless beggars and fluttering pigeons and gawking visitors. He followed the signs for BART and went down a flight of stairs to catch the subway.

He got on a train, went two stops west, then got off. Caught another going back downtown, and did the same thing. Got out and walked around South of Market, enjoying the sunshine that had battled the usual morning fog to a standoff the other side of Twin Peaks.

He went in the lobby of a hotel and exited through its parking garage. He went into a restaurant, hid in the restroom for a while, then exited through the kitchen. He went down alleys and up steps and through parks and around corners and he felt like a jackass, taking these precautions, but he wanted to make absolutely sure no one followed.

He hailed a cab and asked the driver to take him to an address on Townsend, near Sixth Street, not far from Pac Bell Park, where the Giants play. Solomon removed the baseball cap and wiped his sweaty scalp with his handkerchief. He opened his aluminum briefcase and put the cap inside and got out his suit jacket and shook the wrinkles out of it and laid it across his lap, ready to put it on when he reached his destination.

Partly because of the new ballpark, Townsend was gentrifying. Once an industrial area in the shadow of the elevated freeways, now it was starting to look like the rest of the city—offices and chic shops and trendy cafes. Hell, there was even a Starbucks on the corner. You could practically *hear* the real estate prices shooting skyward.

In the middle of the block stood a sooty brick storefront with papered-over windows. A narrow parking lot and loading dock flanked the building on one side, ringed by razor-wire fences. On the other side was a gutted building surrounded by scaffolding.

The brick storefront could've been mistaken for an abandoned building, if it weren't for the constant thrum of the presses inside. The glass door bore the plant's only signage—peeling gold-leaf letters that said, "Valu-Rite Printing Inc." above the address. Valu-Rite didn't advertise; the company had more business than it could handle, much of it from Sheffield Enterprises. A multinational corporation requires a lot of printed matter, everything from business cards to letterhead to innumerable forms. The Sheffields had used Valu-Rite for years. The shop often ran seven days a week.

The owner, Clyde Merton, was a harried, nervous man with thinning black hair that he slicked straight back. He usually wore an apron that had once been white, but was covered by years of spritzed ink and spilled coffee. His hands were so stained by ink, they looked purple. The little finger on his left hand was missing, and Solomon always had to fight the urge to stare as Clyde gestured and smoked and took notes with his busy, busy hands.

Clyde was in the front when Solomon entered. A smile flickered on his face, exposing his pointy teeth, then he came over, held out a grimy hand for Solomon to shake.

"Solomon Gage," he shouted over the thundering presses, his voice like sandpaper on rust. "Been a long time."

"Haven't needed your services for a while, Clyde. Keeping busy?"

"Always, always. Do you, um, need to see me in private?"

"If you've got time."

"Sure, sure. Come back to my office."

Clyde scurried away, and Solomon followed, weaving between presses and copying machines and huge rolls of paper and a dozen busy workers. The concrete floor was gritty and littered.

Cobwebs dangled from the ceilings. The high windows were filmed over with yellow crud.

About the last place in the world you'd expect to turn out pristine printed goods, but Clyde's products were perfect. That was the main reason Valu-Rite had been the company's printer for twenty years. The other reason, known to only a handful of people at Sheffield Enterprises: Clyde Merton was a master forger. If someone needed travel documents or a birth certificate, even credit cards, Clyde was the man to see.

His office looked like the aftermath of a disaster—papers strewn everywhere, overflowing ashtrays, dust on everything. It smelled like a smoker's dirty underwear. The phone was an old-fashioned model with light-up buttons for each line. Three were blinking, but Clyde ignored them as he sat behind his battered desk. Solomon lifted some catalogs out of a chair and set them on the floor as Clyde said, "Just throw that shit anywhere."

Solomon sat, his briefcase on his knees. Clyde seemed to have developed a twitch in his right eye. The man always had been a bundle of tics and flinches, and apparently it had only gotten worse.

"What can I do for you, Solomon?"

"I need a new identity."

"Ah." Clyde's head bobbed up and down. "Passport?"

"Just domestic for now," Solomon said. "Driver's license, Social Security card."

"That's easy. Credit cards?"

"Are they hot?"

"Not at all." Clyde looked insulted. "We'll open accounts under your new name. All completely legit. We can even have them go to a real address, if the company wants to pay the tab."

"This one's not for the company. It's personal."

"Ah. Not a problem."

Solomon reached inside his jacket, pulled out the packet of hundred-dollar bills. "How much?"

"You get the corporate rate. Least I can do, as much business as you've thrown my way over the years. Say, five hundred bucks? Have 'em ready for you in two hours?"

"Perfect." Solomon peeled off the bills and handed them over. "I'll get something to eat and come back."

He noticed a camera on a tripod against a wall. "You need a picture of me?"

"Nah. We've got you all on file. I'll pull the photo, get started right away."

Clyde stuffed the money in his shirt pocket with his mangled hand.

"This one's just between you and me, Clyde. If anyone asks."

"Sure, sure. Don't worry about it. Happy to do it."

Clyde's beady eyes roamed the room. He looked to be mentally assembling everything he'd need, eager to get started. Solomon showed himself out.

CHAPTER 52

●●●●●●●●●●●●●●●●●●●●

Three hours later, Solomon used his new driver's license and Visa card in the name of "Seth Maxwell" to check into an old motel a couple of blocks south of Market Street. He'd walked there from the printing plant, taking a roundabout route, careful not to be followed.

The motel was ready for the wrecking ball. Its stucco walls were blistered and faded, looked like scarred skin, and the sun damage must've occurred a long time ago, because the squat building was surrounded by skyscrapers and hadn't seen the sun in years. The railings along the steel stairs and the balconies were rough with rust and peeling pink paint. Inside Solomon's upstairs room, the floor felt spongy underfoot, as if it could give way at any moment and drop him into the room below. He moved gingerly, plugging in the cell phone, taking off his jacket, hanging his clothes and setting up his laptop. Stalling. He dreaded what he must do next.

He'd decided to call Dom and tell him about his out-of-control sons. Time was running out before the Nigerien election, and there wasn't much Solomon could do to stop them. It was up to Dom.

He stared out the window at a sliver of blue sky, sorting through what he knew about Niger and uranium and the Sheffields, piecing together the arguments he'd present. If Dom would listen. If he'd even take the call.

Finally, he couldn't find another reason to put it off. He dialed Dom's number at Cutthroat Lodge. The old man answered it himself.

"Dom, it's Solomon. We need to talk."

A long silence. Finally, Dom said, "Why?"

"It's about Michael and Chris." Solomon paused, but Dom said nothing. "What they're doing. In Africa."

"I told you, Sheffield Enterprises doesn't operate anywhere on that continent. I guess I'd know if—"

"It's uranium, sir."

"The hell are you talking about?"

"They're trying to take over the uranium industry in Niger. Two mines and a refinery, currently run by the French. Your sons are planning to overthrow the government so they can get the uranium franchise."

Another long silence. Then Dom said, "Start at the beginning."

Solomon told him about his meeting with Victor Amadou. Laurent and Boudreaux and Goma and the elections. Bart Logan's connections in Africa. The federal agents who'd come to visit the night before. Lou Velacci's mysterious murder. Even Solomon's theory that Abby's death was somehow related to the Africa mess.

When he couldn't think of anything else, Solomon said, "That's it."

"You're done?"

"I'm sure there's more, but they've blocked my access to the company computers, which makes it hard to develop any solid proof."

"My thoughts exactly," Dom said. "Where's the proof? Can you prove Michael even went to Africa? I understand that's what

Grace is saying, but wouldn't she say any goddamned thing? You sure you're not letting her attorney fill you with ideas?"

"None of this came from her," Solomon said tightly. "Ask Michael. Ask Chris. See if they can tell you straight-out that they're not involved in Niger."

Silence.

"They're working behind your back, sir. Taking Sheffield Enterprises to places you never wanted to go. And they're breaking federal laws."

"It's always about my sons. You can't stand that they're going to be running things before long, so you try to take them down with you."

"You don't believe that, sir."

"The hell I don't. They told me how you went on a rampage at Embarcadero Center and had to be escorted out at gunpoint. I think you've lost your mind, Solomon. You've gone paranoid."

"Paranoia didn't kill Abby, sir. Paranoia didn't slash Lou Velacci's throat."

"No, but maybe that was you, too. Logan called last night and said the police are looking for you."

Solomon sat on the foot of the ratty bed, elbows on knees, staring at a round stain on the carpet between his feet.

"I'm sure Logan and your sons did everything they could to convince the police that I killed Velacci. But I didn't, sir. You know me better than that."

"I don't know anything anymore," Dom said. "But I can tell when a man's got no proof of what he's saying. All you've got is conjecture and speculation."

"Check it out yourself. There must be travel vouchers. Receipts. If they're pouring money into Niger, you should be able to track it. If Logan is behind this, then you should—"

"Good-bye, Solomon."

Click.

Solomon took the cell phone away from his ear and stared at it until its readout screen went dark. Then he hurled it across the room.

CHAPTER 53

• • • • • • • • • • • • • • • • • • • •

Dominick Sheffield sat in the leather chair in his study at Cutthroat Lodge and stared out the window at the evergreens at the edge of the clearing. A spring wind had kicked up, and the feathery branches rippled in green waves.

He pressed his palms against his forehead. A migraine was building, a storm inside his skull. Solomon's words flashed through his mind like lightning.

Africa? *Could* Michael and Christopher be pulling an end run, leaving Dom out of the loop on the biggest deal they'd ever made? Backing a coup on foreign soil? Would they take such a huge gamble?

Managing a corporation was like steering a ship. A man needed a sure hand and a long view. He'd taught that to his sons, taught them that sometimes you pass up the short-term profit for the long-term gain. That the responsibilities of command were more important than individual egos. That every decision made at the top affected hundreds, even thousands, of lives.

If Solomon was telling the truth, then Chris and Michael were steering the ship into the icebergs. Wresting control from the French made a certain amount of business sense—the company that controlled that ore could influence agendas and markets in other countries—but the risks were huge. Plus, you'd have the whole world watching. International regulations and government meddling and United Nations monitoring and God knows what else. Every ounce of ore tallied, every minute of refinery time tracked. Dom hated that kind of scrutiny. It didn't allow room for the kind of corporate creativity that had helped him make his fortune.

Overthrowing a government? That made him itch all over. When he plotted an acquisition, he wanted complete control over the result. You couldn't put your business in the hands of some juju man with medals on his chest or trust it to a government that could change, top to bottom, overnight.

God, his head was pounding. Dom rang a bell. Fiona came into the room, and he asked her to bring him some Tylenol and a glass of water. She hurried away.

He walked over to the windows, feeling unsteady, as if his world had shifted under him, as if its solidness had been an illusion all along. He stared out at the forest, looking in the direction of Solomon's cabin, though he couldn't see it for the trees.

Dom decided he'd call Chris and Michael, demand that they come see him at the lodge. He wanted to look into their eyes when he asked them about uranium and Africa and Abby.

He wanted the truth.

CHAPTER 54

• • • • • • • • • • • • • • • • • • • •

At his ranch outside Niamey, General Goma sipped from a tumbler of Chivas Regal, taking it slow, making it last. It was very late, and he had a big day tomorrow.

He sat in an upstairs office, maps and charts and photographs spread out before him, remnants of an hours-long strategy session with his unit commanders. The other chairs around the long wooden table were empty now, but Goma felt as if he could still hear their chattering voices, debating Sunday's attack.

The majority advocated frontal assault—using surprise and superior firepower to storm the city and take the stone garrison that sat two blocks from the *Palais Presidentiel* on the banks of the Niger River. But Goma had another plan, one he hadn't revealed to anyone, not even Reynard.

A small force would attack the garrison. Another squad would lob grenades at the palace, pinning Boudreaux and friends inside. But these assaults would be mere distractions. The real prize was the convention center, the concrete-block monstrosity Boudreaux erected a few years ago near Niamey's ancient bazaar. That was where the ballots were to be counted.

Goma didn't intend to seize the garrison or the palace or the television station or the airport. Troops loyal to Boudreaux would fight to the death to protect such traditional targets. Goma didn't want buildings. He didn't need to control air traffic or the airwaves. All he needed were the ballot boxes.

Once he'd seized them, all the delicious options would be in the hands of General Erasmus Goma. He could declare martial law. He could declare a winner, if one side or the other could produce enough money and political concessions to make him happy. He could even declare himself the winner of a surprise write-in campaign.

He gleefully anticipated the horse-trading to come. The ballots were the key to power. They were the key to riches. And they'd make a nice victory bonfire.

Goma yawned. He topped off his drink with the last ounce from the bottle he'd cracked open only hours before. Definitely his last drink of the night. He should go to bed. He looked at the Patek Phillipe on his wrist, then did the math for the nine-hour time difference between Niger and California. Afternoon in San Francisco, a good time to call.

General Goma hated getting telephone calls. He always assumed they were bad news. He liked to be the one dialing the phone, the one swooping into another person's life. The element of surprise on his side.

Goma dialed the old black rotary phone. So many numbers to reach Bart Logan. It didn't help that the general misdialed a couple of times, and had to start over. Finally, the phone on the other end rang.

"Hello, Bart."

"General! I was just thinking about you. Everything ready?"

"We are ready. In twenty-four hours, the capital will be ours."

"Excellent! The arms arrived all right?"

"They're here. No mortars, and many of the rifles were missing, too. But we will manage."

"Good, good." Bart paused, waiting for the general to get to the point of this call. Goma was happy to oblige.

"The men are unhappy," he said. "They are nervous."

"Sure they are. That's only natur—"

"They want more money."

"What?"

"There is no guarantee that the battle will go our way."

"But you said—"

"I do not believe we will lose. But the men, they worry. Most of them have families. They need their Army salary. If they're on the wrong side of this conflict, they could end up starving to death. They want more up front."

"But General, we had a deal—"

"No bullshit! The deals come after. First there is bloodshed, then there is talk. But if there is no more money, the bloodshed never comes, eh?"

Silence. Just as the general was starting to think he'd lost the international connection, Bart said, "How much?"

"A million should do it. For now."

"A million dollars. For bonuses for your men."

"To ease their worries."

"I see. You hand out a million dollars to your men, and every-one happily trots off to battle."

"Something like that."

"How am I supposed to deliver a million in cash? On a weekend?"

"Just wire it to my account," Goma said. "I'll take it from there."

The general took a slug of his Scotch while he waited for Logan to make up his mind.

"I'll have to talk to the Sheffields," Logan said at last. "It's awfully late in the game to be asking for more money."

"Not too late, though. Your Sheffield brothers are wealthy men. They can make people jump."

"Yeah, sure." Logan sounded distracted, as if already mentally rehearsing the speech he'd make to his bosses.

"Go get the money, Bart. I'm going to bed now. When I get up in the morning, I'll check my account. If the money is there, we will launch our attack. If not, I cannot guarantee anything."

Goma hung up the phone and let a laugh rumble up from his round belly.

CHAPTER 55

●●●●●●●●●●●●●●●●●●●●

Bart Logan hesitated outside Chris Sheffield's apartment building in Pacific Heights. He was bringing bad news, and he dreaded the brothers' reaction. Bastards thought "kill the messenger" was the Golden Rule.

Michael, who was staying with his brother temporarily, curtly answered the intercom and buzzed Bart inside.

Bart had been to Chris' apartment many times, but he never got over the luxury. The elevator walls were brass, so highly polished he could see his unhappy reflection. When the doors opened on the top floor, Bart stepped onto a carpet so thick, it felt like it came to his knees. Sconces along the corridor threw scallops of muted light onto oak-paneled walls.

Michael was waiting for him, standing in his sock feet in the open door of the apartment, fuming.

"Now a bad time?" Bart asked.

Michael didn't answer. He went back inside, leaving the door open. As Bart crossed the threshold, he felt like he was stepping off a cliff.

Chris sat across the living room at a desk, leaning forward on his elbows, Saturday casual in a loose green shirt that made him look like a fat toad. Michael, in jeans and a red polo shirt, crossed over to the desk. Beyond the brothers, a window looked out at Angel Island and Alcatraz and the shimmering bay.

Michael picked up a sheaf of papers and thrust them at Bart. "Have you seen this?"

"What is it?"

"That bitch attorney filed another motion shortly before the courts closed yesterday. She wants specifics on any Sheffield operations in Niger. She even mentions uranium. Somebody's fed her information."

"Aw, hell," Bart said.

"How are we supposed to keep it a fucking secret now? As soon as the courts open on Monday, our lawyers will be all over this. They'll tell Dad."

Bart stared at the floor, wondering how Lucinda Cruz got the information and if there was any way to cover it up. Grace's attorney was a problem. Was it time to take her out of the picture? He looked up at Michael, who stared at him, waiting.

"Think Solomon tipped her off?" Bart asked.

"Son of a bitch. I'll bet you're right." Michael wheeled on his brother. "I warned you, goddamnit. Solomon doesn't need to kill us. He'll ruin us instead."

Chris' cheeks flushed, but he didn't take the bait. "The question now is what, if anything, we can do about it."

"Hell, it's too late now!" Michael steamed. "The horse is out of the barn! The fucking barn's on fire! Closing the door won't do much good."

Chris sat back and knitted his fingers together over his paunch, looked as if he were trying to keep from strangling his brother.

"We can still manage this," he said. "We can keep it tamped down until it's too late to turn back. The election's tomorrow. If Dad doesn't find out about the court filing until Monday, then Goma will have already—"

Bart moaned. It slipped out before he knew it was coming. Both brothers froze in place.

"I was bringing bad news," he said. "About Goma."

"For shit's sake," Michael said, his angry face reddening. "What now? Did they lose the rest of those weapons?"

"No, no," Bart said. "The arms arrived. But Goma says his men want more money. They're worried the coup will backfire."

"Nothing's going to backfire," Chris said tightly.

"Try telling that to some African soldier, squatting in the dust at Goma's ranch, thinking he might die tomorrow."

"How much?"

"Not that much," Bart said, trying to give it a rosier spin. "A million bucks."

"Fuck that," Michael said. "A million dollars? That's extortion. Goma waits until the last minute, then—"

"Goma probably will rake off half," Bart conceded, "but the rest would be enough to make the soldiers happy. I know a million's not peanuts, even for you guys, but we've come this far—"

A phone on the desk rang. Chris barked a hello, and his eyes went wide. He looked at Michael and mouthed the word "Dad."

"Oh, shit," Michael muttered.

Bart had a pretty good idea what the old man was pumping into Chris' ear. He must've gotten wind of the uranium deal, probably from his lawyers after that goddamned Lucinda Cruz—

Chris' face glowed like a coal fire.

"Yes, sir," he said. "But if I may say—"

Whatever he was going to say, he never got the chance. Bart guessed the old man didn't want to hear excuses.

Chris said "yes, sir," a couple of times and "no, sir," once, and finally ended with "right away." His hand trembled as he hung up the phone.

"He's heard about Niger," Chris said. "He wants us to come to Cutthroat right now. He's pissed."

Michael ran a hand over his scalp and down his face, as if he could wipe away his anxiety.

Worry boiled up within Bart, too. The old man could blow up the whole plan, just by waving his hand. Bart wouldn't get his share. Hell, he might not even get to keep his job. Goddamnit.

"We'll stall him," Michael said. "We'll fly to Cutthroat and bullshit our way out of it. It'll be okay."

Chris didn't look as if he believed it.

"But first," Michael said, "what do we do about Goma?"

"We can't afford not to pay it," Bart said. "We're too close."

"But Dad's going to nail our asses," Chris said. "If he finds out we've sent another million over there—"

"Maybe that'll be the tipping point," Bart said. "Maybe, if he sees how much you two have poured into it, he won't cancel the whole thing. If he'll just let it play out, it'll be fine."

The Sheffield brothers shook their heads, but Bart knew that wasn't their final answer. They'd pony up the money. It was too late to quit now.

"Go talk to your dad," he said. "I'll take care of things here. Give me the authorization, and I'll make sure the money gets to Goma in time. You two keep Dom from ruining everything."

"Maybe he's right," Chris said. "Maybe we could get Dad on board. If he sees how much we've already spent, and what the potential return is, maybe he'll green-light Goma. If it goes wrong, we can back out in a hurry, cover our tracks. Keep our involvement under wraps."

"Oh, yeah?" Michael snapped. "What about Lucinda Cruz? She's telling the whole fucking world about it."

"Don't worry about her," Bart said. "I'll handle her."

They stared at him a moment, but neither said anything. Bart recognized the tacit permission.

"Go," he said. "I'll get things squared away, then I'll come up to Cutthroat myself. Maybe I'll bring you a gift."

The brothers didn't touch that. Instead, they got busy with the phones. Chris started making arrangements for the money. Michael hit the speed-dial on his cell and ordered up a helicopter.

Bart stood watching them, thinking how much these dumb bastards could accomplish with a phone call. They didn't know how lucky they were. Money can fix anything, because there are always guys like Bart, willing to do anything for it.

As Bart turned to leave, Michael said, "You better be right about this."

"Trust me. It's going to be fine."

"Easy for you to say," Chris snorted. "You're not the one facing Dad."

"He'll come around."

Bart closed the door and walked down the silent corridor, thinking: Dom better fucking come around. Or the brothers will get their inheritances sooner than they expect.

CHAPTER 56

●●●●●●●●●●●●●●●●●●●●

The bedsprings squawked as Solomon shifted his weight. He'd stared at the ceiling for nearly an hour, reliving his conversation with Dom. Depressed as hell.

Now what was he supposed to do? About Chris and Michael and Goma? About his job? His *life*?

A phone chirped. Not the room phone. And not the one he'd thrown against the wall. It was his personal cell, which sat on the desk next to his laptop. He hauled himself to his feet and answered it.

"This is Mr. Gage?" A French accent.

"Amadou?"

"Yes. I am calling you, as promised. I have your proof."

Solomon's pulse quickened. "What do you have?"

"A photograph. Documents. Sent in the diplomatic pouch from Niamey."

"What kind of photograph?"

"It shows Michael Sheffield talking to General Goma. It's not the best photo because it was shot with a very long lens at Goma's ranch. But you can tell it is them."

That, Solomon thought, might be all it takes to convince Dom.

"I need that. Right away."

"Have you talked to Dominick Sheffield?"

"I did, but he didn't believe me. He thinks his sons would never go behind his back on something like this."

"Then he is a fool," Amadou said.

"No, he's just a father. He wants to believe they'd never lie to him. I can take the photo up to the lodge, show it to Dom—"

"I want to go with you," Amadou said.

"Dom wouldn't like me springing a stranger on him."

"I represent my country. How can he deny the truth, if I'm standing there before him?"

The man had a point, but Solomon said, "Let me think about it. How soon can I get that photo?"

"I have a meeting now," Amadou said. "With the ambassador. I can't escape for an hour or two. Where are you?"

"Paradise Motel, on Ninth Street south of Market."

"Paradise, eh?"

"More like Hell, but you'll see it soon enough for yourself."

"Six o'clock?"

"Six will be fine. I'm in room fourteen. Upstairs."

"Very well. I'll see you then."

"Make sure you're not followed," Solomon said, thinking about the federal agents who'd photographed him with Amadou. He'd have to warn Victor about them, but the details could wait. "Be careful."

"You, too. See you at six."

Solomon looked at his watch. Two hours to kill. He couldn't just sit here, waiting for Victor Amadou. He'd go crazy. But there wasn't anything more he could do about Niger or the Sheffields. He'd tried everything he could think of, called everyone who'd know anything. And it hadn't been enough for Dom. He hoped Victor's evidence would be enough to persuade the old man.

Solomon went to the window, but saw nothing suspicious in the motel parking lot or the street beyond. He wondered whether the feds had tapped his cell phone, whether they were on their way here now. All his efforts to hide might've been ruined by the call from Amadou, but that wouldn't matter if they could stop the Sheffields in time. The rest could be sorted out later.

He still had his phone in his hand, and he thought of Lucinda Cruz. He'd promised to call her today, but he'd been so busy, eluding tails and finding a hiding place and haranguing Dom, it had slipped his mind.

He dialed her cell. It rang once. "Lucinda Cruz."

"That sounded awfully official," he said. "You at your office on a Saturday?"

"Always a lot of work to do, even on the weekend. But I find I'm having trouble staying focused. I keep thinking about a certain man I met recently."

That made him smile. "Maybe we can act on those thoughts, as soon as this business with the Sheffields is over."

"Might be a long time," she said.

"Maybe not. I'm meeting with a guy who might sort it out. He's bringing me some stuff that should show Dom that I've been telling him the truth."

"About Michael?"

"And his brother. But I don't want to talk about—"

"Would this be about uranium?"

He nearly dropped the phone. "How do you—"

"I've got sources of my own," she said. "After I talked to you yesterday, I filed a motion asking that they disclose Michael's business dealings in Niger. He's sending a good chunk of the family fortune there, and I want to know why."

"Pretty good source?"

"I think you know him," she said. "Victor Amadou."

"He talked to you, too."

"He called me after reading about the divorce in the newspaper. Is that who you're meeting?"

Solomon hesitated. "I'd rather not say."

That made her laugh. "Mm-hm. You're pretty easy to read, you know that?"

"Even over the phone?"

"I wouldn't become a poker player, if I were you. I can't wait to get you on the stand. All your secrets will come out in court."

"That's what I'm afraid of."

She laughed again, but cut it off abruptly. For a moment, he thought he'd lost the connection. Then she said, "Hold on a second. There's someone at the door."

Five minutes passed, and Solomon began to think the call had been dropped. He said "hello" a few times, but there was no answer. Finally, he disconnected and redialed. Four rings, then voicemail picked up: "You've reached Lucinda Cruz. Please leave your name and number and I will return your call as soon as possible."

Hmm. He hung up, waited a few seconds, tried again. Same result.

A shudder of nerves ran through him. He hit "redial," but he was pulling on his jacket while he listened to it ring. Voicemail again.

Then he was out the door, sprinting for the street, his head snapping back and forth in search of a taxi.

He loped all the way to Market Street before he found a Yellow Cab. He gave the driver Lucinda's office address and waved a hundred-dollar bill so the driver could see it in the mirror. The driver, a scrawny white guy who needed a shave, didn't bat an eye. He stomped the accelerator, and they raced toward The Avenues.

They made it out Geary Boulevard in record time, and Solomon gave the cabbie the hundred and leaped out in front of Lucinda's office. He looked up and down the sidewalk, but didn't see anything out of the ordinary. He checked the law office door and found it unlocked. He had his hand on the .45 under his arm as he went inside.

No one. No sign of a struggle. No strewn papers or overturned chairs. He checked two doors that opened off the reception area. One was an empty bathroom. The other was a closet full of file cabinets. No Lucinda.

She wouldn't leave him on hold and walk out the door, not even lock the place up. He went to her cluttered desk to see if it held some clue. On the blotter sat her cell phone, next to a color photograph, the one taken outside the courthouse. Lucinda up on her toes, kissing him.

"Aw, hell."

CHAPTER 57

• •

Victor Amadou tapped his foot on the worn carpet in the consulate hallway. Ambassador Mirabeau had kept him waiting for more than an hour while various functionaries filed in and out of the consul's office. None had more urgent business than Victor, but the ambassador liked to make the point that he, not Victor, set the agendas.

Finally, the ambassador's secretary, a young fop named Barre, told Victor that Mirabeau would see him now. Victor stood and straightened his brown suit jacket, and tried to wipe the impatience off his face.

The ambassador sat behind the consul's desk, the Nigerien flag draped on the wall behind him. He was dressed in full regalia—a black suit and tie and the green-red-and-white sash of his office diagonally across his chest. No one else was in the office, which surprised Victor. He'd assumed all the ambassador's people would be in the meeting. The ambassador gestured Victor into a chair across from him.

"I've been on the phone with the president," the ambassador said. "I gave him your information about Goma. Our military is ready."

"Goma owns the military," Victor said.

The ambassador held up a hand. "Not all of it. The commanders who are loyal to the president assure me they'll withstand whatever attack Goma brings. They will arrest him, and this crisis will be past."

"What of the elections?"

"They will go as scheduled," the ambassador said. "In fact, the uprising could be very good for President Boudreaux. Once people see he is still a strong man, that he is the only one who can keep revolutionary forces from—"

"They still will vote him out. Laurent is leading the polls."

Mirabeau smiled slyly. "Polls mean nothing. Laurent will come in a poor second, I assure you."

"So," Victor said, his temper getting the better of him, "you will steal the election."

The ambassador scowled. "Be careful how you speak to me, Amadou. I will not stand for—"

"I've run all over this city, trying to derail the Sheffields' plan before the election. Why did I bother? Nothing will change. It doesn't matter whether Boudreaux or General Goma runs the country. Not if the crooks stay in charge."

"Insolence!" the ambassador shouted, stabbing a finger toward Victor. "I will not stand for it!"

Victor caught himself before he said more. He took a deep breath.

"I'm sorry, Monsieur Ambassador," he said. "I have been under a lot of strain. Of course, you are right. Of course it is better to stay our present course. General Goma would ruin our country."

Mirabeau sat back and straightened his sash. Victor knew he must mollify him. It was the only way to keep this meeting short. If Mirabeau started orating, Victor would never make his appointment with Solomon Gage.

"What about the Sheffields?" he asked.

"The president feels we must make an example of them. We must show the world that outsiders cannot come into Niger and meddle in our affairs."

"As the French have been doing for years." The words were out of Victor's mouth before he could stop them. He regretted them immediately.

"You mean the businessmen who run the mines? They have proven to be our friends. Without them, we would have no modern industry at all."

Yes, Victor thought, and we wouldn't send what little money that industry generated out of the country. But he kept it to himself. He couldn't have spoken anyway, not without interrupting the ambassador, who still lectured about the splendid friendship between the consortium and the Boudreaux administration.

When the ambassador paused for breath, Victor cut in: "The Sheffields?"

"Ah, yes, the Sheffields," Mirabeau said. "This is an example how our friendship pays off. We don't have to do anything to make an example of these Americans. The French are taking care of this for us."

Victor's pulse pounded inside his head. "What do you mean?"

"The French have sent people to address this problem." The ambassador made a point of looking at his wristwatch. "Any time now."

"Address it how?"

The ambassador briskly brushed his palms together. "Gone."

"They've sent people to kill them? Here in the States?"

"At the Sheffields' compound north of here. It's quiet there, isolated."

"Impossible."

"What better way to send a message?" Mirabeau said smugly.

"If they kill the Sheffields, the entire force of the United States will turn against us. The Americans will send their armies, their bombers. They will leave a blank spot where Niger used to be."

"Nonsense. We've been assured no one will connect us—"

"We must warn the Sheffields," Victor said, jumping to his feet. "We cannot let this happen."

He fumbled inside his coat, and came up with his phone. He punched buttons, trying to find the number he'd recorded for Solomon Gage.

"What are you doing?" the ambassador said. "Put that away!"

"You are insane," Victor muttered. "All of you. You'll do anything to keep Boudreaux in power. Anything."

"Give me that phone."

Victor backpedaled as the ambassador hurried around his desk. The taller man tried to grab the cell, but Victor yanked it away from him. The ambassador grasped Victor's lapels and slammed him against the wall. Victor held the phone at arm's length, still trying to push buttons with his thumb.

Too late, he realized the ambassador wasn't reaching for the phone. He was jerking Victor's gun from its shoulder holster. He tried to twist away, but the ambassador took a step back, and pointed the pistol at him.

"Drop that phone now," the ambassador growled.

Victor stared at his own gun in Mirabeau's hand.

"You wouldn't dare."

The pistol cracked, and a bullet punched Victor Amadou hard in the chest.

CHAPTER 58

•••••••••••••••••••••

Solomon went to the receptionist's desk and flipped through her old-fashioned Rolodex until he found a card with Lucinda's home phone number. He dialed it while trying to flag down a cab on Geary, but got no answer.

He got the attention of a passing gypsy cab. The green taxi looked as if it could rattle apart at any moment, but the swarthy driver had a heavy foot. As they rocketed through traffic toward downtown, Solomon sat in the back seat, redialing Lucinda's numbers, not finding her anywhere.

He could call the police, but what would he report? He had no proof the Sheffields had snatched her, other than that photograph on her desk, and that could've been delivered anytime. The cops would tell him to take it easy, that she probably just went for a walk or got called away for an emergency. But he knew better.

He took a deep breath, fought off the sudden adrenaline burst. He needed to stay calm, to think. Maybe it wasn't too late to save Lucinda Cruz. But he was damned if he could think how to start.

Solomon looked out the cab's back window, checking whether anyone followed him from her office. He didn't see any tails, but he no longer trusted that he was any good at spotting them. He'd been followed for days without noticing; maybe he'd never lost them. He'd covered his tracks, used the fake ID—

A thought hit him so hard, he groaned aloud. The cabbie stared at him in the rear-view mirror.

"Change of plans," Solomon said. He gave a different address. The driver shrugged and wheeled the taxi through a sudden right turn, headed south.

Why had Solomon thought Clyde Merton would help him without tipping off the Sheffields? The rat-faced printer owed his whole livelihood to Sheffield Enterprises. If he alerted Bart Logan to the new identity, then all Solomon's efforts to hide were a waste of time. Had Logan been tracking him the whole time? Did he know about Amadou?

The cab stopped in front of the brick printing plant, and Solomon paid the driver. Most other buildings along the street were locked up for the night, but lights still glowed behind Valu-Rite's papered-over windows. Solomon pushed his way through the front door, and was buffeted by the noise of a running press. Someone pulling Saturday overtime, finishing a job.

Solomon didn't see Clyde anywhere. He started back toward his office in the rear of the building, but was waved over by a pressman who had a shaved head and a biker mustache. The sleeves of his gray coveralls were cut away at the shoulder, showing off beefy arms covered in black tattoos of skulls and chains.

"Help you?"

"Here to see Clyde," Solomon shouted back. "Is he in his office?"

"I haven't seen him leave."

"Okay to go back?"

"Sure." The printer turned his attention back to the pages flying through the press.

Solomon couldn't see into Clyde's office until he was almost at the door. The upper half of the door was glass, but it was filthy and smeared with inky fingerprints. He could make out Clyde slumped over, his head on his desk.

He went inside, reached across the desk and gave Clyde's shoulder a shove, but the man didn't move. Solomon stepped around the desk, and saw blood puddled around Clyde's chair.

Shit. He grasped Clyde's shoulder and sat him up. His head tipped over backward, and his mouth hung open, exposing his pointy teeth. Clyde's face was ghostly pale. The front of his shirt and his filthy apron were soaked with blood. The black hilt of a switchblade knife protruded from his chest.

"Hey."

Solomon turned to find the tattooed pressman in the doorway. The guy's eyes widened.

"Holy shit. What happened to Clyde?"

"Looks like someone stabbed him."

"Holy shit," the guy said again. His press still rumbled behind him, its noise like a repetitive drum solo. "When did that happen? I didn't hear nothing."

"How can you hear anything with that goddamned press running?"

"Hold on." The man hustled over to the printing press and flipped a switch. The drumming slowed to a stop as he came back to Clyde's office.

"I'll call the police," Solomon said. "But not on this phone. Might be fingerprints. In fact, let's stay out of his office until the cops arrive."

Solomon called 911 on his cell and reported the murder. The pressman stood in the doorway, staring at Clyde. When Solomon flipped the phone closed, the man said, "You found him like that?"

"He had his head down on his desk. I thought he was asleep. How long had he been back there?"

"I dunno. Hour or two? Some guy came in to talk to him, and they went back to the office. The guy left a few minutes later."

"What did he look like?"

"Just some guy. Had on a Raiders cap. I noticed because I'm a fan. Raider Nation, y'know?"

"White guy?"

"Yeah. Regular clothes. Regular sized. I barely paid him any attention."

"Anybody else here who would've noticed more?"

"No. Couple of other printers worked today, but they left mid-afternoon."

Solomon looked at his watch. Almost time for his meeting with Victor Amadou.

"I've got to go."

"Hey, man. You're not going anywhere. You need to stay here and tell the cops about finding him."

"I'll give you my card. You can have them call me. I've got a meeting."

"Fuck that. Your meeting's canceled. This is more important."

"Nothing I can do for Clyde now. But I might be able to save somebody else."

"The fuck are you talking about?" The pressman took a step sideways, cutting off Solomon's exit.

"Get out of my way."

"You want to walk out of here," the beefy pressman said, "you're gonna have to go through me."

Solomon stared at the floor, shaking his head. He didn't have time to play footsie with Mr. Raider Nation. The guy stood planted in front of him, his thick arms crossed over his chest.

Solomon drew the Colt from its shoulder holster and pointed it at the pressman's face.

"Rethink your position," he said. "I told you, I can't be late."

The guy's eyes crossed as he stared at the gun.

"Okay, man. You'd better hurry then."

"Good answer."

The printer backed away, hands raised, all the way to his ticking press.

Solomon hustled out the front door into the fading evening light. He holstered the gun as he hurried up the sidewalk, just as a police car rounded the corner ahead, red and blue flashers going. Solomon ducked his head as the squad car sped past. He turned another corner and walked quickly toward the Paradise Motel.

Whoever killed Clyde might be waiting for him at the motel. But he had to take the chance. He needed that evidence from Victor Amadou.

While he walked, he used his phone to dial the numbers he had for Lucinda Cruz, but still got no answer. He tried to call Amadou, too, to tell him he was running late. No answer.

Solomon hurried along the darkening streets, feeling isolated. Feeling vulnerable. And nervous as hell.

CHAPTER 59

•••••••••••••••••••••

Solomon had almost reached the motel when a shadowy figure came reeling out of the mouth of an alley. He leaped back, at first taking the man for an attacker, then for a wino or a junkie, some vomit-spewing denizen of the streets. But the staggering man called Solomon by name.

Victor Amadou. Sweaty and haggard. He stumbled against Solomon. Was he drunk? Drugged? As Solomon caught him, his hand found warm, sticky blood.

"Inside," Amadou whispered. "Take me inside."

Solomon got an arm around him and half-carried him across the motel's parking lot.

"It's upstairs. Can you make it?"

Amadou nodded and lifted his foot onto the bottom step, but Solomon took most of his weight as they climbed up. He dragged him along the rickety balcony to his room, then balanced him against the wall while he dug out his key and got the door unlocked. It was like handling a drunk, except there was blood all over them, and Amadou's breath came in abrupt wheezes.

Solomon hauled him inside and lay him down on the bed. He went back to the door, stuck out his head and checked the parking lot. No one. They'd gotten lucky.

Amadou moaned. Solomon flicked on the light and bent over him. He tore open Amadou's blood-soaked shirt and found the bullet hole under his left breast, not far from his empty shoulder holster. Blood bubbled up from the hole. A lung shot.

"I'll get an ambulance."

"No," Amadou said. "It's too late. I had a choice. Go to the hospital or come here. This is more important."

He feebly reached across his chest, and pulled a long envelope from the inside pocket of his jacket. The envelope was soaked with blood, but Solomon took it from him and opened it. Inside was a sheaf of bloodied documents, folded length-wise around a color photograph. The photo showed Michael Sheffield, wearing sunglasses, talking to a fat black man in a khaki military uniform. They were on a whitewashed balcony, with an expanse of sandy rangeland beyond.

"Goma?"

"That's him," Amadou rasped. "They are mounting the offensive on Niamey any time now. Using Sheffield money."

Solomon hurried into the bathroom. He came back with a towel soaked with cold water and used it to sponge the sweat off Amadou's forehead.

"We need to get you some help," he said.

"Yes, okay," the Nigerien said. "But first you must leave. If you're here when the police come, you will never get away—"

"I'm not going anywhere," Solomon assured him. "I'll make sure that you—"

"But you must warn the Sheffields. The mercenaries are on their way."

Solomon froze. "Mercenaries? On their way where?"

"To the old man's property."

"Cutthroat Lodge?"

Amadou nodded feebly. "They will kill everyone."

"Why didn't you call me?"

"I dropped my phone when I was shot."

"Who shot you, Victor?"

"Mirabeau."

"The *ambassador*?"

"I was trying to call you, to warn you. He shot me with my own gun. I knocked him down and ran away."

"Stop talking. Save your strength."

"They plan to steal the election. They plan to defeat Goma and—"

"Sshh. I'll take care of it. Let's get you to a hospital."

"There's no time—"

Solomon got up from the bed and went over to the motel phone. His hands were so bloody, it was as if he were wearing sticky red gloves. He picked up the receiver to dial 911. Amadou coughed and sputtered. Solomon turned toward him, saw that Amadou was staring at him with wide round eyes.

"No time," he rasped.

Air escaped his mouth in a ragged exhalation, and he went limp. His eyes still stared at Solomon, but now they saw nothing.

Solomon hung up the phone and went to him. He felt his neck, hoping for a weak pulse, but there was none.

"Goddamnit."

Solomon tore off his bloodied jacket and threw it on the floor. He went to the bathroom and scrubbed the blood off his hands, muttering curses.

Victor Amadou had seemed like a good man, the only one in this whole cluster-fuck who wasn't strictly out for himself. They'd known each other for less than two days, but Solomon felt as if he'd lost a friend.

He added Ambassador Mirabeau's name to his mental list of people who should pay. It was becoming a long list.

CHAPTER 60

•••••••••••••••••••••

As soon as Solomon got the worst of the gore off his hands, he used his phone to call Cutthroat Lodge.

"Hello?"

"Who's this? Michael?"

"This is Michael Sheffield. Who's calling?"

As if Michael didn't recognize his voice after all these years.

"It's Solomon. Let me talk to Dom."

"He's busy right now."

"It's an emergency."

"How did I know you'd say that?"

"Look, Michael. Killers are on their way to the lodge. You guys need to get out of there."

"Killers, huh?" Disbelief in his voice. Dismissal.

"The French consortium has sent mercenaries here from Niger. They're on their way to Cutthroat."

Silence. Finally, Michael said, "I don't believe you."

"You know Victor Amadou? He gave me this information."

"You can't believe him. He works for Boudreaux."

"He was telling the truth."

Another pause. "Is he there now? Put him on the phone."

"He's dead."

Michael laughed bitterly. "Nice try, Solomon. But I don't believe a word you're saying. If anybody's trying to kill us, it's you."

"I tell you, they're on their way there right now. I don't know how much time you have."

"*I'm* telling *you* that you're full of shit," Michael said. "No way their people would come up here. If they even existed."

"You're running out of time."

"Hell, even if you're telling the truth, let 'em come," Michael said. "We've got security guards. We've got weapons. We can take care of ourselves."

"You're wrong. Let me talk to Dom."

"Fuck you, Solomon. I'm tired of you twisting the old man's mind. Chris and I nearly have him convinced that the Niger deal never happened. We don't need you screwing that up now. Take your imaginary mercenaries and stuff them up your ass."

Click, then a dial tone.

"Bastard!"

Solomon hit redial, but the line went directly to voicemail. Michael had left the phone off the hook. Solomon tried to keep his voice calm as he repeated his warning. Maybe he'd get lucky. Maybe Dom or one of the servants would find the message.

He still felt sticky with Amadou's blood. He took off his holster and stripped off his shirt and washed himself in the sink from the waist up, trying to think of ways he could prevent a bloodbath at Cutthroat Lodge.

Calling the cops wouldn't do any good. Jurisdiction at the lodge belonged to the Mendocino County Sheriff's Department, which didn't have the manpower or the resources to take on a team of mercenaries. If Solomon could even persuade them an attack was imminent.

Nobody at the FBI would believe one man's strident alarms. Not in time anyway.

His only option was the spooks. Patricia Hart and her silent sidekick, Gallegos. They already knew the situation. Hell, they might already know about the mercenaries.

Solomon toweled off and got his phone. He fished Hart's business card out of his wallet and dialed the number that looked like it belonged to her cell phone.

"Hart."

"Ms. Hart, this is Solomon Gage.

"Yes, Mr. Gage. We've been looking for you."

"You have?"

"You seem to have vanished."

"I'm at a motel, but I won't be here long. Victor Amadou showed up here. He'd been shot. He's dead."

Only the slightest hesitation before Hart said, "Who shot him?"

"He said it was Ambassador Mirabeau. I guess it happened at the consulate, and Amadou managed to escape. He said the French have sent mercenaries to kill the Sheffields at Cutthroat Lodge. Dom and both his sons are there."

"Did you warn them?"

"I tried. Michael wouldn't believe me. He took the phone off the hook."

"As if that lodge isn't isolated enough," she said.

"They're sitting ducks. You've got to do something."

"Why us?"

"You know what's at stake." He took a deep breath before playing his trump card. "Keeping the Sheffields alive is in the national interest, no matter what the boys have been up to in Africa."

Hart let silence build for several seconds. Solomon squeezed his eyes shut, waiting for her to decide.

"All right," she said. "I can get a team together. We'll take a chopper, fly up there and check for mercenaries running around in the woods. But you'd better be right about this, Mr. Gage."

"Let me go with you."

"Not a chance. Call the local cops and have them baby-sit you until I get back to town. I'll call as soon as we know something."

He started to object, but the line went dead.

CHAPTER 61

•••••••••••••••••••

No way Solomon would sit on the sidelines. He'd invested too much in the Sheffields, his whole fucked-up life, to trust that Hart and her agents would get to Cutthroat Lodge in time.

He pulled on a clean shirt and strapped on his shoulder holster. The gray jacket in the closet was rumpled, but at least it didn't have blood all over it. Lou Velacci's revolver still sat on the desk, and Solomon pocketed it. He plucked the Giants cap off the dresser.

He found a clean motel envelope in a desk drawer and put the photo of Michael Sheffield and General Goma inside it. The bloodied documents probably were important, too, but the photo was enough for now. He stashed the envelope inside his jacket.

Solomon checked himself in a mirror. No blood spatters, no lingering evidence of violence. Just a big guy in a baseball cap and a wrinkled suit, his pockets loaded with a gun and a phone and proof.

He needed transportation. If he were still with Sheffield Enterprises, he could've made a single phone call and someone would've picked him up, taken him to the airport, put him on a ready-to-go helicopter. None of those resources were available to him now. He could rent a chopper himself, but how long would that take? Better to drive there, as quickly as possible.

He went back to where Victor Amadou lay, his eyes still open, all the life leaked out of him. Gingerly, trying not to get blood on his hands, he reached into Amadou's pants pocket and felt what he'd hoped to find—car keys.

The key fob said "Honda," and it had push buttons to unlock the doors. Solomon hoped it was the type that made the car's horn beep; it would help him find the vehicle faster.

He gathered the last two clean towels from the motel bathroom and tucked them under his arm. Then he went out onto the balcony, making sure the room's door locked behind him. He hated to leave Victor's body unattended, but he had no time to deal with it now.

He clanged down the stairs to the parking lot and walked among the cars, pushing buttons on the key fob, hoping for headlights and honking. Nothing. He went out to the street, then along the sidewalk toward the alley where Amadou had accosted him. He pushed the button, and was rewarded with a quick beep-beep from the alley. He turned the corner and saw lights glowing inside a car.

Solomon hustled over to the compact and looked inside. Bloody handprints on the dash and steering wheel, but not much blood on the seat. He cleaned up the blood as best he could, then spread a towel over the seat before he squeezed behind the wheel. Even with the seat pushed all the way back, he barely fit.

The car was several years old, and the upholstery was worn and there was a crack in the windshield. But the engine started right up, and the gas tank was nearly full. He threw it into gear and rocketed out of the alley and onto the street.

It took fifteen minutes to reach the Golden Gate Bridge, dodging in and out of evening traffic. The little car's tires thrummed over the steel joints in the bridge's roadbed as Solomon pushed it past the speed limit. Oncoming traffic was a sea of headlights, cars backed up a mile from the tollbooths. Five bucks a vehicle to enter the magical kingdom of San Francisco. Departure was free.

On the north side of the bridge, Highway 101 widened to eight lanes, and he drove as fast as he dared. At this speed, it would take two hours to reach Cutthroat. Freeway all the way to the sleepy town of Willits, then the winding county road into the mountains. Would Hart get her people assembled and up there any faster than that? What would they find when they got there? If Amadou was right about the mercenaries, the feds might arrive just in time to clean up the mess.

He used his phone to alert the cops to Amadou's murder, hanging up when the dispatcher asked his name. He repeatedly tried Lucinda's numbers, but no one answered. He tried to call the lodge, but couldn't get past voicemail. Goddamnit.

As he raced north, the towns got smaller and the spaces between them got larger. Vineyards and pastures, forests and mountains, all illuminated by the silvery light of a three-quarter moon. Solomon barely noticed any of it, too busy with thoughts of mercenaries and murder, money and betrayal, Lucinda and Abby, Amadou and Dom.

CHAPTER 62

●●●●●●●●●●●●●●●●●●●●

Jean-Pierre Chatillon rolled down his window as he pulled up to the guard shack in the silver pickup truck. Robert sat in the passenger seat, the guns propped against the seat between them. The four mercenaries Jean-Pierre had hired were in another truck back on the county road, squeezed into its "king cab." He'd instructed them to hang back while he dealt with the sentry.

The guard was a roly-poly white man in a gray uniform, a pistol on his hip. He slid off a wooden stool to open the wood-and-glass door of the small, well-lit building. He had to look up at Jean-Pierre in the truck.

"Can I help you?"

"Yes," Jean-Pierre said. "Is this the way to Willits?"

The guard frowned and leaned out the door of the concrete-block shack, glancing back toward the road. Jean-Pierre resisted the urge to look, and hoped that the other truck was out of sight.

"Willits is back that way," the guard said. "This is private prop—"

Jean-Pierre lifted the AR-15 rifle off the seat and fired a three-round burst into the guard's chest. The man flailed backward, knocking over the stool, falling into a heap on the concrete floor.

Headlights behind them lit up his truck and the shack. Jean-Pierre stuck his arm out the window and lifted his hand in an "OK" signal.

As planned, Robert jumped out of the truck, carrying long-handled bolt cutters. He went to a junction box beside the road and cut the lock off its metal door. Robert opened the door and squatted before the box, reaching inside and yanking loose the telephone wires that served the property.

Jean-Pierre gunned the truck's engine, and Robert got the message. He threw the bolt cutters into the pickup's bed, and climbed into the cab. Robert's face had that dreamy look he got whenever there was killing to be done.

Jean-Pierre shifted into gear, but hesitated. What was that noise? He leaned his head out the open window and listened. A steady bass note—whump-whump-whump—echoed around the canyon. A helicopter, getting closer.

"*Merde!*"

He threw the pickup into gear and roared along the private road, the other truck right on his rear bumper.

"The airstrip?" he shouted to Robert.

"Another five hundred meters," Robert answered. "On the left."

Jean-Pierre slowed when he saw the turnoff.

"The lodge is straight ahead," Robert said. "On this road."

"The Sheffields may be at the airstrip already," Jean-Pierre said. "Perhaps that helicopter is their ride back to the city. Or perhaps it's bringing more guards."

Robert grimly picked up his rifle and angled its barrel out the truck's window, watching the dark forest.

Jean-Pierre turned onto the side road. Two boxy hangars were up ahead, each illuminated by a light suspended over its wide door. He slowed the truck to a crawl.

"Take out those lights," he said, and Robert leaned out the window and started shooting. The lights popped out, and darkness cloaked the area.

Jean-Pierre turned off his truck's headlights. The truck behind them got the message, and turned off its headlights, too, leaving only its amber running lights lit. Jean-Pierre eased forward until he could see around the corner of the nearest hangar

A large helicopter, perhaps a U.S. military Huey, hovered in the sky above the runway, two hundred meters away, a search-light under its belly probing the darkness, checking the airstrip and the nearby woods. Its rotor beat the air, and Jean-Pierre knew the noise would keep those on board from hearing anything on the ground. He might still have surprise on his side.

He jerked a thumb at Robert, and they climbed out of the truck. Jean-Pierre signaled at the other truck, holding up two fin-gers, and the two men in the back seat of the king cab jumped out, rifles in hand. Both were dressed in black jackets and blue jeans, all but invisible in the shadow of the hangar.

Jean-Pierre signaled for the driver and the other passenger to stay with the trucks, then led Robert and the two riflemen to the trees alongside the airstrip. They hurried along the fringe of the forest, watching the helicopter as it slowly dropped from the sky. The chopper's searchlight still danced around the airstrip, but they were far enough away not to be caught in its beam.

By the time the helicopter's runners were almost to the tar-mac, Jean-Pierre and his men were within range, weeds tangled around their knees. Gunfire would alert the Sheffields to the pres-ence of his team, but he couldn't take the chance of them escaping on this helicopter. He lifted his rifle to his shoulder and opened fire on the Huey. Robert and the others did the same.

The chopper set down hard as bullets shattered its wind-shields. Side doors slid open and several dark figures jumped out and threw themselves to the pavement. Immediately, they began returning fire, flame leaping from the ends of their guns.

"Fall back," Jean-Pierre shouted in English. "Into the trees."

One of his men spun around with a shriek as bullets ripped into his torso. Jean-Pierre and Robert and the other hired gun sprinted for the trees, gunshots splitting the air around them. When they reached the trees, they wheeled around to find that a couple of the men from the helicopter were on their feet, charging their way. They were dressed in black, wearing helmets and military-style boots, and Jean-Pierre cursed as he pressed the AR-15 to his shoulder and opened up on them. This was more of a fight than he'd expected.

Robert and Jean-Pierre stood on either side of a thick tree trunk, exchanging fire with the black-clad soldiers, who had no cover out there on the empty tarmac. One of the charging men fell backward, his gun flying out of his hand. The other one appeared to be hit, too, but he kept shooting.

A bullet ripped into Jean-Pierre's thigh, knocking his leg out from under him. The hot lead burned through and through. He dropped his gun and grabbed at his leg with both hands.

"Robert!"

Robert fired another burst at the men on the tarmac and the nearest one dropped. The others still were on the ground near the helicopter.

Robert crouched beside Jean-Pierre, feeling around in the dark, finding the wound, dipping a finger in the bullet hole. Pain flared, and Jean-Pierre thought for a second he'd lose consciousness. He heard a ripping sound, then felt Robert tying a tourniquet around his thigh, near his groin.

The shooting halted. Jean-Pierre had no idea where the other mercenary had gone. Perhaps he'd run off through the woods. Not, at this point, a bad policy. They'd come here to commit murders, not to have a firefight with a well-armed force. Perhaps they should fall back and—

Another sound erupted in the night. An engine roaring. Jean-Pierre pushed up to look. The king-cab truck was screaming down the runway toward the helicopter, its headlights illuminating the men on the ground.

A man sitting in the passenger-side window sprayed automatic rifle fire toward the helicopter, the bullets sparking and singing off the asphalt. One of the men on the ground raised up on his knees and threw something at the onrushing truck.

"No," Jean-Pierre gasped, but it was too late. An explosion lifted the truck into the air. The truck turned halfway around, bursting into flames as it thudded to the tarmac.

Then hands slipped into his armpits and lifted him up. The pain in his leg was like a flame as Robert dragged him backward, into the shadows of the trees.

CHAPTER 63

....

Solomon's heart thumped as he neared the turnoff to
Cutthroat Lodge.

The guard shack at the entrance was lit up, inside and out, but
he couldn't see anyone through its large windows. He turned onto
the paved private road and stopped. The door to the guard shack
stood open. Inside, a uniformed guard sprawled in a splash of dark
blood.

Shit. Solomon was too late.

He stomped the gas pedal, and the little car shot up the hill.
After a mile, he neared the turnoff to the airstrip and slowed almost to a stop. He smelled smoke. In the distance, where the
airstrip sliced through the forest, an orange glow rose above the
trees. A sudden noise, carried on the wind. The crackle of small-
arms fire.

He killed his headlights as he turned onto the narrow driveway that led to the hangars. The buildings were dark, which was
unusual. An empty pickup was parked near one.

More shots cracked in the distance. He stopped the Honda
behind the nearest hangar, and used the hefty Colt to smash the
car's interior light before opening the door. Then he slithered out
into the cool night air, keeping low, straining his eyes in search of
gunmen.

The orange glow came from farther up the runway. Solomon ran in a crouch to the shelter of the nearest trees, then picked his way among them, moving parallel to the airstrip.

Another burst of gunfire. Sounded like automatic weapons. The mercenaries might have other military gear, too. Kevlar. Night-vision scopes. Grenades. Did Solomon, with his two pistols, stand a chance?

He had one advantage. He knew every inch of these woods. His morning runs took him along the airstrip, beside the trout stream, around the lake. No one was more familiar with this forest. Or so he told himself as he trotted along, ducking branches and dodging the trunks of oaks and pines.

He covered a hundred yards, slipping through the trees, before he could get a good look at what was burning. A pickup truck, totally consumed, a scorched, steaming husk. Nearby sat a helicopter, a Huey, painted black. In the glow from the smoldering truck, Solomon could see that the chopper's windshields had been punctured by bullets.

Several dark figures lay on the tarmac near the chopper, and Solomon assumed they were Hart and her agents. He thought they might all be dead until one prone shadow lifted a rifle and unleashed a fiery blast toward the woods.

Trees were kept cleared about fifty feet on either side of the tarmac, and that area was thick with weeds and wildflowers and brambles, a knee-deep tangle. A dark shape rose from the weeds forty yards away. The man came up onto his knees and fired toward the helicopter, then dropped back down as return fire came from the men near the chopper.

Solomon crept from tree to tree, getting closer to the action. He watched the spot where he'd seen the gunman emerge from the weeds. He got as close as he dared, and knelt behind the thick trunk of a pine. Still a long shot for a pistol, but he didn't want to walk into a crossfire.

He watched the rustling weeds, his gun poised. When the dark shape appeared again, rifle to his shoulder, Solomon squeezed off a round and the man pitched sideways with a yelp.

Shouts rose from the chopper about the gunshot coming from their flank. Time to speak up.

"Agent Hart! It's me, Solomon Gage! Tell your people not to shoot!"

"Gage?" A woman's strained voice. "What the hell?"

"I just got here. Are there more shooters?"

"They went into the trees," she shouted.

Solomon ran from his hiding place and dropped into a squat in the weeds. No shots followed him. He moved through the jumbled plants in a crouch, expecting bullets to fill the air, but he apparently was in a lull of his own creation.

He hit the tarmac running and covered the sixty feet to the chopper in record time. No gunshots. At the helicopter, he dropped to his stomach next to an agent dressed in black.

"Hey," Solomon gasped, but the man didn't respond.

He took a closer look, and realized it was Gallegos, the body-builder from the Hotel Blue. The lower half of his face had been shot away. With a shudder, Solomon rolled away from him.

"Hart?"

"Over here."

Solomon crawled to her, past two other prone agents who kept wicked-looking machine guns trained on him as he passed. They, too, were dressed all in black, including shoeblack on their faces, but their fierce eyes reflected the last of the pickup truck's glow.

Hart was near the rear of the chopper, lying on her back. She'd pulled her black shirt away from her left shoulder, checking on a bloody wound there.

"You're hurt," Solomon said.

"Just a graze. My people weren't so lucky. Only three of us left."

"What happened?"

"We flew right into an ambush. As the chopper set down, they started shooting. A truckload of them came racing down the runway, guns blazing."

"You should've gone back into the sky."

"Pilot was the first one hit. We set down hard. All we could do was jump out and grab pavement. Gallegos managed to hit the truck with a grenade before they shot him. Two of our people ran for the grass. They're dead."

"Jesus Christ."

"Yeah." Hart gasped, prodding at the bullet wound. "I got on the radio. Reinforcements are on the way, but it could be a while."

"What about the Sheffields?"

"Haven't been able to raise them. The lodge is back over that way, right?"

"About half a mile. Through those redwoods."

"Surely they heard the shots. Maybe they're hiding. Have they got guns?"

"Hunting rifles. Shotguns. But they're no match for—"

"I know," she said tightly. "But I'll be damned if I'm losing more agents on their account."

"You think the mercenaries went that way?"

"Don't know how many are left," she said. "But it looked like a few melted into those trees."

Solomon rose to a crouch.

"Gage? The hell are you—"

He didn't hear the rest. He was running for the trees again, headed toward Cutthroat Lodge.

CHAPTER 64

●●●●●●●●●●●●●●●●●●●●

Robert Mboku helped Jean-Pierre limp out of the trees and onto the moonlit pavement. They were taking a chance, using the road, but he couldn't get Jean-Pierre through the snatching trees, not with him dragging the wounded leg.

The bullet had missed the bone, and Robert had staunched the bleeding with a tourniquet made from a sleeve from his own shirt, but Jean-Pierre was shivering and sweaty and dizzy. Robert needed him alert. Still killing to be done.

No gunfire the past few minutes. Probably none of Jean-Pierre's hired men left. Idiots. They could've kept to the trees, sniping at the soldiers, but someone had to play the hero and charge the helicopter. All their supplies and spare ammo had been on that truck.

Jean-Pierre moved slowly, his face twisted with pain. If he died, Robert would be alone, stranded in an unfamiliar country where he didn't speak the language. No money, no contacts, no way to get home. Jean-Pierre was his lifeline.

"Lean on my shoulder," he whispered. "It's not far to the house."

Jean-Pierre grunted and put more weight on Robert. Together, they hobbled up the long driveway. The pace reminded Robert of the three-legged race, a game the missionaries had taught the village children when he was very young, before he became a boy soldier.

Robert watched the trees, expecting the flare of gunfire. He carried his AR-15 in his left hand, could shoot one-handed if need be. Jean-Pierre's rifle was slung over his shoulder, but Robert wasn't sure the wounded man could aim it if he tried.

If they could reach the lodge without stumbling upon a patrol, Robert could plant Jean-Pierre somewhere—preferably in a place where he could offer covering fire—then move through the dark forest, see if the Sheffields were still home. He hoped they were. He wanted to kill them all.

Once the job was done, he'd go back to the airstrip and get the silver pickup. Haul Jean-Pierre into the little town down in the valley. Find a doctor. Find a way out of this mess.

Jean-Pierre moaned as his boot scuffed against the pavement. Robert shushed him. No time for sympathy. Just keep moving.

After three hundred meters, the lights of the lodge appeared between the trees. Robert helped Jean-Pierre limp off the road and into the woods. They came upon the game trail Robert had used when he was here before, and soon they reached the edge of the clearing around the big house.

Robert helped Jean-Pierre settle onto the ground beside the trunk of a giant tree. Jean-Pierre leaned his shoulder against the tree's alligator-hide bark and unslung his rifle. Robert squatted beside him, silently pointing out the two sentries on the lodge's front deck. They carried shotguns.

The sentries stood at the corners of the wooden deck, staring out at the forest, their backs to the lodge, which was ablaze with light. Through the house's huge central windows, Robert could see men moving around, carrying long guns, preparing to defend the lodge. As if that would do them any good now that Robert Mboku was here.

Robert pointed to his own chest, then to the two sentries. Jean-Pierre nodded, and raised his rifle to show he was ready to cover him. Robert set his own gun down and slipped the machete from his belt.

He glided from tree to tree until he was well beyond the nearest sentry. Then he hurried across the clearing to where two cars were parked in the shadow of the house. Robert peeked over the cars, but the guard apparently had heard nothing. He stood staring at the woods in the direction of the airstrip, expecting any trouble to come from there.

Robert slipped behind him and stepped up onto the end of the porch. He made no sound, but the sentry sensed him there. As he tried to turn, Robert grabbed his hair and yanked his head back. The machete sliced through his throat before he could make a noise.

Robert dragged the guard off the edge of the porch, and crouched in the shadows next to the body. He peeked around the corner in time to see the other sentry swing his shotgun around.

"Jim?"

The guard's boots clumped on the deck as he came near, calling Jim's name again. A burst of gunfire erupted from where Jean-Pierre waited in the trees. The sentry danced with the impact of the bullets, then fell backward and lay still.

Robert took the first guard's shotgun and ran for the safety of the trees. The Sheffields knew the mercenaries were here now, which posed its own problems, but Robert had a smile on his face. Jean-Pierre still was with him, still protected him. Together, they'd kill these bastards. Each and every one. They'd burn down this house. Set fire to this miserable forest.

Leave nothing but ashes.

CHAPTER 65

•••••••••••••••••••

Solomon had nearly reached the lodge when he heard the shots. He'd run along the beaten path from the airstrip, between the fat trunks of the redwoods that stretched toward the moonlit sky. His heart pounded, and his breath came hard. He needed to stop a moment, regain his stealth, but the echoing gunfire made it difficult to go slow.

The path emerged into the clearing on the north end of the lodge, opposite the long driveway. Solomon stopped before he was clear of the trees, watching for muzzle flashes, listening for rustling footfalls.

The wings of the lodge were dark, but light spilled from the window walls of the great room. Solomon couldn't see inside from this angle, but a man lay unmoving on the front deck. Solomon feared he was too late, that everyone inside the lodge was dead, too. Had the mercenaries reached the lodge before the helicopter arrived? Were they on their way out of here, their bloody work done, when they ambushed Hart and her people?

He skirted the clearing, keeping to the trees, trying to get a better view. He hoped Dom had gotten his message. But would Dom have gone into hiding, even if he knew the mercenaries were coming? Probably not. He'd stand and fight.

Solomon slipped from tree to tree, trying to be silent and invisible. His dark clothing helped, and he was glad for the black Giants cap that covered his shaved head. As he got broadside of the house, he was relieved to see Dom's silvery head moving near the stone fireplace. The leather furniture had been pulled into a horse-shoe shape around the hearth, and Dom and others were crouched behind it. He'd hoped that they'd made a strategic retreat. Instead, it appeared Dom was commanding the fucking Alamo.

Heads poked up from behind the furniture fort. Michael. Chris. Armed with rifles and shotguns, the barrels pointed at the high ceiling.

The guns wouldn't be much of a match against automatic weapons. But then, neither was his pistol. His only advantage was that the mercenaries didn't know Solomon was here. He was the wild card. Would that be enough?

•••

Inside Cutthroat Lodge, Dom calmly watched the woods, waiting. The other men hunkered down behind him. Bart Logan barked into a walkie-talkie, unable to raise any of his men. Michael Sheffield hammered at a phone, trying to get a dial tone, though it was clear the lines had been cut. Chris cowered behind a heavy chair, trembling. He looked ready to burst into tears.

They were clustered near the huge river-rock fireplace, which provided the best protection in the lodge. They could've hidden in the kitchen with the servants, but Dom knew that could only end badly. The attackers would have them trapped there; they easily could torch the place, then pick them off as they fled the flames.

Instead, Dom had ordered his sons and Logan to take up arms to defend Cutthroat Lodge. Michael and Chris had hunting rifles, Dom and Logan shotguns. They pointed the guns at the windows, but could see nothing to shoot. Only darkness.

"Logan," Dom said. "Give up on that radio and get over to the light switches. It's too bright in here."

Logan set the radio aside and did as he was told, crawling on all fours, keeping low. He went faster once he cleared the furniture barricade, but no shots rang out. When he reached the far wall, he slowly got to his feet. As he reached for the light switches, gunfire split the night. The giant windows shattered, sending blades of glass flying everywhere. Bullets hammered into the wall near Logan, spitting splinters into the air.

Logan dropped to the floor and covered his head with his hands. Michael cursed and crouched lower. Chris mewled and rolled onto his back, his fat torso trembling with each ragged breath.

Dom peered over a leather chair. The shooters must be around the corner, with an oblique angle to the great room. The perfect spot to see without being seen.

"Logan!" he shouted. "Try it again. Turn off those lights."

"Fuck that," Logan called from his spot on the floor. "You want 'em out, you come do it."

Shit, Dom thought, I have to do everything myself. He pivoted and aimed his shotgun at the expensive chandelier fashioned of deer antlers. *Boom!* The buckshot ripped the chandelier off the chain that held it to the ceiling, and the huge lighting fixture crashed to the floor, its bulbs shattering. Two floor lamps still were lit at the far side of the great room, over by Logan, but it was darker at this end now.

Machine-gun fire erupted outside, shattering the glass wall on the east side of the house. Bullets whistled and ricocheted and pocked into the stone fireplace.

Dom fell flat, clutching his shotgun. Someone screamed. One of the lamps exploded, throwing more of the room into darkness. Bullets ripped into the furniture, throwing white stuffing flying into the air.

The shooting stopped. The sudden silence was a like a blow to the head.

Dom sat up, pointed the shotgun out into the darkness and fired. Pumped in another shell. Fired. Pumped. Fired. He lay flat again, waiting for the incoming fire to resume.

He hadn't seen where the shots were coming from, hadn't bothered to aim. His only hope was that he'd get lucky, that his overlapping patterns of buckshot might hit whoever was out there. Or at least force them to back off. Dom trying to buy some time.

He stared out at the dark, wishing Solomon were here. At this moment, with death staring him in the face, his fractured relationship with Solomon was the thing Dom regretted most.

"Dad!" Michael's voice, filled with alarm. "Chris has been hit!"

•••

Once the automatic weapons fire ended, Solomon saw Dom blast buckshot into the darkness on the far side of the house. The old man was the only one inside with any guts.

No one fired back from the woods, and Solomon couldn't see any movement among the trees. The glass on both sides of the building was shattered, the jagged remains dangling like broken teeth, the floor covered in glinting shards.

Solomon eased around the clearing counter-clockwise, pausing every few steps to listen and watch. A couple of dark cars were parked at the south end of the lodge, but they looked empty.

Another burp of gunfire from the forest, just as Logan had started to cautiously sit up. He threw himself back to the floor as the bullets thudded into the wall. Solomon didn't know whether Logan was hit, didn't care. He'd gotten what he needed. The muzzle flash among the trees was thirty yards away, near the southern end of the lodge. From there, the shooter likely couldn't even see Dom and the others by the fireplace. The angle was wrong. But he could see Logan by the far wall, could keep him pinned there.

Solomon slipped through the trees, his pistol ready, creeping toward the spot where he'd seen the flash. Between the moonlight and what little light still glowed from the lodge, he could just make out a white man with a scruffy beard sitting at the base of a tree. He had his rifle to his shoulder, sighting along it, watching the lodge. The rifle bucked in his hands as he unleashed another round toward the lodge.

Enough. Solomon stepped around a tree trunk, so he had an open shot. The scruffy man froze for a second, then swung the rifle toward Solomon.

Solomon squeezed the trigger. The .45 jumped in his hands. Once, twice, three times. The man slammed backward, his rifle flying out of his hands.

Solomon spun away, back into the trees. He went into a crouch and crept back the way he'd come, staying near the edge of the clearing.

One down. He wished he knew how many others left.

CHAPTER 66

••••••••••••••••••••

Solomon crept halfway around the clearing without locating the other shooter. He stood still for a few minutes, straining his eyes and ears, and finally risked a run to the lodge.

He covered the ground between the trees and the kitchen wing as quickly as he could, knees bent, the pistol held out before him. He froze in the shadow of the building, squatting next to a wall, waiting.

He heard weeping from inside the kitchen. The servants must be terrified, locked in there in the dark, with all the shooting outside.

His back against the wall, Solomon stepped up onto the wooden deck and peeked through a large window into the dining room behind the free-standing fireplace. The room was dark and empty.

He edged forward, the planks creaking under his weight. Inside the great room, a shotgun racked in answer. Solomon hated to give away his position, but he'd hate it worse if Dom blasted him to kingdom come.

"Dom," he said, his voice low. "It's me, Solomon. I'm alone."

A pause.

"Thank God," Dom said. "Get in here. We need your help."

Solomon smiled. Despite his pounding heart, despite the anguish in Dom's voice, it felt good to be needed. He slipped into the great room through the shattered windows, keeping low, glass crunching under his feet as he made it to the cluster of furniture.

Michael, dressed in jeans and a polo shirt, squatted behind a chair with a white-knuckle grip on a hunting rifle, his eyes wide in the half-light. He gave Solomon a glance, then returned to scanning the trees. Good. Somebody needed to stand watch.

Bart Logan was no good to anyone. He lay on the floor across the room, still on his stomach, his arms wrapped around his head. His khaki pants were soaked in blood. The broken windows had spilled across his legs. Bloody shards stuck up from his wounds.

"Don't move, Logan," Solomon called to him.

"Don't fuckin' worry, I won't," Logan said through clenched teeth. "Just get me some help."

Solomon crawled between sofas to reach the interior of the barricade. He found Dom sitting up with Chris' head in his lap. Chris lay on his back, sightless eyes staring at the ceiling, blood soaking his green shirt. Tears streamed down Dom's cheeks.

"He's dead," Dom said.

Solomon crawled over to them, and rested a hand on Dom's shoulder.

"I'm sorry, sir. But you need to get lower. You're a target, sitting here."

Dom met his eyes. "I wish the bastards would shoot me. Put me out of my fucking misery."

"You don't mean that, sir. Come on. The only decent shelter is the fireplace."

Dom gently set Chris' head on the hardwood floor. Then he and Solomon stretched out next to the stone hearth, propped up on their elbows.

"I'm glad you're here, Solomon. Did you kill those bastards?"

"One. But there's still at least one out there. We need to keep our heads down."

Dom wiped at his eyes with the back of hand. "I was thinking about you. During the shooting. Before I even knew you were here. I'm sorry, Solomon. I'm sorry for all of it."

Dom squeezed his eyes shut. Solomon couldn't remember the last time he'd seen the old man cry. After Rose was killed, nearly twenty years ago?

"Later," Solomon said, his own voice thick. "Help is on the way. We just need to survive until it arrives."

"Sounds good to me." Michael crawled toward them, glass snapping under his knees. "Let's hide in the kitchen."

"No, Michael," Dom said. "We'll stay out here and take our chances."

"But, sir, that doesn't make any sense," Solomon began.

"None of this makes any fucking sense. Some jackasses on the other side of the world decide to overthrow a government, and Chris winds up dead? That's like saying a butterfly fart in California caused a hurricane in Bermuda. I can't believe that—"

Gunshots ripped through the room. Everyone flattened, hands over heads, as glass and hot lead filled the air.

CHAPTER 67

•••••••••••••••••••

Robert Mboku fired his rifle until it was empty. He tossed it aside and bent over to retrieve the shotgun he'd taken off the guard. Fired it five times until it, too, clicked on empty. Rage filled Robert, and he didn't care if he wasted ammunition. He didn't care what happened next. With Jean-Pierre dead, he had no future. All he wanted was to kill the men in that big house, to *annihilate* them.

He picked up Jean-Pierre's AR-15 and sprinted along the tree line, getting a better angle on the cowering Sheffields. The big man with the shaved head, the one they'd followed all over San Francisco, raised up from behind a chair and shot at Robert with a pistol. The bullet winged past, much too close. Robert ducked into the cover of the shadows.

He peeked around a tree and opened fire on the house. Bullets chipped the fireplace and thudded into the floor, but he didn't think he'd hit anyone. Michael Sheffield popped up from behind a chair and fired a single rifle shot in his direction. Robert felt a tug on his shirt, as if someone was trying to get his attention, but the bullet did not bite into flesh.

Robert got off another burst before this rifle, too, went empty. He cursed and threw the hot gun aside.

He still had his machete. His stealth. The camouflage of his dark skin. He would slip through the night and take out the

Sheffields one at a time. Slit their throats. Hack off their limbs. Cut out their evil tongues.

Robert might have no future, might be outnumbered and alone, on the wrong fucking continent. But he would have his revenge.

CHAPTER 68

••••••••••••••••••••

Silence. Solomon stayed on the floor, his head down, listening. After a minute or two, Michael said, "Maybe I hit him."

Dom rose to his knees and peeked over the nearest sofa, his shotgun pointed out at the night. Solomon knelt beside him and searched the forest for movement, first on one side of the lodge, then on the other. Nothing.

"Who are these guys, Solomon?" Dom asked.

"Mercenaries, sent by the French who run the mines in Niger. I warned Michael they were coming—"

"You did what?"

"I called up here hours ago. Michael didn't believe me. He took the phone off the hook."

Dom swiveled around to look at his son. "Is that true, Michael?"

"I thought he was lying," Michael said. "No reason to believe that they'd send people to kill us—"

"Tell that to your brother," Dom said sharply.

Michael muttered something, but Solomon wasn't listening. He was looking around the lodge, measuring distances and risks, trying to decide what to do next.

Bart Logan groaned. He still lay on the far side of the room. Solomon needed to get him some cover. He holstered his pistol and moved away from Dom.

"Where are you going?"

"I'll drag Logan over here."

Dom, scowling, looked as if he'd be happy to leave Logan as a target, but all he said was, "Be careful."

Solomon started across the room on all fours, leaving little bloody prints where his knees were cut by fallen glass. His skin crawled, anticipating bullets, but no shots came.

Logan's face was red and sweaty. Solomon got hold of his feet. Scooting backward, he dragged him across the hardwood floor toward the furniture fort. The strain made the bandage pull against the bullet wound on his chest. His knees stung from the cuts there.

Logan hung onto his shotgun, but he moaned and cursed as they progressed through the broken glass.

"Shut up," Solomon said through clenched teeth. "You're lucky I don't leave you to die."

Once within the shelter of the circled furniture, Solomon yanked the largest of the glass shards from Logan's legs as Logan grunted with pain.

"Roll over," Solomon said.

Logan managed to sit up, his back against a chair.

"Cover me," Solomon said. "I'm going back out there."

"Stay here with us," Dom said. "We can watch each other's backs until help arrives."

"Might be another hour, sir. You want to sit here that long, waiting to get shot?"

Dom had no answer for that.

"Watch the woods," Solomon said. "If anyone fires toward the house, shoot back. But don't shoot at just any movement. It might be me."

"Don't risk your life, Solomon," Dom said. "We'll find a way to—"

"Just sit tight. I'll be back as soon as I've killed these assholes."

He crawled quickly out onto the back porch and toward the kitchen wing, expecting to draw fire, but none came.

Solomon eased along the wall, keeping low, pistol in hand. One of the kitchen windows was open slightly, and he rose up enough to speak through it.

"Juanita?"

A squeal from inside, and a frying pan came crashing through the window. Solomon ducked in time.

"Juanita! It's Solomon."

"Oh! So sorry, *mi hijo*. Are you okay?"

"I'm fine. Stay where you are. This will be over soon."

"We're not going anywhere. This is crazy business."

He moved to the corner of the lodge, where a fieldstone column supported the roof, and peeked around it. Nothing.

Solomon crouched by the two cars that were parked near the servants' entrance. He saw another Sheffield security guard sprawled dead on the ground by the end of the front deck. Solomon slipped between the two sedans. Moonlight flooded the clearing, but he got his feet under him and ran as fast as he could, bent over. No bullets chased after him, and he threw himself down onto the spongy needles and brittle twigs that covered the forest floor. He waited a full minute for any sound, any motion. Nothing but the pounding of his own heart.

He stood and moved clockwise around the lodge, pausing behind tree trunks every few steps to listen and look. Someone still was in the forest with him. He could *feel* it.

He reached the bearded mercenary's body. A shotgun and an automatic rifle lay on the ground near him. Both were out of ammo.

Solomon left the guns and moved through the trees, his pistol in front of him, pointing wherever he looked. As he passed a fat pine, a black shadow leaped at him from behind the tree, swinging a glinting blade downward.

The machete hit the top of Solomon's gun, knocking it out of his hand. The blade bit into his right hand just behind his index finger, snapping the bone and sending a blaze of pain up his arm.

Solomon went low as the machete came swinging at his head, just missed him. He threw himself sideways, rolling toward the clearing, his injured hand clutched against his chest. One roll, two, then back up onto his feet.

His attacker was wild-eyed, and his teeth were bared. He was a shirtless black man in cuffed-up blue jeans, so skinny that Solomon could've snapped him in two with his bare hands if it weren't for that machete.

The man charged, swinging the machete, carving a big "X" in the air. Solomon dodged backward, fully out into the clearing now, trying to keep out of reach of the singing blade.

His ankle twisted, but didn't give way. He kept backpedaling, limping now. If he fell, the machete man would hack him to pieces.

The man spat French at him, but Solomon had no idea what he was saying. Didn't matter anyway. The only sound that mattered was the whir of the big knife as it swung past, an inch from Solomon's nose.

Before the man could swing it back the other way, Solomon lunged forward, going low, tackling him. The skinny man folded in half over his shoulder. The machete smacked across Solomon's back, but it was the flat of the blade, not the razor-sharp edge, and he kept driving with his feet until his attacker hit the ground, all of Solomon's weight upon him.

The mercenary huffed as the air went out of him, but his arm cocked back the machete. Solomon blocked his wrist, and the machete flew into the darkness.

The attacker screamed in frustration and went at Solomon with his hands, punching and clawing. Solomon slammed his left fist into the man's ear. His head snapped sideways, and his crazed eyes rolled around in their sockets.

Solomon tried to hit him again, but the man managed to get hold of Solomon's sliced hand and dug his thumb into the wound. Solomon howled and yanked his hand free and rolled away.

The mercenary crawled after him, punching and gouging. Solomon tried to roll away, but the man pinned him to the ground, sitting on Solomon's chest, clawing at his eyes.

Solomon swatted at him with his good hand, but it was as if the madman didn't feel the blows. His hands wrapped around Solomon's throat, and he pressed down with all his weight, cutting off his air.

Solomon hit him again and again, but the mercenary's grip didn't loosen. His eyes glowed in the moonlight, and his teeth were bright. As spots danced before his eyes, Solomon thought the crazy grin might be the last thing he'd ever see.

Why didn't someone shoot this son of a bitch? Surely, Dom and the others could see them out here. A quick bullet could do more good than all the punches in the—

A thought flashed in his oxygen-deprived mind. He had Lou Velacci's revolver in his jacket pocket. He fished around with his left hand, got hold of the gun.

His attacker didn't seem to notice. He was too busy choking the life out of Solomon, savoring the moment.

Solomon brought the gun up and pressed its muzzle against the mercenary's head. The man froze, his grip on Solomon's throat relaxing as he realized the mistake he'd made. The gun bucked, and blood erupted from his head as he pitched sideways.

Solomon lay there a minute, trying to breathe, pain rocketing up his arm, fireworks exploding inside his head. As his vision cleared, wisps of moonlit clouds came into focus in the black sky above. He could see the stars.

Time to move. Clutching his bleeding hand to his body, he clambered to his feet and ran for the lodge as best he could on his twisted ankle. He gripped Lou's pistol, ready to fire if shots came from the woods. He reached the deck, rolled onto it, and crawled the rest of the way into the great room, broken glass eating into his elbows and knees.

Only when he was inside did he realize that Dom had been shouting at him the whole time. His vision was loopy, too, the world going in and out of focus. Blood loss, he thought. Shock. He took deep breaths, trying to stay conscious.

Dom ripped off his own flannel shirt and used his teeth to tear it in half. He wrapped one half around Solomon's hand, pulling it tight, tying it off. Solomon winced against the pain. He knew it was necessary. They had to stop the bleeding. But *damn*.

"Good job, Solomon," Dom said as he wiped blood off his hands onto the white T-shirt he still wore. "I think that was the last of them."

"How do you know?"

"If there were more, they would've shot you just now. Listen. It's quiet."

Solomon listened, but all he could hear was his own ragged breathing.

CHAPTER 69

●●●●●●●●●●●●●●●●●●●●●

The cut on Solomon's hand was nasty, and a bone clearly was broken, but Dom didn't think he'd lose any fingers.

"We need to get you to a hospital," he said. "We can't call an ambulance. The phones are down."

"Give it a minute," Solomon said through gritted teeth. "Make sure we're safe."

Dom peered at the woods on both sides of the lodge, but he was pretty sure it was over. He sat next to Solomon, their backs against a ruined sofa.

"Seems you were right about these mercenaries," Dom said. "That last one was screaming in French."

Michael slid across the floor, coming closer. He had the rifle in his hands, but he wasn't watching the forest anymore. His attention was on Dom.

"The whole thing's a crazy misunderstanding," he said. "We didn't do anything to—"

"Shut up, Michael," Dom said. "No more lies."

"*I'm* the liar? Why not Solomon? You always choose to believe him over me or Chris—"

"Stop," Solomon said.

Dom looked over at him.

"Reach inside my jacket, sir," Solomon said, his voice raspy. "The inside pocket. There's an envelope."

Dom fished out the envelope, lifted the flap and pulled out the photograph. He studied it, tilting it to the catch the light.

"I don't know what that is," Michael said, "but this is all a bunch of—"

"That's Logan's friend General Goma," Solomon said, talking over him. "The one who's trying to overthrow the government in Niger."

Dom glanced at Logan, but the security chief wouldn't look at him. He sat at the far end of the herded furniture, plucking glass out of his skin.

"I'll tend to you later," Dom said. Turning to Michael, he added, "To both of you. Your lies nearly got us killed tonight."

Michael snorted. "Like you've never told a lie yourself. Look around, Dad. You owe everything to cheating and scheming in business. Chris and I were trying to do the same."

"It's not the same," Dom said, but he felt a knot in his throat. He hadn't set the best example.

He turned to Solomon and said, "I'll make it right. There's got to be a way to fix this."

"Not much time," Solomon said. "It's already Sunday in Niger. The election's under way."

Michael stood and stalked across the room, muttering under his breath.

"Christ, Michael," Dom said. "Get down. You could get shot."

"Nobody's out there," Michael snapped. "You said it yourself. Your beloved Solomon killed off the last of them. It's all mop-up now. Hiding the bodies."

"Too late for that," Solomon said. "Everyone knows about this now. Who do you think was doing all that shooting over at the airstrip? Federal agents."

"What?"

"That's who landed in the chopper. You heard it, right?"

Michael said, "We thought it was the mercenaries—"

"No, they drove in. The feds flew up here, trying to cut them off, and got cut down instead. There are bodies all over the airstrip. And the feds sent for help. More are on the way."

Dom felt himself scowling. Once word got out, everything would turn to shit. It would take years to set business right again. He looked around the room, at the shattered glass and the crashed chandelier and the bullet holes in the walls. His lodge, his hiding place from the world, was ruined. The world had come to his doorstep, brought here by the sins and omissions of his own sons. Christ, what had they been thinking?

As his eyes roamed the room, he noticed someone was missing. He said, "Where did Logan go?"

CHAPTER 70

●●●●●●●●●●●●●●●●●●●

Solomon saw a trail of blood snaking across the back porch. While they'd been busy arguing with Michael, Bart Logan had sneaked out into the darkness, taking a shotgun with him.

"I'll get him."

"Let him go," Dom said. "He won't get far."

Solomon stood, feeling unsteady. "Didn't he drive here?"

"Yeah," Michael said. "His car's around back."

"Then he's trying to run. I don't want him getting away."

"Leave it," Dom said. "We'll find him later."

Solomon wasn't so sure. Logan clearly had connections overseas. And, after this mess, the Sheffields' reach wouldn't be what it once was.

"Give me that shotgun," he said. "If I have to shoot him, I'd rather not have to aim."

Dom handed him the Remington pump. Solomon held it with his left hand and let the barrel rest on his right forearm, away from the bloodied shirt wrapped around his hand.

"Keep watch on the trees," he said. "I'll be right back."

He followed the trail of blood off the porch toward the south end of the house, where the cars were parked.

Soon as he rounded the corner, he saw Logan. He was at the back of the nearest car, illuminated by light from the open trunk. His shotgun sat on the ground, its barrel leaning against the bumper.

"Freeze," Solomon said, striding toward him, his shotgun leveled at Logan's gut.

Logan went for his gun, but the barrel slipped in his sweaty grip and he fumbled the grab.

Solomon swung the Remington up one-handed and drove its wooden butt into Logan's forehead. He reeled backward and hit the ground hard, out cold.

A noise came from the open trunk. Solomon wheeled, shotgun at the ready, to find Lucinda Cruz curled up inside, rope around her wrists and ankles and silver duct tape over her mouth. She wore jeans and a sweatshirt, and her eyes were wide with panic. Solomon wasn't sure she even recognized him looming over her. All her attention was on the shotgun in his hands.

He set the gun aside, bent over and got his hand under her and helped her sit upright. He pulled the tape off her mouth, as gently as possible, but it still must've stung like hell. She winced and took a deep shuddering breath.

"Boy, am I glad to see you."

"Same here," he said. "I thought you might be dead."

"I nearly was. That bastard said he'd use me as a shield."

Solomon glanced at Logan, who hadn't twitched since he hit the ground. "He was trying to salvage something from a situation that's gone really wrong."

"All that shooting?" A note of hysteria crept into her voice. "I thought bullets would come right through the car and—"

"Easy. You're okay now. It's all over."

An open pocketknife lay beside her in the trunk, where Logan must've dropped it when he realized Solomon was coming for him. Solomon cut through the ropes and helped Lucinda out of the trunk. She nearly collapsed when she put weight on her feet.

"I'm numb," she said. "I've been in that trunk for hours. I need a bathroom."

"We'll go in the house. Juanita will take care of you."

He helped her over to the windowless kitchen door and kicked it a few times.

"It's Solomon. Open up."

Latches clicked and rattled, and the door finally opened a crack. Light spilled from inside, and Juanita peeked out.

Solomon still grasped Lucinda's arm, holding her up. He said to Juanita, "Help her."

"Is she shot?"

"No, but she needs help walking."

Juanita came down the two steps to the ground and slid an arm around Lucinda's waist. "*Pobrecito.*"

Lucinda answered her in Spanish, but Solomon didn't follow it. Fiona, the red-haired maid, came down the steps and got on the other side of Lucinda, and helped carry her into the kitchen.

Solomon closed the kitchen door and went back to Logan, who moaned and shifted on the ground, coming around. Solomon gave him a kick in the side.

"Get up."

He picked up the shotguns while Logan struggled to his feet. He tucked one under his right arm, and held the other with his left. He prodded Logan with the barrel and marched him back around the lodge.

Solomon called out to Dom and Michael before they walked up to the broken windows; he didn't want an accidental shooting this late in the game. Logan, his head hanging, stepped onto the porch. Solomon said, "Hold it."

He set one shotgun aside, dipped his hand into Logan's hip pocket and pulled out his wallet. Then he pushed him forward, and they walked into the wrecked great room.

CHAPTER 71

•••••••••••••••••••

Solomon handed the Remington to Dom, then slid into a sitting position next to him, saying, "Watch him."

Dom pointed the gun at Logan, who remained standing in his bloodied clothes, ten feet away, weaving a little with dizziness.

Solomon tightened the makeshift bandage around his hand. The bleeding had slowed. That was good. His head had cleared, too, and he felt answers clicking into place. He fished through Logan's wallet. It wasn't easy one-handed, and he tossed credit cards and business cards and other crap aside as he looked for a particular item.

"Hey," Logan said, still sounding groggy. "The hell do you think you're doing?"

Solomon ignored him. Logan took a step forward, but Dom pointed the barrel of the shotgun at his face, and he remembered to stand still.

In an inside pocket of the wallet, Solomon found what he was looking for. He turned it around for Dom to see.

"A fake driver's license."

Dom said, "How do you know it's fake?"

"Because it's got my name on it, and I've never looked like that."

Dom looked closer. Solomon knew he probably couldn't read it without his glasses, but there was no question that the thumb-nail-sized photo showed Logan, though he wore a Raiders cap and a fake mustache.

"This is what he used to get Abby out of rehab," Solomon said. "The night nurse's description threw me because she said he was bald. But all she saw of his head was the sides, where it's shaved around his ears, because he was wearing a baseball cap. He pretended to be me, got Abby released, then dropped her off in Oakland where she could get high."

Dom's face darkened. "But why?"

"He didn't want her talking to anyone. I think he kept watch on her. Waited for me to show up outside that crack house, so he could shoot me, too. That way, it would look like I was the one who took her out of rehab and I wouldn't be around to question it."

Dom got to his feet. Logan shrank from the anger blazing in the old man's eyes.

"I'm guessing he got Clyde Merton to make this driver's license," Solomon said. "I went to Clyde myself this morning to get fake ID. Clyde seemed even more nervous than usual. Probably thought I was there to confront him over this driver's license. He must've known Logan was up to no good."

Michael took a step closer to Logan. He had his rifle trained on him. Both the Sheffields looked ready to gun him down.

"Clyde's dead," Solomon continued. "Somebody stabbed him this afternoon. The killer wore a Raiders cap. Clyde probably called Logan and told him I'd been there. Logan must've thought I was getting too close to finding out the truth. That's why he kept people following me the whole time, too. After Lou Velacci was murdered—I'm guessing by our friend out there with the machete—he tried to pin that on me, too."

Logan stared at the floor, but didn't try to deny anything.

Solomon shuddered and a chill ran through him. Shock. His hand throbbed. He needed a doctor. He needed to get this finished.

"Logan got your sons involved with the Africa deal, then covered their tracks for them," he said. "I'm guessing they promised him a cut of the profits."

Dom looked at his son. "Is that true?"

Michael hesitated, then said, "I didn't know about the killing, Dad. I swear it. I didn't know Bart killed Abby or anybody else."

"What about all the killing in Niger?" Solomon said. "Goma's ready to kill plenty of people in his coup. That's okay with you?"

Michael scowled. "They're halfway around the world. They're nobodies. They're not family, like Abby."

"That makes it all right?" Solomon said tightly. "It's okay if lots of people end up dead, as long as they're not Sheffields. Other people don't count?"

"Aw, don't get whiny about it," Michael said. "You know what I mean. Family is what matters."

"Yeah?" Solomon said. "Tell it to Grace. Tell her how much family means while you're beating her."

"You son of a bitch. I'm sick of you." Michael pointed his rifle at Solomon. "I ought to shut you up once and for all."

"Michael!" Dom said. "Don't threaten Solomon. He's family, too."

"No, I'm not," Solomon said. "Never have been. I'm the hired help, expendable and replaceable. You've all made that perfectly clear."

Solomon glared at Michael until he turned away, muttering.

Dom still had his shotgun pointed at Logan's gut. "As for you, you bastard, you'll pay for killing Abby."

As the old man's finger tightened on the trigger, Solomon said, "Don't do it, sir. Wait for the police. He's better off in prison."

"He should be shot down like the dog that he is," Dom said.

A latch clicked behind them. The dining room door opened and light flooded through. Standing in the doorway, the light behind her like an aura, was Lucinda Cruz.

"Solomon?" she said. "Are you out here?"

"Over here."

"Good Christ," Michael said. "What's *she* doing here?"

"Logan brought her," Solomon said. "I found her in the trunk of his car. He was planning to use her as a bargaining chip."

Lucinda walked unsteadily into the great room, glass crunching under her shoes. She looked at the Sheffields with their guns, Michael glaring at her, Dom gaping in surprise. Her gaze settled on Solomon, on the bloody shirt wrapped around his hand. She knelt beside him and said, "You're hurt. Let me see."

"It's okay." He didn't want his hand occupied. He wasn't sure this situation wouldn't deteriorate into a gun battle. Dom's shotgun still was aimed at Logan; only a little more pressure on that trigger, and Logan would be cut in half.

"Don't kill him, sir," Solomon said. "Too many witnesses. I'll testify against you. So will she."

Michael sensed an opening. "Maybe that's the answer, Dad. Let's get rid of all of them. We can say the mercenaries killed them, that we had nothing to do with—"

"Shut up, Michael," Dom snapped. "You're embarrassing yourself."

Michael froze with his mouth hanging open.

"You're embarrassing *me*," Dom said. "You make me sick. Your greed and your lying have ruined us. Your brother's dead. Your niece is dead. And all you can think about is covering your own ass."

Tears filled Michael's eyes. He still had the rifle in his hands and, for a second, Solomon thought he might shoot his own father.

But he tossed the gun aside and stomped off to the far end of the room. He stood facing a wall, hugging himself.

"My God," Lucinda said under her breath.

Dom's gun never strayed from Logan, but he seemed to lose interest in blasting him. The moment had passed. His shoulders slumped.

"Now what, Solomon? What do we do now?"

"We need an ambulance," Lucinda said.

"I didn't ask you anything," Dom said. "You're as much to blame for this mess as—"

"No, she's not," Solomon said. "She didn't do a damned thing, except her job. It's you people who fucked everything up."

Dom's mouth snapped shut. His face glowed with anger.

Solomon swallowed hard and his eyes burned, but he matched Dom's glare until the old man looked away. In that moment, Solomon knew he'd changed his life. For the better.

"Come on," Lucinda said quietly. "I'll drive you to a hospital."

She helped Solomon to his feet, and they turned away from the Sheffields and Logan and the shattered glass and the spattered blood.

Before they could take two steps, an amplified voice came from the forest.

"Federal agents!" Hart's voice. "Drop your weapons!"

Solomon couldn't see them among the trees, but he felt their guns trained on the trashed lodge.

"Do it, sir," he said. "Put the gun down."

Dom grumbled, but he tossed the shotgun away. It clattered across the floor and slid into the shadows.

Solomon tilted his head at a noise, off in the distance, a deep-throated thumping, like a rapid heartbeat. Helicopters, headed this way.

CHAPTER 72

●●●●●●●●●●●●●●●●●●●●

General Goma stood on the balcony of his white-washed house, binoculars to his eyes, watching trucks lumber off into the distance on the rutted road. Yellow dust swirled in the air, and the engines of the overloaded trucks grumbled and moaned. He could hear some of the men cheering, pumping themselves up for the lightning strike on Niamey.

An hour from now, the trucks would reach the city, and his soldiers would fan out, spreading fire and lead and terror. A core group would go straight to the convention center, swoop down on the election headquarters. The ballot boxes soon would be in his hands. After that, Goma would call the shots in Niger.

He lowered the binoculars and squinted against the setting sun. The dust hung in the windless sky. What a godforsaken country, Goma thought, it's dying of thirst.

"General, sir?"

Reynard stood in the arched doorway, looking terrified.

"What is it?"

"A call for you." Reynard offered the cordless phone to his commander, holding it gingerly, as if he were handing Goma a snake.

"I do not wish to speak on the phone. Not now."

Reynard's face was coated in sweat. He looked ill.

"Sir, I must insist."

Insist? Reynard did not insist. No one *insisted* anything to General Erasmus Goma. How scared must Reynard be, to speak to Goma in a way that could cost him his life?

He took the phone and cautiously put it to his ear. "This is Goma."

The connection wasn't great, but the voice on the other end was deep and strong. "My name is Dominick Sheffield."

Oh. Now Goma understood what had frightened Reynard. His own bowels felt a little loose after hearing that name.

"I understand my sons have funded your little Election Day adventure," the voice said. "I want it stopped. Now."

"I don't know what you—"

"Don't lie to me, you fucker. I've had enough of lies. Just call off the revolution."

Goma swallowed and said, "You're too late. It has begun."

"Find a way to make it stop."

"Why should I?"

"Because you'd rather live a rich man than die a poor one."

Despite the heat on the balcony, Goma felt a chill run down his back. He took a deep breath, drawing himself up, and tried a bluff.

"You have no power here, old man."

"My money paid for your guns and your graft. I'd say that gives me a stake in this mess. Almost cost me my life as well. French mercenaries tried to kill me."

"I know nothing of that."

"They killed my son—"

"Michael?"

"No, Chris. Michael's standing right here."

"Let me speak to him."

"Fuck you, General. Listen to me. You've already got a million dollars of my money sitting in your bank account. I can put another million there if you call back your troops."

Goma's breath caught in his chest. Two million dollars? To walk away?

"Or," the old man, "that same million bucks will become the price on your head. Costs me the same either way. How long do you think you'd stay alive in Niger, once word got out that your death was worth a million dollars?"

Goma had been staring at the stone floor. Now he looked at Reynard, who still stood in the doorway, sweaty and apprehensive. Hell, he thought, for one million dollars, Reynard himself would kill me in my sleep.

Goma held the phone away from his ear, but close enough that he was sure the old man could hear.

"Get Colonel Abideau on the radio," he said to Reynard. "Cancel the attack. Immediately."

Reynard stiffened and saluted, then hurried away.

"There," Goma said into the phone. "Did you hear?"

"Good decision, General. Maybe I won't use your skull for a soup bowl after all."

CHAPTER 73

●●●●●●●●●●●●●●●●●●●●

Two weeks later, Solomon was propped up in his hospital bed in San Francisco when Lucinda arrived, carrying a copy of the Examiner.

"Have you seen this?"

The newspaper was folded open to an inside page. The brief article at the bottom of the page was the sort of international story that wouldn't interest most stateside readers, but it was fascinating to Solomon:

> NIAMEY, Niger—After a full recount, overseen by international monitors, election results in Niger have certified that Jacques Laurent is the new president.
>
> Laurent narrowly defeated Ibrahim Boudreaux, who'd served as president the past ten years. During Boudreaux's term, the country has fallen to the worst poverty level in the world, amid growing allegations of government corruption.
>
> Laurent's election follows an aborted government overthrow by elements of the Nigerien military led by Gen. Erasmus Goma. His planned Election Day attack on the capital was called off before a single shot was fired. Goma

fled the country and reportedly is living in exile in the Bahamas.

In his acceptance speech, Laurent pledged a number of reforms, including a plan to nationalize the uranium industry.

Solomon tossed the newspaper onto the blanket that covered him from the waist down.

"Son of a gun. It turned out the right way. Just as Victor Amadou wanted. He ought to be recognized as a national hero."

"It'll probably be hushed up," Lucinda said. "You'll notice there's no mention in there of the Sheffields."

"The reporters are still piecing it together. It's a long way from Niger to a shootout in Mendocino County. But it'll come out eventually."

The newspapers already had made a big deal about the arrest of Bart Logan, who was charged with the murders of Abby Maynes and Clyde Merton and the attempted murder of Carl Jones, and the fact that Logan was chief of security for Sheffield Enterprises.

Getting less attention was the arrest of Ambassador Mirabeau, who fled the United States only to be taken into custody as he got off a plane in Niamey. Officials in the new government pledged to go hard on him for the murder of Victor Amadou.

Lucinda sat on the edge of the bed and rested a hand on Solomon's chest. She was still dressed for work, and she kicked off her high heels.

"I keep thinking we should help it along," she said. "A well-placed phone call or two, and every reporter in the country will be all over the Sheffields."

Solomon shook his head. "We should stay out of it. I'm done with that family."

He'd maintained that position since that night at Cutthroat Lodge. He and Lucinda were repeatedly questioned by cops and feds and diplomats, and they'd always told the truth. But neither of them spoke to the news media about the Sheffields and the shootout.

Grace, too, had agreed to keep quiet, after Dom made her a generous settlement offer. She and Lucinda both would become multimillionaires, simply by accepting a quick divorce. Michael had been removed from his leadership positions at Sheffield Enterprises, and Grace apparently felt that was enough punishment. Mainly, though, she was swayed by her fondness for Dom, and her sympathy over his losses.

Solomon had heard from Dom only once, shortly after he was moved by ambulance from the little hospital in Ukiah to the medical center at the University of California-San Francisco. Dom had said that he of course would pay all the medical bills, including the weeks of occupational therapy needed to restore Solomon's damaged hand to full use. Beyond that, Dom hadn't had much to say. He'd seemed distracted, too busy salvaging his empire to waste time patching things up.

Solomon had hoped to be out of the hospital by now, but an infection had delayed his release and dropped him into several dizzy days of fever dreams. He was better now, felt ready to start his new life.

He wasn't certain where he'd live or what he'd do for a job. He supposed he'd stay in San Francisco, at least for a while. Do his physical therapy. Spend time with Lucinda, who'd come to visit him every evening in the hospital. They needed time alone together, someplace where they didn't have to worry about nurses bursting through the door.

Lucinda stretched out beside him, and rested her head on his chest, careful of the still-healing bullet wound there. He ran his good hand through her curly hair, traced her jaw with his fingers.

"Long day?" he asked.

"Aren't they all?"

"You probably need bed rest more than I do."

"Hmm." She snuggled against him, and they fell into a comfortable silence.

Solomon stared out the window at a fog-bound sky, his hand in her hair. Her breathing became more regular, and soon she was asleep.

He closed his eyes, too, and let his worries slip away. Focused on the warm woman cuddled up next to him instead. He might not know what the future held, but this seemed a good place to begin.